Had she thou **Maybe in pro** **was a solid w** under his battered jeans and chambray shirt.

He was nearly a foot taller than she, even in her heels, and he smelled of pine and woodsmoke and mountain air.

His chocolate-covered cowboy hat was pulled low over hair that was as black as night and in need of a trim, and the lower half of his face was darkened by a couple days' worth of stubble. But it was his eyes that were the most startling, a pale, clear green that seemed to open a window into his soul. And that soul looked to Mia as if it were even darker and more brooding than the rest of him.

The minute his gaze connected with hers, he slammed that window shut, but not before Mia got a glimpse of something that sent a shiver both scorching hot and icy cold shooting down her spine. Silas Crockett, she could already tell, was about as far removed from a kindly cowboy as a man could be.

"Silas, this is Mia Hawthorne," she heard Miss Sylvie say. "She's gonna be in your hands for the next two weeks. You treat her nice now, you hear?"

Mia really wished that Miss Sylvie hadn't used the phrase *in your hands* to introduce him. Because that made her gaze automatically drop to his hands—his big, sun-bronzed, callus-roughened hands—and that made her mind race right into thoughts of what those hands could do under the right conditions.

And no, her brain wasn't thinking in terms of ranch work just then.

Dear Reader,

Not long ago, a couple of family members went on a cattle drive in Wyoming for—wait for it—the fun of it. I know, right? Two weeks on horseback, cooking outdoors, surrounded by cattle and coyotes and cowboys, and...

Cowboys. Right. Okay, I guess I see the attraction.

So does bubbly Mia Hawthorne when she meets crotchety Silas Crockett. Maybe she's not at Whispering Winds Ranch by choice—she's more suited to swanky (but not too expensive) boutiques and restaurants. It isn't long, though, before the ranch—and the cowboy—start to grow on her.

Crusty Silas has never met anyone quite like always-look-on-the-bright-side-of-life Mia. But she sure is cute—in a city-slicker kinda way. If he can just get past all that daggone perkiness...

It's gonna be a long two weeks.

I had *so* much fun writing *Capturing the Cowboy*. I hope you have fun reading about them, too.

Enjoy!

Elizabeth Bevarly

CAPTURING THE COWBOY

ELIZABETH BEVARLY

Harlequin

SPECIAL EDITION

MIX
Paper | Supporting responsible forestry
FSC
www.fsc.org
FSC® C021394

Harlequin®
SPECIAL
EDITION™

Recycling programs for this product may not exist in your area.

ISBN-13: 978-1-335-18038-4

Capturing the Cowboy

For questions and comments about the quality of this book, please contact us at CustomerService@Harlequin.com.

TM and ® are trademarks of Harlequin Enterprises ULC.

Harlequin Enterprises ULC
22 Adelaide St. West, 41st Floor
Toronto, Ontario M5H 4E3, Canada
www.Harlequin.com

HarperCollins Publishers
Macken House, 39/40 Mayor Street Upper,
Dublin 1, D01 C9W8, Ireland
www.HarperCollins.com

Printed in Lithuania

Elizabeth Bevarly is the *New York Times* and *USA TODAY* bestselling author of more than eighty books. She has called home such exotic places as Puerto Rico and New Jersey but now lives outside her hometown of Louisville, Kentucky, with her husband and cat. When she's not writing or reading, she enjoys cooking, tending her kitchen garden and feeding the local wildlife. Visit her at elizabethbevarly.com for news and lots of fun stuff.

Books by Elizabeth Bevarly

Harlequin Special Edition

Seasons in Sudbury

Heir in a Year
Her Second-Chance Family
Keeping Her Secret

Lucky Stars

Be Careful What You Wish For
Her Good-Luck Charm
Secret under the Stars

The Fortunes of Texas: Fortune's Secret Children

Nine Months to a Fortune

Visit the Author Profile page
at Harlequin.com for more titles.

For Liz Orndorff and Susie Shear.
Giddyap and happy trails.

Chapter One

Mia Hawthorne adjusted her sunglasses and stepped off the shuttle bus from Jackson Hole Airport to get her first real glimpse of Whispering Winds Ranch in Serenity Valley, Wyoming. And all she could think was, *Wow*. Nestled in a rolling patch of green at the foot of the Tetons, the massive mountains in the distance soaring into the clearest, bluest sky she'd ever seen, the summer sun gleaming like a white-hot diamond... Just *wow*. That was all she could manage. In the distance, a bunch of cattle—A drove? A herd? A coalition? Just what was the proper word for a bunch of cows, anyway?—meandered from one end of the horizon to the other, accompanied by a trio of riders and a couple of hound dogs following at the same laconic pace.

She was one of a dozen other people exiting the shuttle, all of them bound for different plans during their stay. Whispering Winds Ranch, she had read on its website before leaving St. Louis, was both a working cattle ranch with real cowboys and -girls going about their jobs and a dude ranch for wannabe cowboys and -girls who were escaping their jobs in the big city. She'd overheard conversations on the shuttle about how her fellow travelers were here for everything from a once-a-year family vacation to a first-time-ever cattle drive.

All of the other guests who'd arrived with her seemed to be looking forward to their next two weeks here with joy and excitement. Mia, however? Not so much.

As the others kept moving forward away from the shuttle, she stood back to observe her surroundings. She always had to do that—look around first to assess the situation. Even if she'd been told what to expect in advance for an occasion—and she had been for this—she always needed to get her bearings and suss everything out for herself before she could take even one step into the fray. And this fray... This was so far removed from her regular reality that she might as well have just landed on Mars.

But that was okay! She would make the best of it! She always made the best of things. Because the things Mia Hawthorne had plenty of were a can-do attitude and a positive outlook that overcame all odds and adversities.

As the now-empty shuttle trundled off, she turned to take in the rest of her surroundings. Blue butterflies danced in the yellow flowers bunched along the front porch of a massive log cabin she assumed was the main house, but they had nothing on the butterflies that were carousing through her belly. She still couldn't believe she was here. And not because she was about to embark on the dream vacation of a lifetime like so many of her fellow travelers today, since the last place she'd ever want to visit was a ranch, breathtaking scenery or no. She'd grown up on the outskirts of St. Louis, with nary a mountain in sight, had never much cared for the great outdoors thanks to its bugginess and her allergies, and was a teeny bit, oh...terrified of horses...after a pony mishap at a birthday party when she was five. Give her a city full of museums and theaters and gourmet—but not too expensive—restaurants and she was good to go. This? She didn't care how beautiful it was here. This was *way* too much outdoors for her liking.

But that was okay! She would make the best of it! She always made the best of things. That was Mia, through and through.

So what if her reason for being at Whispering Winds Ranch was a tad different from the other ranch guests? Now that she was here, she would take advantage of her time to enjoy what was sure to be a new experience. New experiences were always good, right? Everyone should have an opportunity to experience new things. So Mia was not going to waste this one.

Even if she was here for an—she made mental air quotes as she thought the next three words—*anger management program* dictated by her boss at the car dealership where she'd been the service advisor for more than a decade. Mia didn't need anger management. That was silly. She never got angry. What had happened that day at work had just been a big misunderstanding, that was all. One bad day. She'd had one bad day. Which, okay, had culminated in a bit of an altercation with a coworker—Perpetual Salesman of the Month Jeff Oberstrom—something that was completely unlike her. And, okay, yes, it had kind of found her grabbing Jeff by the Tom Ford necktie he was screaming about having paid full price for at the Neiman's in Frontenac. And okay, *fine*, there might have been a moment where she'd screamed something about how she was going to make him relive his birth by pulling him through its perfectly Windsor-knotted loop—breech.

It really was a misunderstanding. Mia had never been mean to *any*one in her entire life, and *every*one at work loved her—just ask them. And she'd just been under a lot of pressure lately. And, oh, did she mention she was provoked? And it would never happen again, she promised, 'cause it was totally out of character for her, she was such a nice person—seriously, ask anyone. Besides, Jeff was twice her size and weight, so how much harm could she have done anyway, even if, by the end of it, she was halfway up his back, palm over his scalp, pushing with all her might and shouting something about how he was crowning.

It really was a misunderstanding. Really. It was. And he really did provoke her. Really. He did. And she really was normally *such* a nice person. A total team player and all-around people pleaser. Just read her annual performance reviews.

Unfortunately, her new boss at Carrigan Auto hadn't seen it that way, even after some of her coworkers—especially the women—backed her up. He'd told her in no uncertain terms that the only way she would be able to keep her job would be to complete an anger management program, and he'd set it up with HR that very minute.

Mia's stomach tumbled again at the memory of that meeting. Patsy, the HR lady, had been sympathetic—and maybe even a little impressed?—by the whole thing, but had told Mia that yes, this was customary with the national auto chain when their valued employees went a little cuckoo, even temporarily. But she knew just the place for Mia, and it wasn't actually an anger management program per se, but a dude ranch in Wyoming that had a number of programs for people who were, ah, a little high strung for a variety of reasons. Carrigan Auto had used them before, with excellent results, to get their troubled employees back to their normal selves, and she was sure Mia would benefit nicely. She'd be paired with a sweet old cowboy named Beau, who was the epitome of kindness and patience and who could show her the way to maintain a perfectly balanced frame of mind in a world full of...well, Windsor-knot-wearing jackasses.

Mia just hoped Beau was as nice as Patsy promised. Because in spite of her one bad-day episode, she was terrible at confrontations and would normally do any-thing—*anything*—to avoid uncomfortable situations. She really was a people-pleaser, and not just at work. And maybe some people's thesauruses lumped that term in with others like *bootlicker* and *doormat*, but she didn't see it that way. Mia just wanted everyone to be happy, that was all. And she wanted to make her world—hey, the whole world—as free of contention and disorder as it could be.

She gripped her weekender bag more firmly, brushed a hand over her totally-inappropriate-for-ranch-life white blouse and dove-gray palazzo pants—they'd told her to bring casual clothes, and this was as casual as she got—and adjusted the tortoiseshell sunglasses perched on her nose. The warm June wind kicked up, stirring her ash-blond bangs and chin-length bob around her face, but she smoothed her hair aside, too. She could do this, she told herself. It was only two weeks. In a beautiful—if way too outdoorsy—place. With a kindly old cowboy who sounded like he'd just moseyed on out of an old-time Western movie. How hard could it be? Squaring her shoulders, she strode toward the main house of Whispering Winds Ranch and up its three wooden steps. One, two, three, quick as you please. After inhaling one last fortifying breath, she pushed her sunglasses to the top of her head and made her way inside.

Strangely, the interior of the house was somehow even more outdoorsy than the outside. The honey-colored log walls rose up two stories and then some, with wide floor-to-ceiling windows on the opposite side of the room that offered a panoramic vista of more green, more mountain and more blue sky. And, it went without saying, more cattle, horses and riders. A colossal chandelier that appeared to be fashioned from antlers—surely they weren't *real* antlers…were they?—hung from the main rafter, surrounded by a mezzanine on all sides that offered a glimpse of the second floor. The furniture appeared to be wrought from more logs and upholstered in woolen blankets with brightly colored geometric designs. Similarly patterned rugs of varying sizes were scattered about the room over well-worn hardwood. All the artwork featured—gosh, what a shocker—horses and cattle and cowboys, all of them backdropped by what looked like the very scenery beyond the windows.

"Well, hello there," someone called from her left. "You must be Mia."

She turned to find a woman entering the room who looked as if she might have been a part of this place since its genesis. Whatever that genesis might have been, because, honestly, Whispering Winds Ranch felt like it was as much a natural part of the landscape as the mountains behind it. The woman had white hair woven into a thick braid falling over one shoulder to nearly her waist, and she was dressed completely in denim, from the collar of her Western-style shirt to the hem of her flared jeans. Working denim at that, faded and battered in a way that suggested they'd come from a tractor-supply place and been worn daily instead of from a department store for the sake of style. The only thing that broke up the blue fabric was a wide brown belt with an even wider brass buckle and the cowgirl boots peeking out from the over-long jeans. Those boots were battered and dusty, too, as if the wearer had just come in from a long afternoon ride on the range.

Clearly, this was a woman unbothered by seasonal allergies or malevolent party ponies. Or anything else, judging by her relaxed vibe. She smiled at Mia and took a few more steps forward, extending her hand as if it were the most natural thing in the world to do. Mia envied her that. Even after working so long in a male-dominated business like car sales, she had yet to master the comfortable handshake. Or even the uncomfortable handshake. She wasn't much one for physical touching at all, really.

But that was okay! A lot of people weren't comfortable with physical touching. That didn't mean they weren't still people people. And Mia was totally a people person.

"I'm Sylvie Sage," the woman introduced herself. "I run this operation."

Mia smiled back and took her hand, and Sylvie Sage gave it a few very confident pumps. "It's nice to meet you, Ms. Sage," she said. "And yes, I'm Mia. Mia Hawthorne. I'm here for the—" She couldn't even say it. That's how foreign anger was in her repertoire. Mia simply was not an angry person. She wasn't. Honest.

Somehow, though, she managed to finish. "The anger management program."

Sylvie Sage smiled. "Which isn't technically an anger management program," she replied as she released Mia's hand. "Whispering Winds Ranch has just partnered with some corporate entities and nonprofits to provide a little R and R for people they think seem to need it. And call me Miss Sylvie. Everyone does."

She took a step backward, giving Mia a full up-and-down assessment. Then she shook her head. "Funny, but you don't look like the people we usually get for the, um, anger management thing. Just how tall are you, anyway?"

"Five foot six," Mia lied.

"Without the heels, I mean," Miss Sylvie said with a knowing smile. "Which, by the way, are gonna have to stay in your cabin while you're here unless you wanna break your neck."

Fine. "Five foot four," Mia told her. "And a half."

The other woman nodded, but Mia wasn't sure if she bought the *and-a-half* part or not. "Well, I sure hope you packed some work clothes, five-foot-four-and-a-half Mia Hawthorne."

"These are my work clothes," Mia said.

"Not for the work you're gonna be doing around here, they're not."

"It's fine," she assured the other woman. And it was. Honest. "Everything I brought with me is stuff I don't really wear that much. It'll be okay if it gets messed up."

Even if she had packed every piece of non-work clothing she owned, because she didn't own much clothing that wasn't for work. But, hey, if these got messed up, she could just live her nonwork life in pajamas for the foreseeable future. That wasn't so bad, was it? A lot of people would love to live life in their pajamas. Mia would be fine if something happened to anything she'd packed. She was always fine with whatever happened, good or bad. She was. Honest. That was why she never got angry. Ever.

"If you say so," Miss Sylvie said. Still smiling. Still knowingly. But that was okay! Mia didn't mind when people got knowing with her. She didn't. Honest.

"We'll just see how things go," Miss Sylvie added.

Mia gripped her weekender even harder. "Okay. That's fine." And it was. Fine, she meant. Honest.

She was about to ask when she would be meeting with Beau, but Miss Sylvie got there first. "So, about your stay. Normally, Beau would be the one showing you the ropes around here and getting you back on track, but he unfortunately had a little accident over the weekend that's going to make that impossible. He's okay," she hurried on to reassure Mia. Probably because she thought Mia was panicking. Even though Mia was *not* panicking at all, and everything was fine. It was. "He's just gonna be on crutches for a little bit because he tore a ligament in his ankle tripping over a stray piece of fencing."

"Oh," Mia said. Still not panicking, on account of how she was totally fine. Honest. "Well. I see. So. Um, how is that going to work now?"

"Fortunately, we have another cowboy at Whispering Winds who's experienced in this sort of thing and has filled in for Beau a few times. I told him to meet us at your cabin in…" She turned her wrist to look at a state-of-the-art smartwatch that was completely at odds with her Annie Oakley attire. "Actually, we should start heading over that way now. Silas isn't one to abide tardiness." She grinned even wider than before. "In fact, Silas Crockett isn't one to abide much of anything."

Hmm. That didn't sound like someone who had much in common with kindly Beau, who'd seemed like a Sheriff Woody knockoff. Silas Crockett sounded more like an old, grizzled cowpuncher smudged with creosote, who gobbled down hardtack and quaffed rotgut and called everybody he didn't like—which, of course, was everyone—a yella-bellied jack wagon while he cleaned his Peacemaker with a tumbleweed.

But that was okay! Mia would be A-OK with someone like that. She would.

Her stomach surged with anxiety again as she lowered her sunglasses back over her eyes and followed Miss Sylvie through the door she'd just entered. They made their way back down the porch steps and to the right, toward a trio of well-spaced log cabins that were mini versions of the main house. As they drew nearer to the one at the farthest end, another figure emerged from behind it, tall and lanky and as denim-clad as Miss Sylvie was, only his attire was even more rugged and dusty and worn. The man wore a battered cowboy hat tugged low over his head, keeping his face in shade, and he loped along with the dexterity and nonchalance of a coyote.

Drawing nearer still, Mia saw that the man wasn't as old as she assumed someone named Silas Crockett would be, nor was he in any way creosote-smudged. He did, however, appear to be every bit as grizzled-looking, and although he wasn't currently armed with a Peacemaker, she could totally see him cleaning one with a tumbleweed. It was only when she and Miss Sylvie finally arrived at their destination, and when he turned to look at them full-on, that Mia's heart plummeted nearly to her toes. Had she thought he was lanky? Um, no. Maybe in profile, but full-on, Silas Crockett was a solid wall of muscle and sinew and man under his battered jeans and chambray shirt. He was nearly a foot taller than she, even in her heels, and he smelled of pine and woodsmoke and mountain air.

His chocolate-colored cowboy hat was pulled low over hair that was as black as night and in need of a trim, and the lower half of his face was darkened by a couple days' worth of stubble. But it was his eyes that were the most startling, a pale, clear green that seemed to open a window into his soul. And that soul looked to Mia as if it were even darker and more brooding than the rest of him.

The minute his gaze connected with hers, he slammed that window shut, but not before Mia got a glimpse of something that sent a shiver both scorching-hot and icy-cold shooting down her spine. Silas Crockett, she could already tell, was about as far removed from a kindly cowboy named Beau as a man could be. There wasn't a hint of warmth or good humor about him.

"Silas, this is Mia Hawthorne," she heard Miss Sylvie say, her voice seeming to come from a million miles away. "She's gonna be in your hands for the next two weeks. You treat her nice, you hear?"

"Yes, ma'am," he replied obediently, without a trace of obedience in his tone.

Mia really wished Miss Sylvie hadn't used the phrase *in your hands* when she'd introduced him. Because that made her gaze automatically drop to his hands—his big, sun-bronzed, callus-roughened hands—and that made her mind race right into thoughts of what those hands could do under the right conditions. And, no, her brain wasn't thinking in terms of ranch work just then.

Before she realized what she was doing, Mia took a step backward, the heel of her shoe landing on something uneven, making her lose her balance. She righted herself gracefully enough, but not before Silas Crockett smirked a bit at her momentary gaffe. He quickly returned to his stoicism, though. And his grizzledyness. And his wall of musclyness.

When Miss Sylvie said Silas Crockett had *experience with this sort of thing*, Mia thought she'd meant with counseling angry people. Even though she herself was, of course, *not* angry. Evidently, though, his experience lay more in the *angry* part than in the *counseling* part. It was pretty clear he didn't spend a lot of time being happy about anything. Including the fact that he had to fill in as a babysitter for a city slicker. His antagonism toward Mia couldn't be more obvious.

Her stomach lurched again. She really hoped that wasn't the case. She'd grown up in a house full of belligerence and acrimony. Her parents had constantly been at each other's throats, hurling insults and threats and venom at each other on an hourly basis. It hadn't been uncommon for her two older brothers to have fistfights, they'd resented each other so much. She'd done her best to escape whenever she could to the library or the park to avoid the constant discord. Those times when she'd had to be at home, she had just done her best to stay out of everyone's way. She learned at an early age how to make herself small and invisible to avoid becoming a target, and that had—usually—worked. The day she turned eighteen, she took every nickel she'd saved from the three part-time jobs she worked in high school to move into her own place and enroll at community college. She hadn't seen or spoken to her family since.

But that was okay! A lot of people didn't see or speak to their families! Mia was just happy now—really, she was totally happy now—to have left all that in the past.

It was why finding herself in any kind of anger program was so laughable. She just couldn't possibly be angry. She knew better than anyone how destructive anger could be and how badly it could upend lives. She did everything she could to ensure that her life now was completely empty of contention and strife. She thought only happy thoughts. She saw only the best in everyone. She found lightness in every dark corner and the silver lining around every gray cloud. She was happy and cheerful and upbeat. Every damned day. There was nothing to be angry about in Mia's life. Absolutely nothing. Everything was awesome. Everything was fine. It was. Always.

Honest.

"You're gonna wanna find yourself some better footwear," Silas told her by way of a greeting, bringing her out of her gloomy—No! She meant *happy*!—thoughts. He hooked his hands on his lean hips, shifted his weight to one foot, and ran his gaze slowly from her feet to her face. And boy, oh, boy, did Mia feel that gaze on every inch of her body where it landed. Then he added, "And I hope you brought some work clothes with you, cause those—" he gestured toward her outfit as if she were wearing rotting lunchmeat "—ain't gonna cut it around here."

"Silas," Miss Sylvie interjected. "I said, 'Be nice.'"

His gaze never leaving Mia's, he told Miss Sylvie, "I am being nice."

But Mia would not be cowed by Silas Crockett. Much. "These are my work—" She stopped herself before she could get contentious and expelled a resolute breath. "My clothes are fine," she said more evenly, smiling her brightest smile. "It's fine. I'll be fine." And she would be. Everything would be fine.

Silas nodded once, in a way that contradicted what he was obviously thinking. That her attire wasn't—that *she* wasn't—fine at all.

Whatever. He didn't look as if he were much older than Mia's own twenty-nine years, but there was an air about him that made him seem much older. Like age-of-the-earth older, as if he'd clawed his way out from the mountains behind him and wandered the planet alone for eons before settling back here. Not that he seemed in any way settled. But judging by his and Miss Sylvie's familiarity, he'd clearly been a part of Whispering Winds Ranch for some time.

"I mean it, Silas," Miss Sylvie said. "You be nice to Mia."

"I'm always nice," he assured her. In a way that was no way reassuring. Or, you know, nice.

Miss Sylvie turned to address Mia. "Since you arrived so late in the day, you and Silas won't get officially started on things 'til tomorrow morning. But he'll help you get settled in here and then bring you to the main house for dinner later on. It'll give y'all a chance to get to know each other a bit before things get underway." She gave her a quick smile before adding, "I hope you're looking forward to the next two weeks at Whispering Winds as much as we're looking forward to having you. You're gonna love your time here. Everyone does. We've had more than a few people tell us their stays have been life-changing. A lot of them come back every year to recharge."

"Thanks, but I don't need my life to be changed," Mia told her. "My life is perfectly fine. I'm only here because I had one bad day at work. It was all a big misunderstanding."

Miss Sylvie nodded. "I'm sure it was. It always is with the folks who come through here for the anger thing."

Mia started to explain how it really, truly, was a misunderstanding, honest it was, but Miss Sylvie gave her a brief salute and turned on her heel to head back to the main house. Something that left her alone with Silas Crockett. Silas Crockett and his amazing, haunting, pale green eyes that suddenly seemed to be peering into Mia's soul, too.

Silas Crockett looked at Mia Hawthorne, for whose well-being he was responsible for the next two blasted weeks, and he somehow refrained from smacking himself upside his own head. He knew he should've told Miss Sylvie no when she'd stopped him and asked him for a favor, since, too often, that favor ended up being something he didn't want to do. But he owed Miss Sylvie more than he could ever repay, so whatever she needed from him, whenever she needed it, Silas always said yes, even before she officially asked.

And hell, when Miss Sylvie had told him it was for a "dude" coming in to deal with some anger issues, Silas had figured it would be a walk in the park. No, it wasn't his usual gig here at the ranch—he'd much rather be managing the livestock as he generally was or, even better, out on the range with the cattle—but he'd stepped up a couple of times when Beau wasn't able to, and it had always been as easy as tying a honda knot. Some guy comes in, he's mad as hell at life and the universe, and Silas spends a couple weeks with him, showing him how to deal with the anger and move on, pretty much by doing the same things Silas would be doing around the ranch anyway. Then the guy goes home to live the rest of his life without burning every bridge and smacking every person he encounters.

Silas was always real successful at that, 'cause that was pretty much his life, too. He'd been mad as hell at life and the universe for more than a decade, and he would stay mad as hell at them until the day he died. But he'd learned to live with that. No reason others couldn't learn to live with it, too.

He looked at Mia again. She was nothing like the other folks that had come to Whispering Winds for their anger. But damned if Silas couldn't feel it roiling off of her like a kettle about to blow. Even the dark glasses hiding her eyes couldn't make her look cool and calm. Yeah, she had the appearance of some serene celestial being, with her shimmery, silvery hair and creamy skin and flowy clothes, but there was something smoldering just below the surface that was bitter and jagged and barely contained. No way did this woman know how to live with her anger. Hell, she hadn't even acknowledged it. She was smiling at him in a way she probably thought was agreeable and unbothered, but all he could think was how close she was to erupting. And when she did…

Well, hell. He just hoped two weeks would be enough with this one.

"C'mon," he told her, tilting his head toward the cabin she'd been assigned. "I'll help you get settled."

"It's not necessary," she replied. "I'll be fine."

There was that word again. *Fine.* Even in just the few minutes since he'd met her, she'd used that word a lot.

"Do you have the key to your cabin?" he asked.

She arrowed her brows down. "No."

"Then you're not gonna be fine."

"But—"

He interrupted her by removing a key from his back pocket, attached to a length of rawhide cord with a metal disc engraved with the number 3, just like the one tacked to the front door of the cabin they happened to be standing in front of.

"I'll help you get settled," he said again.

This time, he didn't wait for a reply, just turned and climbed the solitary step to the porch and shoved the key into the lock above the doorknob. It turned easily, and he pushed the door open, not bothering to see if Mia was following. He already knew she wasn't. He would have been able to feel all that anger steaming off her if she had been.

He made his way through the cabin, pushing wider the curtains on the four open windows, switching on one of only two brass lamps, and tugging the string to turn on the overhead fan. All the cabins were the same, from the wrought-iron double beds to the Kiowa rugs to the hundred-year-old sofas, chairs and tables that had all been handcrafted from native bur oak. He'd stopped by earlier to stock the kitchen cabinets with a few snacks and stow some bottled water in the minifridge, but if Ms. Mia Hawthorne of St. Louis, Missouri, wanted other provisions, she could grab them at the main house herself. One of the Whispering Winds housekeepers had put clean sheets on the bed that morning and fresh towels in the bathroom, and housekeeping would stay on top of that, but Mia would be making her own bed and keeping her own space orderly while she was here.

Whispering Winds was a little different from most dude ranches in that only part of it was open to tourists, while the rest of it was a traditionally-run commercial cattle ranch. That was the side of the business where Silas normally worked—as the animal husbandry manager, caring for the livestock and seeing to their daily needs. Whispering Winds had been in Miss Sylvie's family for six generations, and there was a time when it was one of the biggest, most successful, ranches in the entire state. But in the middle of the twentieth century, when her grandfather was in charge, the place started to fail. It was kind of a perfect storm of mismanagement, economics and changing cultural landscape, but little by little, the family had been forced to sell off most of their land to neighboring ranchers and communities until there was only a few thousand acres left. And although a few thousand acres was nothing to sneeze at, it was only a fraction of the tens of thousands the family had owned when the ranch was at its peak.

Silas knew all this because his family had been a part of Whispering Winds for almost as long as Miss Sylvie's had. His own great-granddaddy had come to work here more than a century ago as a cowboy. Silas's granddaddy had been a herdsman, and his mother had been a house-keeper here until her death when Silas was ten years old. He'd been on the payroll himself since he was a teenager, working his way up from assistant ranch hand to cow-boy to herdsman to husbandry manager, where he was content—well, content enough—to stay. He'd tried life in the real world for a while. It had just ended up mak-ing him angry. He wasn't going to make the mistake again of trying to live a life anywhere but the wide-open range, where he could spend most of his time alone and unbothered by the chaos and injustice of "civilized" life.

"You're gonna have to come in eventually," he called over his shoulder to the woman who had at least made it as far as the front door. "We're gettin' into thunder-storm season. They come out of nowhere sometimes. Don't wanna ruin those expensive clothes."

When he turned around to look at her, he saw that Mia had taken off her sunglasses and was now glaring at him. Her eyes, he couldn't help noticing, were as stormy gray as the summer clouds could be, a few shades darker than her ashy hair, and sullied by faint purple crescents, as if she were suffering from a profound lack of sleep. The glare, he thought, was actually a good thing, since it meant she wasn't stifling her true feelings. Well, not as much as she had been up 'til now, anyway. If he told her just then that she was glaring, she would deny it and insist that no, she was *fine*, in spite of the obvious anger burning up the air between the two of them.

Sure enough, the second she realized he was looking at her, she forced a bright smile, ran a quick hand through her hair, and rolled her shoulders as if physically shedding her bad mood. And boom. Just like that, before his very eyes, she gave the appearance of a bubbly, happy little human without a care in the world.

Damn. That was impressive.

"They weren't expensive," she said brightly. "I'm really good at finding bargains."

"Mmm," he replied. Because how else was a person supposed to reply to a claim like that?

She took a few experimental steps into the cabin and gave it a quick once-over. "This is nice," she said.

Hey, look at that. She'd just elevated her world from *fine* to *nice. You go, Mia Hawthorne.*

She went to the bed and set her very-expensive-looking-but-probably-a-real-bargain bag on the mattress and unzipped it. As she unpacked her things, Silas told her where everything in the cabin was and how it worked and where she could find anything she needed that wasn't here already. He watched as the piles of her belongings grew, becoming more disconcerted with every passing minute. She really hadn't brought any kind of work clothes suitable for the next two weeks. Not even sweatpants or T-shirts. And was that actually a *dress*? Just what the hell did she think she was going to be doing while she was staying on a Wyoming ranch? They weren't exactly known for their tea parties and cocktail hours around here.

"You don't have a single pair of jeans in there," he said when she zipped the empty bag, lowered it to the floor and nudged it under the bed with her high-heeled shoe.

"That's because I don't own any jeans," she told him.

Oh, now that was just wrong. "How can a person not own a single pair of jeans?"

"I'm not a jeans person."

He expelled an exasperated breath. Not a jeans person. He hadn't realized folks like that existed. "I'll see if I can rustle some up for you from somewhere."

"That won't be necessary," she told him. "I'll be—"

"Fine," they both said as one.

"So you've said," Silas added. "About a million times. You know what kind of people say everything is fine a million times?"

She smiled again. Almost convincingly this time, too. "Happy people?" she said.

"People who are in no way fine."

"I'm fine," she said. Again. "I am."

Silas looked at Mia. Mia looked at Silas. Neither offering even a hint of what they might be feeling for the other. Not that those feelings weren't obvious. And precarious. And problematic.

Oh, yeah, he thought. It was definitely going to be a long two weeks. He just hoped Mia didn't blow herself to angry bits before then.

Chapter Two

Mia looked at the front door of her cabin—the one Silas Crockett had just closed behind himself—and wondered how she was going to make it through the next two hours never mind the next two weeks. Yes, the cabin was nice, if a tad on the rugged side—but that was okay!—and he'd told her enough about what to expect during her stay that her anxiety levels had ebbed. A little. Dinner was at six o'clock, he'd told her, and it would be followed at eight by a reception for people who were arriving at Whispering Winds for the first day of their visit. Some of those would be like her—in programs to help them through one kind of life crisis or another—and some would be here for the simple pleasure of learning how to be an old-time cowpoke by what had sounded a lot like cosplaying cowboys and -girls and learning how to do cowboy and -girl stuff, like riding horses and roping calves and walking around in lots of denim and leather. Some of them, he'd told her, were even here to go on a full-fledged cattle drive, moving the Whispering Winds herd from here to the mountain pastures where the animals would spend the rest of the summer.

All of which of course sounded like fun for the right sort of person. Unfortunately, Mia wasn't that sort of person. And she had expressed her un-outdoorsyness to Patsy the HR lady before asking if there wasn't some other anger management program she could do closer to home, one that preferably involved things like yoga or chai lattes or spa days or maybe ballroom dancing? Ballroom dancing would be nice. Yes, it would, Patsy had agreed. But Carrigan Auto didn't have any arrangements in place with any dance studios, so off to a dude ranch in Wyoming Mia would be going instead.

But that was okay! Mia would make the best of it!

She looked at the stacks of clothes she'd removed from her weekender and hadn't yet put away. Silas Crockett could not have been more contemptuous of her city-girl trappings. Okay, okay, maybe she should have invested in at least one pair of jeans and a couple of T-shirts before she'd left home. She'd at least brought a pair of sneakers. Even if they were ones she wore for evening walks on urban pavement and not for riding horses and scaling mountains. *Fashion sneakers*, Silas had called them when he'd done one final survey of her belongings, speaking in the same tone of voice he might have used to describe a pile of bear droppings he'd stumbled upon out on the trail.

A bubble of anger—no, annoyance, *not* anger, because she never felt anger—rippled up inside her. It was okay that she wasn't the kind of person who felt at home on the range. There was nothing wrong with being a city slicker. It took all kinds to make a world and all that. She didn't care if Silas thought she was useless. Hey, he was right. Here on a ranch, she was useless. He wasn't exactly suited to her job, either, being the go-between for clients and mechanics at an auto dealership, allaying the fears and suspicions of people whose cars needed servicing and making sure the guys working on those cars did the job right in spite of their boss always encouraging them to cut corners. The work Mia did was different from his, that was all. That didn't make it any less important.

It was no secret that people didn't exactly trust car dealers, and yeah, sometimes there was a reason for that. The joke around the showroom at Carrigan—and it wasn't really a joke, even though the sales force laughed about it all the time—was that their unofficial slogan was *Greet 'em, meet 'em, and cheat 'em.* But not in Mia's department, and not on Mia's watch. She kept everything honest and aboveboard in Parts & Service, and people had come to realize that. They trusted her to ensure the company did right by them. Even the customers who were irascible and wary when they came in were always relaxed and upbeat by the time they handed over their keys. That was specifically because of Mia and her smarts and her bubbly personality. No way would someone like Silas win anyone's trust with his cantankerousness.

But it was okay that he was cantankerous! All kinds. World. Mia would just stay upbeat and keep smiling while she was dealing with him and keep on keeping on. Starting with dinner in—she glanced down at her phone—a little over two hours.

Her stomach tumbled again. She'd always been anxious when she was a child, thanks to the turbulence in her home. After turning eighteen and moving out, though, she'd been determined that she would never be anxious again. She had left that contentious environment behind a decade ago, and now everything was better. It was. Everything. Even so, there were still times when she couldn't quite take things easy. Still nights when she had trouble sleeping, lying in bed wide awake, waiting for the eruption of shouting and the slamming of doors and furniture that never even came anymore. And there were still mornings when she awoke, bracing herself for all hell to break loose at any minute, even though it never did these days.

She made sure it didn't. She did that by leading a life that was as small and quiet as she could make it. She kept to herself and maintained an orderly home and existence. She went to work, did her job, came home, fixed dinner, read or watched TV, and went to bed. Wash, rinse, repeat.

Maybe hers wasn't the most exciting life in the world, and maybe it was lacking in a few things. Things like… oh, Mia didn't know…other people. She'd tried including other people in her life beyond her coworkers. She'd tried friendships and relationships. They had never ended well. Either her friends and boyfriends drifted away or she did. It was fine. It was. She'd come to realize that she was one of those people who *didn't* need people. That was what was supposed to happen when you moved out on your own, right? You discovered things about yourself you never knew before? She'd discovered she was a loner, that was all. A loner who preferred a quiet, orderly, predictable life. Mia was content with the way she lived. She was. She was happy. Enough. She was. At least there was no yelling anymore. No chaos. No fear. And there was no anger. At all. There would never be anger again.

She made short work of putting away her things and went about exploring the small cabin. There was water, fruit and cheese in the minifridge, and crackers and cookies in the cabinets, enough to tide her over for the rest of the week. The WiFi signal was good, so she'd be able to check her email and a few other things online when she needed to. Not that she received a lot of email from one day to the next—at least email that wasn't work related—but still. She didn't even have any of the work-related variety today. No doubt her boss had told everyone to leave her alone while she was gone so that she could enjoy her break. Either that, or having witnessed her trying to pull a man twice her size through his necktie, her coworkers were now thinking twice about bothering her at all. Even if it had just been a misunderstanding.

She made another circuit of the cabin and sat on the bed. It squeaked a bit when she did, but the mattress was firm. Then she stood and walked to the window to look at the view. The mountains were still there. The sky was still clear. The blue butterflies that had been dancing around the flowers in front of the main house had made their way to the ones in front of her cabin. Wind ruffled the leaves in a trio of feathery green trees between her and the big house, then pushed through the screen to ruffle her hair, too.

Late June in Wyoming was a lot different from late June in St. Louis. Back home, it was hot and muggy, the humidity keeping her windows closed and her air conditioner humming. As much as Mia liked living there, the city could be uncomfortable in the summer. Serenity Valley might be too pastoral for her preference, but its summer weather was downright pleasant.

She was about to turn back toward the cabin's interior—she had no idea what she was going to do for the next two hours and really should have brought a book or something—but a movement at the main house caught her eye. Silas Crockett was exiting the front door with Miss Sylvie on his heels. Although they were too far away for Mia to hear them, Miss Sylvia looked like she was giving Silas a bit of a talking-to. She even shook a finger at him at one point. Even so, she looked in no way angry as she did it, and Silas seemed to be taking whatever she was telling him with a grain of salt. But even that small display of controversy made apprehension surge inside Mia. When Silas turned away from Miss Sylvie, and Miss Sylvie grabbed his arm to stop him, Mia even flinched, bracing herself for the swat of the other woman's hand—or worse—that was sure to come. Instead, Miss Sylvie pulled him back toward herself, wrapping her arms around him to give him a fierce hug. Silas stood stiff as a board for a moment, then, with clear reluctance, he looped his arms around her and hugged her back. Kind of. Mia supposed for a guy like Silas, the arm looping was about as close to a hug as it got.

She could scarcely believe her eyes as she watched them. Never in a million years had she seen an altercation with anyone end in what was clearly sincere affection. Not even small altercations. Affection had been absent in her own family, so it was no surprise things had always ended badly there. But even among acquaintances and coworkers, there was never an immediate reconciliation and/or forgiveness after a disagreement. There was always resentment first. And grudges. And lame excuses. And it always took at least a few hours, sometimes days, before people were on good terms again. But this…

Miss Sylvie had just gone from stern critic to mama teddy bear in a nanosecond. From lambasting to embracing. Was that even possible? Well, clearly it was, since that was what Mia was seeing. But wow. Miss Sylvie must be some kind of superhero.

Before she or Silas could catch her snooping, Mia moved away from the window and paced to the other side of the cabin, stopping short when she got to the other side. She was surprised to realize how much smaller it was than her one-bedroom/one-bath apartment in St. Louis. It didn't even have a proper kitchen—just a sink and a microwave with one small countertop and a couple of cabinets—and the bathroom wasn't much bigger than a walk-in closet. Even so, the cabin felt so much more spacious than her place somehow. She told herself it was because of the sparse furnishings—since she was a bit of a maximalist herself—and because of the wide-open spaces beyond the windows. But it was more than that. She'd always been a little claustrophobic in her apartment. Here, she felt surprisingly…uncramped.

But still restless. She paced back over to the window she had left and looked at the big house again. Silas and Miss Sylvie were gone, and the landscape surrounding the ranch was empty. The literature she'd read about Whispering Winds indicated the fun group activities were in a more resort-like area of the ranch, where her fellow shuttle-riders must have gone. These cabins by the house must be for the people who were here for the one-on-one stuff, like Mia. The only sound now was the wind, whispering through the trees in a way that made clear things hadn't changed much in Serenity Valley since the original builders of the ranch had named it.

It was a far cry from the sounds of her own neighborhood. Her apartment was just around the corner from the shops and restaurants of Euclid Avenue, and on a clear night, even with the windows closed, she could hear the thump of live music and the shouts of people greeting one another. Every Thursday, the trash collectors backed into the alley below her third-floor window to raise and pound the dumpster to collect its contents, and nary a weekend went by without the sound of at least one siren. It was a nice neighborhood. But it was a busy neighborhood. And not always a particularly quiet one.

She inhaled a deep breath of Wyoming air. No ripe dumpster. No stale beer. No bus exhaust. Only the mixed aromas of fresh air, warm sunshine and yellow flowers where blue butterflies danced. It was just so peaceful here. So calm. So quiet. So beautiful.

Mia had never felt more out of place in her life.

When Silas saw Mia enter the big room of the big house for the welcome reception, his first thought was that he may have been a bit hasty in judging her so harshly for bringing a dress. Not that anyone else in the room was wearing a dress—in fact, as was usual for these gatherings, the denim industry must have seen a real boom in sales when the current crop of dudes went out to buy stuff for their visits—but that only made her stand out even more. Because moving amid a crowd that was clad in varying shades of indigo and accented by miscellaneous leather accoutrements, she was a bright spot of—of all things—pink. But it wasn't a brash *Look-at-me-I'm-pink!* kind of pink. It was a soft, barely-there pink. The kind of color a person wore when they *didn't* want anyone to look at them.

Unfortunately for Mia, though, she had the kind of looks that would always make her stand out, no matter where she was. Even if she had pulled her silvery hair back into a stubby ponytail and wasn't wearing any kind of makeup that Silas could see. Between that and the nearly colorless dress, she seemed to be doing her best to be invisible.

In fact, considering the way she was picking her way through the other ranch guests, he was pretty sure she thought she *was* invisible. She didn't look at or say a word to anyone she edged around, and she moved through them with the finesse of someone who had been maneuvering invisibly for a long time. Hell, she didn't even seem to notice the room at all. She just glided along until she got to the bar, where she deftly and silently picked up a glass of ice water, then eased into the farthest corner she could find and turned her back to the wall. Silas wasn't the only one who noticed her intent to avoid mingling, though. Before Mia could even lift her glass to her lips, Miss Sylvie latched onto her like a hawk on a mouse.

Silas smiled in spite of Mia's obvious discomfort at being singled out. It wouldn't last. Miss Sylvie could make the most uptight person on the planet melt like butter in a matter of minutes. Sure enough, as Miss Sylvie went into chat mode, Mia began to relax. A little. She sipped her water nervously, but she peeled herself off the wall enough to at least look like she was going to give it her best effort to have as good a time as everyone else. She even smiled about something Miss Sylvie said. Until she glanced Silas's way and saw him. Then the smile fell and the discomfort surged right back up again.

For all of a second. Then she smiled bright as a Sunday morning and lifted a hand in cheerful greeting, as if she were genuinely delighted to see him. Except there was nothing in her sudden perkiness that seemed genuine at all. Save the perkiness itself, he meant, even if it was obviously manufactured. Silas hated perkiness. Bad enough when it came naturally to someone, but to deliberately conjure it up out of nowhere? That was just irritating.

Even though he'd promised Miss Sylvie he'd be Mia's constant companion while she was at Whispering Winds, he'd had to skip dinner tonight to check on a calf that had been born earlier this month with a messed-up flexor tendon he'd had to splint. The splint was off now, but the little guy—Silas had named him Tiny Tim because in addition to the bad leg, he was kinda runty—was still struggling, and his mother hadn't been interested in him since he was born. So Silas had become his de facto mom. He didn't mind, even if it meant missing his favorite entrée from time to time. Like tonight's chuckwagon casserole, loaded with beef and bacon and black beans and green chilis and cheese and... Well, suffice it to say it stuck in a person's mind. And also to a person's ribs.

When Miss Sylvie realized she'd lost Mia's undivided attention, she turned to see where it had gone. Automatically, Silas lifted his hand to tip his hat, then remembered he wasn't wearing it, because he'd hung it on a peg by the door before he'd come into the big house proper. He knew a lot of guys thought it was okay to keep their hat on when they were indoors, as long as they were at a casual function like this one, but not Silas. Although he'd never had the benefit of a father's guidance growing up—his dad had taken off for parts unknown before Silas was even born—Miss Sylvie's late husband, Rye, had stepped in to make sure he at least had a father figure in his life while he was growing up. And Rye had been old school. He'd always told Silas a real cowboy didn't just remove his hat as a sign of respect for things like the national anthem or when the flag was passing by, or only for solemn occasions like funerals and church. A real cowboy was considerate and polite at all times, and removing his hat was a way to show that.

Not that all of the polite stuff had stuck with Silas—he'd learned over time that things like courtesy and respect didn't have to be given unless they were earned—but as a kid, he'd toed the line Rye had drawn well enough that some of it had become habit anyway. Case in point: Hat on peg.

"Silas!" Miss Sylvie called when she saw him. "Come on over here!"

Silas started to make his way in her direction before she even finished speaking, so well did he know what she was going to tell him. What he didn't know was why he glanced down as he went, to make sure his pale green Western-style shirt was tucked into the fresh pair of jeans he'd tugged on before coming and double-checking to make sure there were no remnants of the barn stuck to the boots he'd cleaned reasonably well. Nor did he know why he drove a hand through his dark hair to tame it, or, hell, why he'd bothered to shave earlier that afternoon or—

Well, anyway, he did know that Miss Sylvie was going to call him over, and he knew why. She was going to take him to task for making Mia eat dinner alone, and she was going to emphatically repeat that he better make sure he stuck to Mia like glue from here on out.

She smiled as he drew near, though, and he knew what else she was thinking about. She was noticing he'd cleaned himself up since meeting Mia. But unlike him, she seemed to know why he'd done it.

"Well, look at you," she said in that melt-butter tone she had doubtless been using with Mia. "Don't you look nice tonight?"

"You say that like I don't look nice on other nights," Silas told her.

Her smiled grew wider. "That's because you're usually as dusty as the rest of this place." Before he could take exception to that—not that he would take exception, because she was right—she went on. "You're falling down on the job, son. Mia tells me she had to eat supper by herself tonight."

"I had to check on one of the new calves," he told her. "That's my regular job, after all," he couldn't help adding, to remind her that having dinner with pretty visitors wasn't in his usual job description. Even if, you know, having dinner with a pretty visitor once in a while might not be that bad. As long that visitor wasn't as angry as Mia, he meant.

Before Miss Sylvie could take him to further task, he looked at Mia. "Sorry about missing supper," he told her. And to appease Miss Sylvie, he tried to actually sound sorry, even though sincere apologies weren't exactly part of his usual store of responses to life. "I hope you enjoyed it, anyway. Miss Abby's chuckwagon casserole is one of my favorites."

Mia roused that almost-convincing, perkily-manufactured smile again. But all she said was, "It was fine." She said it brightly, but she still said *fine*.

Fine, Silas echoed to himself. Somehow, he kept himself from curling his lip in contempt. How could someone think chuckwagon casserole was just *fine*? It was nirvana. Next she'd be telling him she didn't like the dessert, either, and that had been Texas sheet cake. He wasn't even going to ask. Best not to see that darkness in her soul.

"And what's Mia doing standing all alone in the corner like this?" Miss Sylvie further demanded.

"Miss Sylvie, it's fine," Mia told her. Perkily. Damn her.

"It is not fine," Miss Sylvie countered. "You're our guest. And Silas made me a promise."

"Mia just walked in," he pointed out. "I haven't had a chance to talk to her."

"Did you see her when she walked through the door?" Miss Sylvie asked him.

Well, hell, how could he have missed her when she walked through the door? She was all soft and pretty and…pink. All he said to Miss Sylvie, though, was, "Yes, ma'am."

"Then you should be the one standing here talking to her, not me."

Case made, she spun around and disappeared into the crowd. Leaving him and Mia alone. Not that they were alone. There was a room full of people behind them. More than fifty for this session, Miss Sylvie had told him earlier. Though a good chunk of those would be leaving tomorrow on the annual cattle drive, and most of the rest would be spending their time in their designated parts of the ranch where a half dozen other programs were going on. Somehow, though, in that moment, Silas felt like he and Mia were in a movie, during one of those scenes where everything suddenly went all fuzzy in the background while the two people in the foreground focused entirely on each other, as if nothing else in the world existed.

Well, hell. This was inconvenient. The last thing he needed was to be attracted to the woman he was supposed to be helping through a rough patch. The next two weeks were going to be tough enough for him to get through, what with him doing a job he didn't normally do in addition to his regular one. Even if probably he was better at the whole anger management thing than Beau was, anyway, since Beau didn't have an angry bone in his body, and Silas's bones—and all his other parts, for that matter—were nothing but angry.

Nah, it was okay, he immediately amended. Just because he thought Mia was pretty, that didn't mean anything. He'd found a lot of women pretty since— Well, he'd found a lot of women pretty in the last twelve years. Hell, he'd even dated a few of them. Not that those dates had amounted to much beyond a few more dates before they started fizzling out. He wasn't going to be dating Mia Hawthorne. So there was no problem.

Especially since she seemed to be looking everywhere in the room right now except at Silas, until her gaze finally settled on the big antler chandelier hanging over the main room.

"Please tell me," she said as she lifted her hand in that direction, "that those are all fake."

Silas turned to look where she was pointing, then back at her. "Nope. Real antlers." Her mouth dropped open in what he would call dismay if she weren't playing at being so damned perky, and he knew what she was thinking. So he added, "They're not hunting trophies, if that's what you're worried about. They were all shed by their owners and found scattered around the range over the years before one of the old-timers turned them into that."

She looked back at Silas. "Shed by their owners?"

He nodded. "Cervids—that's what animals with antlers are called—shed those antlers from time to time."

"What, like they just fall off?"

"Yep."

"Onto the ground?"

"Yep."

"And then people make chandeliers out of them?"

"Among other things, yeah." He nodded toward her dress, whose front was closed from hem to neckline with small brown buttons. "Those buttons on your dress might even be made out of antlers," he told her.

She looked down, her hand automatically going to the top button and fiddling with it, first opening it, then buttoning it closed again. She did it enough times for him to figure it was probably a nervous gesture. She didn't even seem to notice she was doing it.

"You look nice, by the way," he told her for some reason. Making things even more inconvenient than they already were. And even more uncomfortable. For him, at least.

Mia dropped her hand back to her side, but not before unbuttoning that top button. Which he totally didn't notice. Nor did he notice how the skin beneath it was even creamier and rosier than the rest of her. Nor did he wonder if it was as soft and warm as it looked. Why would he wonder any of those things if he wasn't even noticing them?

She seemed surprised by the compliment but not offended. She even smiled again, and this time it didn't seem as forced or as bogus as the last few had been. Her voice was even lightly teasing when she said, "But I'm so inappropriately dressed for ranch life."

Yeah, yeah, yeah.

"Touché, Mia Hawthorne. Touché."

She looked oddly delighted that she'd one-upped him. Then she looked a little abashed. "I'm sorry," she backpedaled. "That wasn't a very nice thing to say."

She closed her eyes, inhaled a deep breath, let it go slowly, and opened them again, as if she were doing a reset, the way she had that afternoon in her cabin. And just as had happened earlier, she suddenly seemed to be a new person.

"Thank you," she said simply.

He was about to tell her she didn't need to apologize for what she'd said, that he'd had it coming, but before he had the chance, she added, "You look pretty nice yourself."

It had been a long time since Silas had received a compliment from a pretty woman. Hell, he honestly couldn't remember the last time. Coming from Mia, the praise threw him for even more of a loop. He was about to say something about how he could clean up okay when he needed to, but that might make her—or worse, him—wonder why he'd needed to clean up for tonight in the first place, and there was no reason to go into all that. Sure, he never came to the ranch's opening receptions in the gritty clothes he'd had on all day. But he didn't normally shave or shower before one of these things, either. Tonight, he'd done both.

All he said in response, though, was to echo Mia's

simple thanks. After that, neither seemed to have any idea what to say. Mostly, Mia sipped her water, and Silas wished he'd had the foresight to grab his own drink so he'd have something to do with his hands, too.

Thankfully, after making a quick sweep of the room with her gaze, she asked, "How many of these people are here for the anger management thing?"

Grateful to be back on course talking about something of significance, Silas looked at the group, too. He wondered how she could think any of them were angry. There wasn't a negative vibe in the room, and it was obvious everyone was here because they were planning on having a good time. Sure, a handful had come for some kind of program, but even those were here by choice, looking forward to improving something in their lives that wasn't especially good at the moment. Only the angry people came to Whispering Winds because they'd been job- or court-ordered to be here.

He looked back at Mia. "Ninety-nine percent of these folks are attending something else. You're the only angry one we have this time."

Her gaze met his, and her brows arrowed down. "Oh." Then her expression cleared with the quickness—and contrivance—that it had before. "But I'm not angry. It was all a—"

"Misunderstanding," Silas chorused with her. "So you've said. A lot. Maybe if you say it a few more times, you'll start believing yourself."

For a bare second, her eyes flashed hotly and her whole body went stiff. Then, just as quickly, she made herself relax again. Damn. She must have been doing the catch-and-release thing with her anger for most of her life to be this good at it.

For the first time, Silas wondered what exactly the source of her anger was. Miss Sylvie hadn't told him much about her *misunderstanding* at work. Only that she'd had an incident with one of her coworkers that had ended up with her putting hands on the guy, and that was the kind of thing that got people sent to HR. Miss Sylvie hadn't given him any details about what, exactly, had led up to that, and Silas hadn't asked. He'd figured it didn't matter. He still figured that. Mia wasn't exactly the size of a sequoia. How much damage could she do to someone else, especially a guy? Anger was anger. The angry people he'd known had all been a lot alike and a lot like him. But although he could see for himself that Mia was definitely an angry person, she also seemed capable of keeping it under control. Just what had happened that one day that had made her go off so badly?

He was torn between asking Miss Sylvie if he could read the report HR had sent over before Mia's arrival—a totally acceptable thing for him to do—and waiting to hear about it from Mia herself. He knew there would come a time when the two of them talked about whatever the incident was in detail, so that he could start helping her figure out the whys and hows of what had caused her reaction and the what-to-do-next-times for when it happened again. Since Silas also knew that it would almost certainly happen again. Anger wasn't something that just went away. It was always lurking, waiting for a chance to strike again. He knew that from experience. Another thing that made him suited to do Beau's job this week.

He and Mia would also work toward pinpointing just

where and when her anger issues started—since, often-times, the outbursts that sent people into anger manage-ment had nothing to do with the incidents that had sent them—so she could start working on either letting them go or putting them in a compartment where they wouldn't cause trouble. He had plenty of experience with that, too.

Mia needed help. The same kind he'd needed in his own life a decade ago. He just hoped two weeks was enough for her to learn to cope with her own anger. And he hoped she ended up in a better place with hers than he was with his. 'Cause twelve years after his own anger *incident*, there were still days when Silas wasn't sure he'd make it through to nightfall without coming apart at the seams.

Her voice was still as phonily chipper as ever when she asked, "So, what other something elses does Whis-pering Winds offer in addition to the, um…"

"The misunderstanding program?" Silas finished helpfully. Mostly because he wanted to see that flash of anger again. He knew Miss Sylvie had told Mia ear-lier that they wouldn't officially start with managing her anger 'til tomorrow, but since Mia seemed to have a lot more to unpack than most, he figured there was no time like the present.

Instead of getting angry again, though, Mia only seemed to sweeten more. "Yes. That."

Ah, well. Tomorrow was as good a day as any, he sup-posed, to get her dander up.

"Our biggest draw for dudes is our annual cattle drive," he said for starters. "That was the first thing Miss Sylvie came up with when she decided to open up the ranch to visitors. That's been going on since I was little. And there's a resort area on the other side of the property that's mostly just a kind of big B and B where people stay and find their own things to do. Hiking, riding, exploring, that kind of thing. That started not long after the cattle drive. But in the last ten or fifteen years, Miss Sylvie has opened the place up for even more stuff to bring in a little extra income."

He told Mia more about the history of Whispering Winds. How it had started off as a hardscrabble cattle ranch of a few hundred acres in the early 1800s, then grew into a massive commercial operation, then dwindled down to its current five thousand acres. And how, by the time Miss Sylvie and her husband Rye took over, the place was on its last legs and in danger of going into foreclosure.

"She knew they were going to have to take drastic measures if they wanted to keep the place from going under," Silas said, winding up. "So, under her guidance, they got the whole dude side going. And when that started working well, she got more creative and started adding some other programs that were geared more toward… What's the word she uses all the time? *Wellness*. That's what she calls it. When that started being a big thing, she hired some folks to help her put some wellness programs into place here. Those have really taken off, too."

"Wow," Mia said. Silas was afraid he might have been boring her, but her fascination with the subject matter was obviously genuine. "Miss Sylvie must be some kind of businesswoman."

"She is that," he said. "She did what she had to do to

keep her family legacy intact, even if it did cause some rifts here and there."

"What kind of rifts?"

Silas really should have stopped talking five seconds earlier. Something about Mia, though, just made him want to keep talking. That was probably why he kept it up now, even knowing he shouldn't. "Some of the old-timers who've been around for a while didn't think she should open the place to outsiders. They still think it was a bad idea, even though the success speaks for itself. One of her grandsons, too, is unhappy about what he calls all the 'touchy-feely stuff' and wants to go back to Whispering Winds being solely a working cattle ranch like the old days."

"Is that possible?"

Silas shrugged again. "Yeah, it is now that Miss Sylvie's managed the financial recovery of the place. It'll never be twenty-five thousand acres again, but it could still turn a nice profit for her, even at the size it is now, if she wanted to go back to strictly raising cattle. Truth be told, I wouldn't mind going back to that myself. But it's not my choice to make."

"Then why doesn't Miss Sylvie go back to that?"

"I think it's probably because she's seen now how much *a lot* of people have benefited from her sharing the place with them."

He hoped Mia would be one of those people by the time she left, but the jury was still out on that this early in her stay. Looking at her now, though, her attention fixed on their conversation, her posture a bit more relaxed than it had been, he might have thought she was here for the resort side of things. At the moment, she didn't seem tense or stressed out or angry at all.

"What kind of other programs besides the, ah, misunderstanding one does Whispering Winds offer?"

Even that mention of the fact that she was here for an "ah, misunderstanding program" didn't ruffle her up.

"Miss Sylvie has arrangements in place with corporate America for a few things and with nonprofits and hospitals for a few things more."

"Nonprofits and hospitals?" Mia asked, surprised. "Why nonprofits and hospitals?"

"There's a program for grief management, for instance, that's kind of like the one you're in. People who are having trouble moving on after the death of a loved one come here to clear their heads and reassess their new reality. There's another program to help people manage their depression and anxiety. Things like that. And we have a summer camp for kids who are neurodivergent and another one for kids who are going through cancer treatment. A couple other summer programs for adults who—" He stopped when he saw her expression change again. But not to angry. This time, she looked sad. "What?" he asked.

She shook her head. "Kids with cancer. That's heartbreaking."

"It can be," he conceded, "if you don't look at the big picture. But when you see those kids and how hard they're fighting and how much joy they still manage to have when they're here, you wouldn't say that. It's not heartbreaking. It's amazing. Those kids can teach us all a lesson."

She still looked sad. But she looked thoughtful, too.

She gazed beyond him at the crowd of people still mill-ing about. He wondered if she was looking around for the kids in question, but it was too early yet for any of them to be here, the children's camps didn't start until July. Even so, there was still a handful of little rugrats running around who had come with their families to spend time on the resort side of the ranch for vacation. Silas turned around when he realized Mia's gaze had lit somewhere and stayed there, and he saw that she had found some of those very kids, a little girl and boy with their parents.

They were too far away to be heard, but the kids were vying for their parents' attention, each trying to tell a story of some kind that seemed Very Important. The parents had stooped down to be at their children's level and were listening intently, trying to guide them both in how to take turns, smiling when each of them seemed unable to manage, then laughing lightly at something one of them said. They listened some more, spoke gently some more, then each parent hoisted up a child, wrapped them affectionately in their arms, and wandered away. Silas turned back around to look at Mia and was startled to see her eyes filled with tears. To the point where one escaped, tumbling down her cheek before she hastily lifted a hand to swipe it away.

Before he could say anything, she mumbled something about needing to get another glass of water and bolted toward the bar. But she only left her nearly untouched glass there and kept going, threading her way through the crowd in that *Pardon me, I'm invisible* way of hers again, until she disappeared through the alcove that led to the restrooms.

Silas watched her go, wondering what had brought

that on. Well, obviously something about watching the family behind him had done it, but he couldn't imagine what. There had been nothing sad in the scene at all. Just a typical family doing typical family things.

Of course, not everyone had a typical family, he reminded himself. Including him. But he *had* had a family—an amazing one—the whole time he was growing up. Everyone at Whispering Winds had been Silas's family when he was a kid. He'd followed his mom around to help her out with her housekeeping chores as soon as he was old enough, doing everything from folding pillowcases to drying silverware. When he was a little older, the cowboys had taken him under their wings and taught him how to ride and rope and take care of the horses and cattle. After his mother's death when he was ten, Miss Sylvie and Rye had become second parents to him. All in all, Silas had had a pretty happy childhood. One with strong family ties. Happier than most, probably, in spite of the early loss of his mother, because he'd grown up surrounded by animals and natural beauty and the quiet and calm that came with both. Not to mention the love and support of everyone on the ranch.

He wondered what Mia's childhood had been like. Not typical, he was guessing, judging by the way she'd just reacted to what shouldn't have even been a noticeable exchange between two parents and their kids. He'd been working under the assumption that her anger was the result of something that had happened to her as an adult, the same way his had been. But maybe it went further back than that. Anger as deep-seated as hers obviously was didn't just come out of nowhere. And it didn't just pop up because someone said something obnoxious at work one day. Anger like hers took a long time to grow.

Just what's your story, Mia Hawthorne? he wondered. *And is two weeks gonna be long enough for you to deal with it?*

Chapter Three

Mia had showered and donned striped pajama pants and a Lewis and Clark Community College T-shirt and was about to open the novel she'd lifted from the couple dozen that were stacked behind the front desk at the big house during the reception—which Miss Sylvie had totally encouraged her to do—when there was a knock at her cabin door. She made her way across the room but hesitated before opening it, not sure what to do. At home, she would have looked through the peephole, but there wasn't one here. And she hadn't closed the front windows, so they were wide open for any miscreant to kick in the screen and climb through. That was something she would have never done at home, even living on the third floor of her building, with or without allergies. But the night was so pleasant and cool and quiet, she hadn't been able to resist.

She was about to berate herself further when a familiar voice called through those windows, "Hey, it's Silas. Sorry to be stopping by so late. I brought you something I forgot to give you at the reception tonight. Something you're gonna need tomorrow morning."

After which Mia did berate herself because, duh, she wasn't at home in a big city where women living alone had to watch their backs every second of the day. She was in one of the calmest, quietest, loveliest—and most likely one of the safest—places on the planet. The only predators around here were the four-legged or sharp-taloned ones. And it wasn't late. It was barely nine o'clock. In St. Louis, on Euclid Avenue, things were just gearing up. Here on the range, though, things had already settled down.

She picked up the door key from the nightstand where she'd left it—well, she wasn't quite that confident about her safety, at least not yet—and unlocked and opened the front door. Silas stood on the other side, somehow look-ing even more handsome now than he had at the recep-tion. And he'd been damned handsome at the reception, his pale green eyes even more penetrating thanks to the way they matched his shirt, his black hair combed back from a face that would have been downright beautiful in a less coarse environment. In the pale yellow light of the cabin that spilled out onto the porch from behind her, his features looked even more defined now, his brows slashes of dark silk, his jawline as rugged as the moun-tains silhouetted against the night sky, his cheekbones sharp enough to slice prime rib. His hat was pushed back enough that the wind had blown a lock of his hair down over his forehead, and it was all Mia could do not to lift a hand and smooth it back into place.

Which she very much wanted to do in that moment. Not just to see if his hair was as silky as it looked, but to trace her fingers over his face, too, to see if it was as buckskin soft as it looked to be. Then over his shoulders to see if they were as solid rock as they seemed. Then over his chest and ribs and torso, then lower still, to his waist and hips and—

"Hi," she said before her thoughts could get away from her.

He'd been less crotchety at the reception tonight than he'd been earlier in the day. At times, he'd *almost* been nice. Okay, maybe that was a bit of a stretch, but he *had* smiled a couple of times. Even if those smiles had never quite reached his eyes, it had been impossible for her not to notice how much more appealing he was when he did smile.

"What's up?" she asked when he didn't seem inclined to say more.

Too late, she realized she'd forgotten to breathe while she was remembering his earlier smiles and taking inventory of his current, um, attributes, and now her voice was sounding rough and raspy as a result. Yeah, that was why she sounded the way she did. Because she forgot to breathe. Not because she'd been thinking about—

Um, never mind.

Even so, she was helpless not to drop her gaze to his midsection. Thankfully, he was holding something at waist level that made it seem like that was what had drawn her attention and not his—

Um, never mind again.

What he was holding was a short stack of clothing topped by a pair of boots over which was draped a cowboy hat not much different from his own. Except that it was smaller. As were the boots. He extended all of them toward her.

"These are gonna be a lot better for what you'll be doing for the next coupla weeks," he told her. "Cody, one of the cowgirls here, is about your size, but she said to make sure you know these are only loaners." He grinned. "So, I guess don't go messing 'em up any more than she would. Which actually gives you a lot of leeway, 'cause Cody isn't exactly what you would call tidy."

Automatically, Mia took the proffered clothing. Two pairs of jeans, some T-shirts, a sweatshirt, and a couple of button-ups were under the hat and boots. At the bottom was a denim jacket that had definitely seen better days.

"You'll probably be needing that in the mornings," Silas told her when she lifted the last article of clothing to reveal it. "Even in summer, it can get down in the forties up here sometimes. Evenings can be pretty chilly, too."

She'd actually already noticed that and wished she'd had the foresight to throw in a sweatshirt with the couple of sweaters she'd added after Patsy in HR had told her to be sure and include some warm clothes. As much as Mia loved the cashmere she'd picked up at Macy's when they had those amazing Black Friday prices, she didn't want to sleep in it. Cody's borrowed clothes were going to come in handy even before tomorrow morning.

A quick look told her they were indeed her size. Another look told her there were socks in the boots that were thick enough to keep her feet from getting raw. Everything reeked of Arm & Hammer washing powder and borax, but nothing was particularly soft or cozy. They were working clothes, plain and simple. But she was grateful for them. After seeing every single person at the reception tonight dressed entirely differently from her, she'd had to concede that Silas had been right in assessing her wardrobe as Not The Thing for ranch life.

"Thank you," she said as she accepted them. "And please tell Cody I said thank you, too."

"Will do," he promised.

Transfer complete, Mia told herself to say good-night and close the door and get back to doing what she had planned to do tonight—be alone. Like she was every night. Like she didn't mind being every night, she hastened to remind herself. Really. She liked being alone. And after what had happened at the reception tonight, in full view of Silas and everyone else, she was craving solitude even more. The last thing she wanted to do was prolong her time with someone who had witnessed that embarrassing display of tears.

And just what had that embarrassing display of tears been about anyway? she asked herself for the millionth time since it happened. Mia never cried. Because she was never unhappy. She couldn't remember a single time as an adult when she'd been moved to tears she'd had to swipe away. But it had been all she could do tonight to get to the restroom before she'd fallen apart. Truly. She'd burst into tears once she was safe inside a stall, and she hadn't been able to stop crying for a good five minutes. Then she'd had to sit another ten after she finally got herself under control, because she didn't want Silas to know how badly she'd been affected by...

By what? A couple of people and their kids? Talking? Why would that hit Mia so hard that she lost control of her feelings? Why would that make her unhappy? Who cared that a family was standing around talking? Total strangers, at that? It didn't make any sense.

Exhaustion, she told herself. Just as she'd told herself at the reception. It had been a long week. A long month.

A long year. She hadn't been sleeping well all week. All month. All year. Exhaustion could make a person crazy. All the more reason why she should tell Silas good-night, close the door, and go to bed.

For some reason, though, Mia didn't want to say good-night and close the door. For some reason, tonight, she didn't want to be alone. Before she could stop herself, she asked, "Do you want to come in for…"

For what? she added to herself. It wasn't like she could play hostess in a place where she was a guest. Especially when she didn't have anything to offer in the way of sustenance or libations save a few snacks. "I mean… I brought a couple of bottles of green tea back with me and stuck them in the fridge. If you'd like to come in for one, I'm happy to share."

Right. Bottled green tea. Silas Crockett, cranky, tumbleweed-cleaning Peacemaker guy, totally seemed like the type to drink bottled green tea. And what had possessed her to extend the invitation in the first place? Her brain was becoming as empty as the wide-open spaces surrounding the ranch.

Exhaustion, she told herself again. Because what else could it be?

Not surprisingly, he looked very much like he wanted to decline the invitation. Then, very surprisingly, he lifted his shoulders, let them drop, and said, "Sure. Hey, I promised Miss Sylvie I'd look after you." As soon as he uttered the words, he sounded like he really wished he'd declined the invitation.

He'd look after her, Mia echoed to herself. As if she were some three-year-old who was likely to get into trouble or hurt herself if someone didn't keep an eye on her.

Wasn't that just the thing a woman wanted to hear from the lips of a handsome cowboy?

He added, "And I can fill you in on what to expect over the next couple of weeks. With the anger—I mean misunderstanding—program and all."

Oooh, that was the second thing a woman most wanted to hear from the lips of a handsome cowboy—the specifics of an upcoming agenda. She told herself it didn't matter. Yes, Silas was a handsome cowboy, but she hadn't come to Whispering Winds to appreciate handsome cowboys. She was here because she needed to keep her job. Which was fine. Really. It was. At least she wouldn't be alone. Tonight, she meant. She'd be alone the rest of the nights that she was here. But that was okay! She liked being alone. She did.

She pulled the door open wider and Silas strode inside. He for sure had the swagger of a cowboy, she couldn't help noticing. Not that she had a lot of experience with cowboys—or, you know, any experience with cowboys—but they did seem to have a swagger about them, at least in movies and on TV. She wondered if it was due to horse riding and boot wearing, then remembered the ones she'd seen in movies and on TV weren't real cowboys but were only actors affecting a swagger. So, if Silas had one, maybe it was just a part of who he was.

She went to the minifridge and pulled out the promised tea, but he shook his head. "Water's fine."

She replaced the tea and withdrew two waters instead, since she didn't need the caffeine this late at night anyway, what with all the exhaustion and lack of sleep. She did at least find a couple of glasses in one of the kitchenette cabinets to pour them into before crossing to give

Silas his. Hey, look at her, hostessing. She found him gazing at the book she'd brought back with her to read, his hat sitting on the table beside it, his dark hair curling around his ears in a way that made her want to reach out again to touch it. When he glanced up from the book, though, she just handed him his glass.

"You'll like that," he said, dipping his head toward the book. "Hank Stallard is my favorite writer."

Even when he was praising something, Silas Crockett sounded annoyed. How was that possible? Mia wondered.

"I've never read anything by him," she said. "I've never even heard of him," she further confessed, even though she was a fairly big reader and read across all genres. "But Miss Sylvie said you guys have all of his books because they're so popular with everybody at Whispering Winds."

"Nobody brings the West to life the way he does. That's a fact. It's a good choice for while you're here."

Again, he sounded kind of irritable when he said it, offering the praise for the book grudgingly, as if he couldn't believe he'd actually enjoyed something at some point. On the other hand, he was kind of being nice at the moment. Or at least making polite conversation, even if he himself wasn't what anyone would call *polite*. She supposed Miss Sylvie was responsible for that, after calling him out at the reception and making him promise to behave. But even now, when she wasn't around, he was being what Mia supposed passed for pleasant where he was concerned. Even if he didn't seem like he wanted to be particularly pleasant.

As if he realized then that he was bordering on agreeable, he suddenly sobered and launched into what the two of them would be covering over the next couple of weeks. Mia gestured toward the sofa on the other side of the room before he got too far along, and they retreated to it. Instead of sitting there, though, Silas folded himself into the chair beside it, as if he wanted to illustrate both physically and mentally that he was keeping his distance from her. So, Mia perched on the edge of the sofa furthest from him. Probably best if she kept her distance, too.

"So, like Miss Sylvie said," he continued, "I'm not the one who usually does this sort of thing. That's Beau's forte. But I've done it a few times in the past when he couldn't and have helped more than one person get to the root of the problem and find a better way to cope with things."

Even talking about how he'd helped people out, Silas sounded irritable. As if helping people put him far outside his own comfort zone. Mia would have thought a person would be proud of themself for doing what he was doing, especially when he was stepping up to do it to help Miss Sylvie out, too. But *noooo*. To Silas Crockett, helping people was some onerous task he had to suffer through. And since, as Miss Sylvie had told Mia, what she was completing here wasn't officially an anger management program, she supposed he didn't have to be a certified social worker or counselor, anyway.

Actually, she was kind of heartened by the fact that he *wasn't* a mental health professional. She'd tried the mental health professional route once, and it hadn't gone well. She'd been having some problems her sophomore year in college, mostly with concentrating and staying focused, and her grades had started slipping. One of her professors had suggested she see the school counselor.

But it hadn't taken long for the counselor to start wanting to talk about Mia's family life, which her problems at school hadn't had anything to do with. By then she'd been living away from home for more than a year and she hadn't spoken a word to anyone in her family. Nor they to her. Her family wasn't a part of her life at all at that point, and they would never be again. But the counselor had kept poking and prodding and wanting to dig deeper into Mia's past, so Mia had stopped seeing her.

Since Silas wasn't a mental health professional, he seemed a lot less likely to want to go digging into her psyche. He didn't seem like the kind of person who would want to do that even if she wasn't in a program for figuring things out. He seemed a lot like her, when she got right down to it. The *live and let live and leave me the hell alone* type. Honestly, she still wasn't even sure what she was supposed to get out of her time at Whispering Winds, anyway, and she told him exactly that before they went any further.

"I mean, what happened that day at work was just a misunderstanding," she said again, in case he'd forgotten that part. "I don't know why I have to be here for two weeks to figure out why what happened happened. There's nothing *to* figure out. I'm not angry. I'm never angry. It happened because I had a bad day. Everybody has a bad day sometimes. I'll have more bad days in the future, I'm sure. Just like everybody else. So why do I have to be here? What am I supposed to get out of this? *It was just a misunderstanding,*" she repeated more emphatically.

She told herself she did *not* sound angry when she uttered that last sentence a little more forcefully than was necessary. She wasn't angry. She wasn't. She was just frustrated because her life—her predictable, orderly, quiet life—had been completely disrupted for no good reason, and the next two weeks were going to be unpredictable and disorderly and unquiet, and she hated hated *hated* not knowing or being able to control what was coming next, and—

Anyway, she wasn't angry. Just frustrated.

Silas looked at her for a moment in silence, as if he were weighing his words carefully. "What you're supposed to get out of the next two weeks is up to you," he finally said. "But know this from the start. The reason you're here isn't because of a misunderstanding. And it's not because you had a bad day. It's because you assaulted someone, Mia."

"I did not assault any—"

"You laid hands on one of your coworkers," he interjected before she could finish.

Oh, please. Like Perpetual Salesman of the Month Jeff Oberstrom hadn't laid hands on her first? Hundreds of times? And also on every other woman who worked at Carrigan Auto? If laying hands on people could land you in an anger—she meant *misunderstanding*—management program, Jeff should be sitting here, not Mia. And for a lot longer than two weeks. But evidently it was only putting your hands on someone in anger, not to sexually harass them, that sent the workers of Carrigan Auto into programs to "correct" their behavior.

Not that Mia had put hands on Jeff in anger. She didn't get angry. Ever. It had just been a misunderstanding.

All she said to Silas, though, was, "He's twice my size. No way could I have done him any harm."

"That's not the point. The point is you lost control and you tried to hurt someone."

"I did not try to hurt him. I did not assault him. I just—"

"You lost control," he interrupted her.

The interruption was fine, since Mia had no idea how to finish what she'd started to say anyway. She hadn't consciously wanted to hurt Jeff. And she hadn't actually hurt him. That much she knew was true. She just hadn't really thought about what she *had* wanted to do to Jeff when she'd gone after him the way she had. She'd reacted without thinking. Okay, fine—she had lost control. She wished she could deny that, but she knew she couldn't. After three decades of keeping it together—most of those years spent in environments that were in no way conducive to keeping herself in check, but, by God, she'd done it—Mia had finally lost her grip on her emotions. And even though it had only been for a matter of minutes, she had lashed out in a way that was unforgivable, even if Jeff was a jerk who'd had it coming.

So maybe for that reason—her loss of control over her emotions—if for no other, she should make an effort to get something out of the next two weeks here at the ranch. She should focus on regaining her discipline and regulating her emotions. On making sure she didn't let the irrational side of her brain overtake the rational. On thinking only about rainbows and unicorns and stardust and ignoring everything else. Be happy. All…the…time. And never, ever, be angry. Never, ever, be anything else. She would spend her time here at Whispering Winds getting a handle on her bad emotions, and she would cram them back down inside herself as deep as she could. Then she would slam the door shut on them, and seal it tight. With a blowtorch. The way she had always done before.

Yeah, that's the ticket.

Wow, she felt better already, having made that decision. She nodded once, fiercely, at Silas. "You're right," she said. "I did lose control. And no matter what that scumbag Jeff—" *Mia, be nice. Be happy.* "I mean...no matter what my coworker Jeff said or did, I shouldn't have...gone after him the way I did. While I'm here at Whispering Winds, I'll work on regaining control. Of my emotions, my thoughts, and myself."

While she felt energized by her declaration, Silas seemed to find it aggravating. "It's not about controlling any of those things," he told her. "Anger is a normal emotion, and it's okay to feel it when something anger-worthy happens. What you need to work on is acknowledging it, working through it, and managing it."

"But I'm not angry," she told him. "I'm just...at loose ends. A little. I'm not in control of my feelings right now. And I need to make sure I fix that. Get back in control again and stay there."

She *wasn't* angry. Her family had been angry enough for the whole world. What had happened at work with Jeff had been because of... Well. Something else. Because Mia didn't get angry. She had left the anger behind in the house where she grew up. No way was she going to bring any of that with her after seeing what it did to her parents and brothers.

Looking at Silas, she could tell he didn't believe her. He really did think she was angry. And that was okay! A lot of people misunderstood others' emotions. He could think whatever he wanted. She'd prove to him over the next two weeks that she wasn't an angry person. That she was just a person who needed to get a better handle on things. And who knew? Maybe getting away from home for a little while and being in an entirely new environment, maybe giving up her day-to-day routine, would help Mia do that. Teach her how to think a little differently. Retrain her brain. But still come out on the other side a calmer, cooler, more controlled person. Maybe HR had been right about that part, at least.

"Okay," Silas said, neither affirming nor denying her assurance that she wasn't angry. "Then I guess we'll just work on things day by day. Start off tomorrow morning on day one the way we usually do for the, um, misunderstanding program for people who aren't angry and see what happens next. I'll meet you at the big house for breakfast at eight and we can go from there."

"Fine," Mia said. "That will be fine."

"Fine," he parroted in a way that sounded even less fine than it had when she'd said it. "Guess we'll have to wait and see about that, too."

Silas arrived at the big house for breakfast before Mia did, even though he deliberately arrived fifteen minutes late, just so the two of them could start her day off with a little irritation for her breakfast appetizer. They'd agreed to meet on the front porch at eight o'clock sharp, and she'd assured him that she was the most punctual person on the planet and was never, ever, late for anything. But it was going on eight twenty now. He went inside long enough to check the main room and the dining room both, just to be sure, but Mia wasn't in either. So he went back out onto the porch and glanced across the way at the line of cabins, eyeing hers to see if there was any sign of movement inside. Nope. Looked like he was going to be the one waiting instead of her.

Well, hell. That was irritating.

The reason he'd deliberately come late was that he'd wanted to see if he could get a rise out of her by making her be the one to wait. The part he hadn't told Mia about when he was telling her what to expect over the next couple of weeks was that he was going to do his best to rile her up whenever he could. He couldn't help her deal with her anger if they couldn't even bring it to the fore for a bit. And after hearing her say last night that what she really needed to work on while she was here was controlling her emotions—and not dealing with her anger—he was more determined to do that than ever. She didn't need to control her emotions. Feeling emotions was a good thing. She just needed to learn how to handle them and not let them control her. Emotions weren't bad things. People had them for a reason. Yeah, they could be inconvenient at times, and they could get out of hand. But pretending you were *fine* all the time wasn't healthy.

And it didn't solve anything anyway. Hell, there had been a time in Silas's life when he'd done the same thing Mia was doing now—making sure he stayed in control of his feelings, especially his anger, and pretending he was fine. All that had ultimately done was make him even angrier, until he'd hit rock bottom. Only after that did he finally learn how to cope.

Well, mostly cope. There were still times when he—

Anyway. Maybe he wasn't the usual anger management cowboy on the ranch, but he hadn't been lying to Mia last night when he told her he had helped more than one person get to the root of the problem and find a better way to deal with things that went wrong. He just hadn't bothered to add that one of those people was himself. The biggest part of managing anger was getting to the root of its cause and acknowledging it, then identifying the things that provoked it. Only after a person did that could they start working through everything and get to a reasonably good place. Or, at least, a manageable place. For some people—like Silas—the origin and triggers were obvious. For others—like Mia—those things might be a little more mysterious. The sooner he could help her figure out what was making her so angry and causing her to react to it so badly, the sooner he could start helping her deal with it.

First thing they needed to do was figure out what had made her go after her coworker on that particular day. Everyone had to work with people they didn't like. Usually, folks just ignored anyone who rubbed them the wrong way or did their best to steer clear of them. Silas couldn't see Mia being the type to go looking for trouble. On the contrary, judging by her invisibility cloak at the reception last night, she went out of her way to avoid it. Miss Sylvie had told him Mia had worked with the guy she'd gone after for more than five years, so it wasn't like one of them was a new hire who was suddenly in a position with an antagonist. Miss Sylvie had also told him that, according to the report, Mia was normally an exemplary employee who was the darling of the car dealership, loved by both her coworkers and their customers.

So, she'd been in her normal environment that day at work, surrounded by familiar people, going about her daily routine. Maybe the guy she went after was a jerk who said or did something he shouldn't have, but he'd probably been doing that for years while everyone else, including Mia, just rolled their eyes and ignored him. So what did he do or say that day that had made her snap so badly? Or, more to the point, what had happened with Mia that day to make her, for the first time, not be able to tolerate whatever the guy had done?

Silas wasn't trying to place blame. He just knew from experience that anger wasn't always the result of what other people said or did in the moment. It was the result of a person's reaction that might have nothing to do with that moment. If Mia was normally even-tempered and had worked with and endured this guy for as long as she had, then it was probably something in her, not her coworker, that had led to her uncharacteristic outburst that day.

So he'd thought maybe introducing some inconveniences into her day while she was here—every one of her days here, if that was what it took—might bring about another uncharacteristic outburst. And that might give him some insight into the things that bothered her the most. Being late for breakfast, for instance. But she was even later than he was, after assuring him how doggone punctual she claimed she always was.

He was about to turn and go into the big house to at least pour himself a cup of coffee when he saw the door to Mia's cabin open, followed by her striding through it. All casual and easygoing, too, as if she didn't have a care in the world. Even when she looked up and saw him standing there waiting for her, she didn't hurry her pace, just lifted a hand in greeting and made her way down the stairs to amble toward him.

Had he not been looking for her specifically, he never would have recognized her in her new—well, in Cody's old—cowgirl duds. The jeans were lovingly faded and molded against her as if they were made for her, and the pale yellow shirt looked like a piece of the sun had splashed down to earth on top of her. Her stride was a little wobbly in the boots, and for a minute he thought—hoped—that might irritate her enough to rouse some anger in her. But she recovered admirably and just kept right on walking.

Damn. She seemed downright chipper when she finally made her way up the steps and greeted him—with a smile, no less—seeming in no way as if she were manufacturing any of it this time. She was cute, too, all wrapped up in her starched cotton, with her silvery hair pulled back into a stubby ponytail. Enough short pieces fluttered around her face to make her look as if she'd just come in from a long ride on the range.

"Good morning," she said brightly.

"You're late," he replied irritably.

Her smile fell. For like a nanosecond. Then she regrouped and beamed at him again. "No, I'm not. I'm right on time." She lifted her wrist to show him her watch. "See? Eight o'clock on the dot. I told you. I'm never, ever, late."

He lifted his watch right back at her. "Eight thirty-two," he shot back.

She looked at his watch, then at hers. Then she pulled her phone from her back pocket and thumbed the screen open. She held that up for him to see, too. It also said eight o'clock on the nose. Silas didn't keep his phone on him when he was working, so he couldn't back himself up. Fortunately, one of the front desk workers came out the door behind him just then, and he asked if she had the time. She glanced at her watch, too, and told him it was just past eight.

Well, hell. Silas never set an alarm. He never needed to. After a lifetime of ranch life, he automatically woke up just before sunrise every morning and went about his regular routine in the house he'd shared with his mother growing up that was a lot like, and only slightly bigger, than Mia's cabin. Miss Sylvie had offered it to him when he took over the animal husbandry manager job. He fixed himself breakfast, checked his email, read the day's headlines, got dressed and strapped on his watch, never bothering to look at the time because he never needed to, since all those tasks took exactly the same amount of time every morning. He'd only looked at his watch this morning because he'd had to be somewhere different from usual, and at a specific time. When was the last time he'd checked his battery...?

He looked at Mia, waiting for a sarcastic *Toldja so* before pushing past him to go inside. But she only smiled at him—a smile that seemed genuinely compassionate and sympathetic—and gave him a soft pat on the arm. "It's okay," she said. "I've done the same thing lots of times."

He knew she was trying to make him feel better. But for some reason, that just irritated him more. What was most irritating of all, though, was that she was being all perky about it. There was no snark or smarmy indulgence. Just someone being nice and trying to make him feel better. While being perky.

Dammit.

"Really," she told him. Still bright. Still chipper. Still perky. "It's fine."

Oh, no. No, no, no. She did not get to use the word *fine* for him. Saying *fine* for her was just another way of shoving her anger deeper inside herself. No way was Silas going to let her get that *fine* crap all over him. He didn't do fine. Even back when he was burying his anger deep inside himself, he never posed it as being *fine*. First thing he needed for Mia to learn was that it was okay to *not* be fine. He sure as hell wasn't *fine* at the moment. And he was getting less fine with every passing minute on his erroneously set watch.

"It's not fine," he told her. Then, because he knew he had to own up to it, he told her, "I was wrong. My bad." Somehow, he even managed to ground out, "I'm sorry."

Silas might be the grumpiest SOB at Whispering Winds, but he owned up to his mistakes. Admitting his mistakes and apologizing for them—and making amends if necessary—went a long way toward keeping him balanced. Well, as balanced as a grumpy SOB could be. And Mia needed to see that if even someone like him could admit their mistakes and apologize for them, if even they could be honest with their feelings and themselves, then so could she.

She tried again. "Silas, it's fi—"

"Let's eat," he told her before she could say that damned word again.

Instead of arguing or taking exception, which he'd kind of hoped she would do, she only smiled her seemingly genuine smile and said, perkily, "Okay."

He looked again for the waves of anger that had been flowing off her the day before, but he couldn't find them.

She seemed like the dozens of other people who were at Whispering Winds to just have a good time. Working girl on her *vacay*. Happy to be here. Good to see ya. Can't wait to get started. It's gonna be so much fun.

It was pretty damned annoying.

What the hell had gotten into her overnight to put her in such good spirits this morning? Her cheerfulness was downright creepy. As much as she'd assured him of her fineness and not-angriness yesterday, it had been clear she was barely keeping it together. Had he been meeting her for the first time this morning, though, he would have sworn there wasn't a single thing wrong with her. That she really was just a bubbly, happy-go-lucky person who was A-OK with everything life had put in front of her, and that whatever had happened at work really was just a big ol' misunderstanding because, gosh darn it, she was just so dang cheerful and lovable. All kittens and confetti she was today. Little Mia Sunshine.

And her cheery façade—he knew it was a façade after the way she'd been yesterday afternoon—didn't crack once over breakfast. Not when she tripped over a chair and nearly went face-first into a tray full of biscuits and gravy before Silas righted her. Not when the only table left for them was a tiny one crowded into a corner of the room with barely enough space to fit them both. Not when they got to the buffet and a little boy in front of her snagged the last three French toast sticks she'd told Silas she was *so* excited about having because they were her *absolute fave*. Not when the busboy who went to refill her water splashed a good bit of the pitcher into her lap.

Every time it was just, *Oh well, these things happen. It's fine.* And every time, she sounded like everything, including herself, really was just fine. Not once did her gray eyes darken like a thundercloud as they had the day before. Not once did her entire body tense up like it had last night at the reception. Not once did she seem *this close* to blowing herself to bits.

Silas had to admit he was impressed. And intrigued. And, truth be told, a little envious.

But as successful as she was in masking it, he knew her anger was still in there. Somewhere. He knew that as well as he knew his own name. Anybody who'd seethed below the surface the way she had yesterday didn't just lose their rage because of a good night's sleep. Mia might hide it well. Hell, she'd doubtless had years of practice. But he knew it was in there as much today as it was yesterday. He'd recognized it then because it mirrored his own. And if it was like his own, she wouldn't be able to mask it for long.

Mia Hawthorne, it was becoming clear, was tougher than he'd first thought. But where he used to admire people who had a tough hide, he knew now that, for a lot of them, that wasn't a good thing.

"So, what are we going to do today?" she asked as she swirled the last of her just-regular-not-French toast over the last bits of scrambled egg on her plate. Still sunny. Still perky. Still irritating. She'd asked the question like he'd prepared a whole agenda of day trips and arts and crafts for her, as if he were some cruise ship recreational director. In fact, there was only one thing on his agenda today: Make Mia mad.

"First, there's some paperwork you need to fill out," he told her. There. That didn't sound like fun, did it?

"What kind of paperwork?" she asked. Cheerfully. Dammit.

"Some stuff for your HR department, some stuff for the ranch, and some stuff for you."

"What kind of stuff for me?"

"Just some questionnaires."

That were actually assessments. Specifically, anger assessments. And maybe one or two tests. Anger tests. But she didn't have to know that. She wasn't angry, after all.

"What kind of questionnaires?"

"What are you, Generation Why?"

She grinned at that. A genuinely happy grin. Dammit. "Just squeaked in to Gen Z, actually. Thanks for asking."

"Mmm."

"You look like a late-stage Millennial to me," she told him. Then she immediately backpedaled. "Even though you *seem* like a Boomer."

He couldn't tell if that was a dig or a compliment. Hard to tell with Gen Zs. "I'm thirty-four, if you're asking. What makes you think I'm a Boomer?"

"You seem pretty set in your ways."

He couldn't help the wry chuckle that escaped him at that. "Oh, what, and you're not?"

And there it was—a flash of annoyance. Just for a nanosecond, but it was there in her eyes like a sizzle of lightning through a storm cloud. It disappeared as quickly as it came, but by God, it was there. Silas was gonna claim it as his first victory on the road to Mia's recovery.

"I'm as flexible as they come," she assured him.

To be honest, he couldn't exactly contradict her there.

She had completely shape-shifted herself this morning from what she had been yesterday. And he couldn't quite let that go.

"You do seem different today," he told her.

She looked a little surprised by that. "I'm exactly the same person today that I was yesterday."

"I didn't say you're a different person. I said you seem different."

"I don't understand."

He could tell she wasn't yanking his chain. She really was confused by what he'd said. That kind of confused him, too.

He tried again. "Yesterday, you were a bundle of tension and—" He checked himself before he used the word *anger*, since she would just deny it. Again. "—exasperation. This morning, you're just a walking, talking, sunbeam."

She brightened. "Thank you. I do my best to always keep a sunny outlook and radiate positivity."

"You weren't sunny yesterday," he pointed out. He still wanted to get a rise out of her. "And you sure as hell didn't radiate positivity."

But she didn't rise to the bait. Her smile fell the littlest bit, but she quickly rallied it. "That's because I had a long day yesterday, what with leaving my life in St. Louis to come here. I'm not a good flyer. I didn't sleep well the night before. I've never been in a place like this. It was a lot to take in. I'm better now."

"You haven't even been here twenty-four hours," he pointed out. "It's still a lot to take in."

"I'm fine. Amazing what a good night's sleep will do."

"So, you don't sleep well at home?"

Her smile fell again. Not a little this time. A lot. But she still rallied well. "I sleep just fine."

Liar, he thought. Every time she used that word *fine*, she was lying. That was one thing about her he knew to be fact. What was also clear was that she didn't even realize she was lying when she said it. She really seemed to think she was fine right now. Just how deeply mired in denial was she? And how was he going to pull her out of it short of tying a rope around her and yanking on it with all his might?

He tried again. "But you got a good night's sleep last night?"

Again, no answer. No change to her expression, either. Between that and the purple smudges still prevalent under her eyes, chances were good she hadn't slept any better here than she did at home. Which was and wasn't surprising. It took most people a while to get used to new surroundings enough to be able to pass the night in comfort. On the other hand, there was something about wide-open natural spaces—be it the open range or the seashore—that made a lot of people sleep like a rock.

Even so, Silas was reasonably certain that her "sunny" mood this morning was more due to her having shoved her emotions down deep inside herself, the way she'd promised last night that she would. She might have even gotten them crammed in there deeper than they'd been before.

"You want to take a cup of coffee to go?" he asked as she crossed her knife over her fork on her empty plate.

She shook her head. "I'm good."

Silas downed the last swallow of his own coffee and pushed his chair away from the table. "Okay then, Mia Hawthorne. Let's get to work."

Chapter Four

Mia turned to the last page of the *questionnaire* Silas was making her fill out and did her best not to get ang— um…annoyed. No, not even annoyed. She was fine. Even if this questionnaire wasn't a questionnaire at all and bordered on being a psych evaluation. Questionnaires just asked specifics about age, employment, education, whatever, or maybe opinions and observations about stuff. *This* questionnaire wanted a peek into her brain. And her emotions. And herself. How did she feel about her future? How did she feel about her past? How did she feel about her failures? How much did other people bother her? Was anything interfering with how she ate, how she slept, and how she worked? Was anything interfering in her social life? Her love life? Her family life?

It was that last one that finally made her snap her No. 2 pencil in two. On accident, of course, because she wasn't expecting all that personal stuff, and it surprised her. Enough to snap a No. 2 pencil in two. But that was okay! Lots of people snapped No. 2 pencils in two when they were surprised by a questionnaire.

At the snap, Silas looked up from whatever he was reading in his chair on the other side of the desk. They were sitting in Miss Sylvie's office in the big house, which was as log-cabin-on-steroids-looking as the rest of the place, surrounded by all things working-ranch-related: maps and weather reports and work schedules, along with a desktop computer bigger and more technically sophisticated than Mia had ever seen. One wall was virtually all windows, looking out onto the vast and gorgeous vista that was Wyoming. It was as bright and beautiful today as it had been yesterday, and the requisite cattle and riders and hound dogs were threading their way through the tapestry of the landscape again, looking as carefree as they had the day before.

Mia couldn't imagine how anyone could get any work done in here. She'd do nothing but stare out the window all day. But Silas hadn't even noticed. After having her sit down at Miss Sylvie's desk, where there had been a good dozen pages' worth of stuff she needed to fill out, he'd picked up something in a blue binder and started leafing through it. That was nearly an hour ago. They'd sat in total silence since then, save the scratch of pencil on paper. Oh, and the snapping in two of said pencil just now.

"Everything okay?" he asked.

"Fine," she assured him, gripping half a pencil in each hand until her knuckles went white. Silas, she noticed, noticed. So she did her best to release them. She even managed to set them back down on the desk instead of hurling them at the wall, which was what she very much wanted to do. "I guess they just don't make pencils like they used to."

Silas craned his neck to look at the page she'd been filling out. She started to cover it with her hand, but he tugged one corner until it was out from under her palm and firmly in his grasp.

He scanned her responses—which she kind of would have preferred he not do, but the questionnaire had pointedly stated at the very top that her responses would be reviewed by appropriate personnel—but only replied, "There's only a few left. Just grab another pencil and finish up."

She grabbed another pencil from a mug on Miss Sylvie's desk with a quote from someone named Fallon Taylor that said, "Dirt is cowgirl glitter." Then she colored in her responses to the last four questions as quickly as she could and shoved it back toward Silas.

He looked at it again. "You didn't answer the one about family life," he said.

"That's because I don't have a family life."

"Everyone has a family life."

"Not if they don't have a family, they don't."

"You don't have a family?"

Her answer was crisp and to the point. "No."

He eyed her warily for a minute, but she could no more tell what he might be thinking than she could have stopped the earth from rotating on its axis. "I'm sorry you lost your parents," he told her. Almost as an afterthought, he added, "Condolences."

His condolences, though, sounded more automatic than they did heartfelt. Then again, that was how most people sounded when they threw out "Condolences" to someone who'd lost a loved one. Not that Mia had lost her parents. She knew exactly where they were—still living in the house where she grew up. Not that they were loved ones, either. That house was still as lacking in love as it had been when she lived there, she was sure. But Silas didn't need to know any of that.

"It can be even tougher when you're an only child and don't have siblings to help carry the load," he added, misunderstanding that part, as well. Not that Mia was going to correct him there, either. Considering the relationship she had with her older brothers, she was absolutely an only child and always had been.

He pushed the page back toward her. "But even losing your parents and not having siblings doesn't mean you don't have any family. Everyone has a family, Mia. Maybe not by blood," he hastened to add when he saw she was about to take exception. "But everyone has someone they consider family. Even if it's just a dog or a cat."

She pushed the page back toward him without looking at it—certainly without answering the question about family. "Not everyone."

"You don't even have a dog or cat?"

"No."

Her parents had never allowed a family pet when she was growing up, saying they were expensive and messy and that no one would take care of them. Not that that had stopped them from having children, who were also expensive and messy, and who they also hadn't taken care of. Mia had considered adopting a rescue when she'd first moved into her own place, and had even gone so far as to visit the local humane society to find one. But she'd taken one look at the animals in the cat room alone, who all greeted her so eagerly at their cage doors, and the minute she saw their little paws and tiny smiles and heard their little meows and purrs, something had swelled up inside her so fast and so fierce and so scary, that she'd bolted from the place within minutes of entering.

The thought of taking care of another living creature had been terrifying to her. What if she wasn't good at it? What if she didn't even know how to take care of another living creature? She hadn't exactly had any examples to follow growing up. Sure, she'd read about how much people loved their pets, but she wasn't sure she could do that, either. She'd never loved anything. Anyone. She wasn't even sure she was able to love. Which, now that she thought about it, was maybe why her attempts at having friends and relationships had failed so spectacularly, too.

Silas studied her in silence for a minute, then gathered up the rest of the pages she'd filled out and put them all in order. Except for the last one she hadn't completed, which he pushed back toward her *again*.

"All the bubbles need to be filled in for this," he told her. "'Cause you'll be filling out another one related to it before you go home, and they need to compare all the responses."

"Who's they?"

"Miss Sylvie, for one. Then she'll put together a report for your HR department where you work, and they'll probably share the results with your boss. They need to make sure your stay here did what it was supposed to do and that you won't be going after any of your coworkers again."

As much as she wanted to repeat that it was just a misunderstanding, Mia said nothing. She only took back the page, bubbled in the option that said *No change* and shoved it back at Silas.

"Thanks," he told her as he took it from her.

"So, what's your family situation like?" she asked him.

He looked surprised by the question. And, to be honest, it surprised Mia that she had asked it. Normally, she didn't pry into other people's lives. Not even after she'd gotten to know them fairly well. Of course, it could probably be argued that there were very few people she knew *fairly well*. Or even *at all*. She and her coworkers shared the usual shallow banter about what they did over the weekend or where they were going for vacation or whose kid/brother/cousin/whatever was getting married/graduating/having a baby/whatever. But that was information that was always volunteered by the person who was doing it. No one really asked much about each other's lives. She didn't know if it was like that in all workplaces, since Carrigan Auto had been pretty much her only employer since she graduated from college, but she suspected it probably was.

Anyway, no one there was especially forthcoming with personal info. And Mia was A-OK with that, because she didn't want to hear about other people's personal lives any more than she wanted to share her own personal life with them.

That was why she backtracked when she told Silas, "I'm sorry. That's none of my business. Forget I asked."

"Nah, it's all right," he told her. He didn't even sound cranky when he said it. "We're gonna need to talk about this stuff at some point over the next two weeks, and I can't expect you to be the only one doing it."

She'd figured before arriving at Whispering Winds that talking about personal stuff would be inevitable in a program like this, but she'd really been hoping they could avoid it and focus instead on things like how to get on a horse and how to get off a horse and how to avoid horses entirely because she sure as hell didn't want to be on one. Or maybe something about leather-tooling her very own cowgirl belt. Or how to build a campfire for s'mores. Or learn how to brew the perfect cuppa Joe from someone named Cookie. Stuff like that.

Silas sighed heavily. "I mean, I hate to sound like a Hallmark movie—" he started, which didn't surprise Mia at all, because god forbid Silas Crockett have anything in his life that could be misconstrued as warm or happy "—but pretty much everybody on this ranch is my family. I lost my mom when I was ten, to cancer, and my dad was never in the picture. Miss Sylvie and her late husband took me right in after her death, and I grew up after that in this very house, in a room upstairs. They did all the parent stuff—made sure I was fed and clothed, helped me with my homework, hosted birthday sleepovers, got me involved in junior rodeo, steered me toward a degree in animal husbandry, all that. All the ranch hands took me under their wing and became like uncles and aunts and cousins to me. Miss Inola, who used to run the kitchen until she retired a few years ago, was like a grandmother to me. She even had me call her *Ni-hina*, which is Cherokee for 'grandmother.'"

Holy moly, Mia thought, stunned. He'd almost sounded human when he'd said all that. He'd even sounded a little—gasp—warm and happy.

Then he astonished her even more by grinning. Well, okay, kind of grinning. It was more like he stopped scowling than anything. But if he'd been handsome before, when he was not-scowling-almost-kind-of-grinning, now he was absolutely… *Wow.*

"Miss Sylvie gave me my first horse when I was thirteen," he added, "and there were always dogs and barn cats around for me to play with and take care of. So, yeah. I have a family. A pretty big one. And, of course, there was a time when—"

He stopped abruptly, and the humanity and warmth that had started to creep into him fled, to be replaced by an iciness and acrimony that exceeded even his earlier irascibility. It was like whatever he'd been about to say had flicked a switch inside him to immediately shut off the words he was about to utter. No, not flicked a switch. More like shoved down the plunger on a TNT box and blew those words into a mushroom cloud of noxious gas. And just like that, he was—

Wow. Angry. Really, really, angry. Way angrier than Mia had ever been. Not that Mia had ever been angry. But if she ever had been, it would have had nothing on Silas's current state.

She wanted to ask him to finish whatever he'd been about to say, but she didn't dare. So she only sat in silence, waiting to see if he would do it anyway. But he didn't. He only stood abruptly and strode toward the other side of the office. Mia honestly thought he was going to just walk right out the door and leave her there, but he stopped short of it and turned back around. When his gaze fell on her, though, he almost looked surprised to see her sitting there, as if whatever *had* been going through his mind had seized his thoughts so thoroughly, he'd forgotten where he was and what he was supposed to be doing.

He didn't cross back to where she was, though. He only leaned against the wall by the door and crossed his arms over his chest. Then he turned his gaze toward the massive wall of windows and looked out at the beautiful day beyond the glass. Little by little, his body relaxed—some—and his expression cleared—a little.

But he continued to stare out the window, not at Mia, when he finally started to talk again. "Anyway, I've always had a big family here at Whispering Winds."

She was grateful for the return to their conversation and even more grateful that he was pretending his drastic change of mood never happened. She was happy to pretend that, too. Anything to avoid the hostility that had spilled off him like toxic waste. The last thing she wanted to experience during this stay was more adversity. Especially in a place like this, one that was so calm and unsullied. Antagonism didn't belong in Serenity Valley. It was much too beautiful.

And so was the man on the other side of the room, in spite of his brief lapse into ugliness. That ugliness now seemed to have ebbed to a place inside him that was more manageable. But he still looked troubled and gritty and...kind of angry.

For the first time, Mia wondered about *why* Silas was the go-to for Miss Sylvie when Beau wasn't able to fulfill his duties as anger manager. His description of his early life had surprised her. Except for the part about not having a father and losing his mother, it sounded like he'd had it pretty good growing up. He'd been a child who was loved and welcomed and accepted, with lots of substitute aunts and uncles and cousins. It sounded like he'd done well at school and had friends, activities, and pets galore. So why was he so crotchety as an adult? Even Miss Sylvie thought so, though her affection for Silas was certainly clear.

Despite that, Mia asked him, "And have you always gotten along with your family?"

"Sure," he replied readily. "I mean, yeah, there have been times when I didn't see eye to eye with everyone. But not to the point where—" he dipped his head toward the desk, where her pencil still lay in two pieces "—I've had to break something."

"That wasn't why I broke the pencil," she told him.

"So you at least admit that it didn't go snapping all by itself and had a little help from you?"

"No, you don't—" She cut herself off and expelled a restless breath. "You misunderstood."

Now he nodded. "Another one of those, huh? Just how many misunderstandings do you have in any given week, Mia?"

"I don't have—" She cut herself off again. "I'm just going through kind of a difficult time in my life right now."

He nodded. "Totally understand that. Comes with living life. What's causing this difficult time?"

She wanted to tell him to stop trying to be her therapist then remembered he was supposed to be kind of a therapist while she was here. What bothered her more, though, was that she couldn't really give him a definitive answer to his question. There hadn't been anything out of the ordinary going on in her life lately that should make it any more difficult than anyone else's. Just like there hadn't been anything unusual going on in her life when she had trouble focusing in college. And, anyway, why did there always have to be some kind of identifiable trigger when things weren't going as well as they should be? Lots of times, things were just...you know, difficult.

But that was okay! Lots of people didn't have triggers in their lives that made it difficult to get through the day.

When she didn't answer, Silas tried a different tack. "Okay, how about this? When was the last time your life *wasn't* difficult?"

She thought about that for a minute. Hard. And then she had to think about it some more. Even harder. But not only could she not pinpoint what was difficult right now, she couldn't remember her life ever being difficult since leaving home. Sure, there had been challenges after she graduated and before she was making a living wage, but none that a million other people didn't have. These days, she was doing pretty well. She could even afford the occasional perk, like dinner out with friends or that cute Coach handbag that had finally been marked down and down and down. Not that she ever actually went out to dinner with friends—and that was okay!—but she did have more than one cute markdown in her closet.

There was nothing in her life that should make her feel challenged. Nothing that should make her feel angr— Nothing that should make her feel annoyed. Nothing that should have made her try to pull Perpetual Salesman of the Month Jeff Oberstrom through his Tom Ford necktie.

Okay, no, she didn't have a lot of friends, and she didn't have any pets, and she didn't have anything she considered family. Big damn deal. She didn't want friends or pets or family. She liked being alone. Friends and pets and family brought obligation and concern and fear, none of which were things she wanted to invite into her life. Mia was a free agent. Free spirit. Free everything. She could come and go as she pleased and do whatever the hell she wanted. Life shouldn't be difficult. Life *wasn't* difficult. So why had she just told Silas she was going through a difficult time?

"It's complicated," she finally said.

He studied her in silence for a moment more, then told her, "Sounds like. Or, it would if you told me anything."

She forced down the ang—she meant annoyance—that surged into her chest at his comment and said nothing. Silas pushed himself away from the wall and crossed back to Miss Sylvie's desk. He moved the pages Mia had signed and filled out front and center, where Miss Sylvie wouldn't be able to miss them. Then he closed the binder he'd been reading for the last hour and shelved it over the desktop where he'd found it. As Mia watched him do it, she wondered what his regular job was here at the ranch, when he wasn't doing the anger management thing.

"So, what would you normally be doing around here if you didn't have to babysit me?" she asked.

She thought he would sidestep the question or at least grumble something about not being her babysitter. Instead, he told her, "I'm the animal husbandry manager here at Whispering Winds. Which is a fancy way of saying I take care of cattle. Lots and lots of cattle."

"Take care of them?" she echoed. "What? Like you make sure they're tucked in at night with a bedtime story and a cup of warm milk?"

She'd hope she would see that not-scowl-almost-smile from him again, but his expression changed not at all. She could sense there were still remnants of his earlier, albeit brief, turmoil lingering just below his surface, and something about that bothered her more than it should. She had no idea why. She barely knew the guy. And he hadn't exactly gone out of his way to put on his best face for her or to be her friend. On the contrary, he seemed to want to be left alone by the outside world even more than Mia did.

She wished she could find his appearance as unappealing as she found his personality. But he was somehow more handsome every time she looked at him. The dark scruff of a beard was back this morning, and he didn't look like he'd bothered to comb his inky hair at all. Where she would have considered other guys unkempt for such oversights, on him, both were...well... The word *stunning* came to mind. Along with a host of others. Like *bewitching*. And *gorgeous*. And *downright sexy*. He was wearing his usual scuffed jeans and boots, along with a chambray work shirt whose sleeves were rolled back over the salient muscles of his forearms, then strained at even more pronounced biceps and shoulders higher up. He had a tattoo on his inner forearm she hadn't noticed the night before, what looked like two skinny pine trees with long trunks before the leaves kicked in, one big, the other little.

His eyes, though, were what caught and held her attention—again. They were like sea glass that had been tumbled and beaten in turbulent waters against rocks and grit and time, only to be made more beautiful by the upheaval and injury. Maybe that was what Silas was, too. Maybe whatever the thing was, or things were, that had made him stop talking a few minutes ago, those things were what made him so surly. Maybe, deep down, he had a legit reason for not having an especially sunny disposition. Unlike Mia, the poster girl for Sunny Disposition, who had no reason at all for going off the way she had that day at work.

"Not quite," he told her, bringing her back to the matter at hand.

Which was what? she wondered, trying to remember. Oh, right. She'd been asking him about his regular job here and whether or not he tucked in the cows at night. Funny how sea-glass green eyes could make a person forget what she was thinking.

He added, "I oversee the breeding, care, and welfare of all the animals. Keep track of all the medical records and vet visits. Make sure they get the right stuff to eat and are moved to wherever they're supposed to be. Make sure all the animals are getting what they need, especially the calves, when they come in the spring. That kind of thing."

He was a caretaker, Mia thought. In the literal sense of the word. Silas Crockett took care of creatures that couldn't always take care of themselves. Never in a million years would she have thought that would even be his disposition, never mind his job. Looked like Miss Sylvie had a good reason, after all, for making him Beau's substitute for this gig. Well, except for the part about Silas having such a cranky personality. Where did that come from? she wondered again.

Just what makes you tick, Silas Crockett?

And why did she even care? She was only at Whispering Winds because she wanted to keep her job. And she was only going to be here for a couple of weeks, which wasn't nearly enough time to make friends with Silas.

Not that she even wanted to make friends with Silas. She didn't care how handsome he was.

"So, are we done here?" she asked him.

He nodded. "For now. You're gonna have to fill out some other stuff as the weeks go on. It's a way to track your progress and make sure you're getting to where you need to be."

"Who's going to be doing the tracking?"

"Miss Sylvie. HR. Me."

Just as Mia had figured. That was why she'd fudged so many of her responses and answers. She didn't want to give anyone any intimate glimpses into her psyche. Not Miss Sylvie, not HR, but most of all, not Silas. Why that was, she had no idea. Miss Sylvie's assessment of Mia's time here could compromise her standing with HR, and HR's assessment could cost Mia her job. Silas's assessment seemed like it held the least amount of weight, so anything he read of her responses would just give him an idea where he needed to focus his attention. There wasn't much risk when it came to what he thought of her. So why did the idea of him learning things about her bother her so much?

Whatever. It was fine. It was! Mia just needed to get through the next two weeks as quickly and as efficiently as possible. Keep a rein on her pesky feelings. Be careful about what she said. Stay upbeat. Which was much the way she lived her life anyway. Piece o' cake.

"Come on," Silas said, tilting his head toward the door. He took a few steps in that direction, not bothering to see if she was following. He just assumed she was, because that was the kind of person he was. The kind people followed without even asking why.

So just to be ornery—even if she did it politely—she asked, "Where are we going?" She couldn't help standing up as she did, though, because, hey, she was human. She'd follow him, too. Eventually.

But Silas just kept walking as he threw the answer over his shoulder. "We're gonna put those cowgirl boots to good use."

Chapter Five

"That's Beanie. She's gonna be your best friend for the rest of your stay here."

Silas watched Mia as she watched the horse he'd brought her to the corral to meet. They were currently on the other side of the fence from Beanie—who, in turn, was all the way on the other side of the corral—but where Silas had his booted feet firmly planted in the dust, Mia had climbed up to the first slat of the fence to get a better look. Even a foot off the ground, though, she still wasn't quite eye to eye with him. Not that she was looking him in the eye, anyway, because she had her gaze glued to the horse instead. And she didn't look happy about Beanie being even a full corral away. He couldn't wait to see how she reacted when she finally got to make her acquaintance up close and personal. He could see her chest already rising and falling in near panic.

Which was ridiculous, because Beanie was the greatest equine ambassador in all of Serenity Valley, a ten-year-old brown-and-white American Paint who was mellow and happy and didn't have an angry bone in her body. Her whole job at Whispering Winds was being a beginner horse for people who had never been around horses before. And she was really good at it. First-timers always did great with the Paints, because they were such patient and friendly animals.

Mia didn't seem to think so, though. In fact, judging by the way she was looking at the horse just then, Mia seemed to think Beanie was an equine Ted Bundy.

All she said, though, was, "That's a gigantic horse."

"That is not a gigantic horse," he assured her. "You wanna see a gigantic horse, I'll introduce you to Big Pierre instead."

That made her turn to look at him. "Big… Pierre? That doesn't sound like a name you hear on a ranch very often."

"He's a Percheron. They're a French breed."

"Then shouldn't he be *Grand* Pierre?"

Silas thought about that. "Yeah, maybe so. But I'm not the one who named him. Miss Sylvie bought him a while back to mostly to pull the hayride wagon, and she had a contest for the kids to pick a name for him. Big Pierre tied with Horsey McHorse Face, so you can see the dilemma."

"For sure," she replied dryly. "Both stellar names."

"Thankfully, Miss Sylvie had the deciding vote, so Big Pierre he is. He's about twice Beanie's size."

Mia's eyes went wide. "No way. That's like a Tyrannosaurus rex."

"Maybe a baby rex. But yeah. He's decent-sized. He's not too far from where we are now. Wanna go meet him?"

"No." Her reply was swift and decisive.

"Well, if you change your mind."

"I won't."

Silas didn't bother telling her—yet—that she'd be meeting Big Pierre anyway. They always ended the guests' stays at Whispering Winds with a bonfire and hayride on the last night. He was already planning to make sure Mia had a seat up front where she could get a *really* good look at Big Pierre. By then, she ought to be able to deal with adversity. And even if that did wind up making her angry, she should have mastered the skills to deal with it in a healthy way. If not… Well, she'd have to take that up with her HR department when she got home.

"Beanie's great," he assured her. "The two of you are gonna be just fine together."

He chose the word *fine* deliberately, hoping that would get her dander up as well as her impending introduction to Beanie clearly had. But she didn't seem to notice. She was too busy looking worried about getting any closer to the horse than she had to.

"Come on," he told her. "I'll introduce you."

She was shaking her head before he even finished talking. "Why do I have to meet Beanie up close?" she asked.

"Because in about half an hour, you're going to be riding Beanie up close."

She closed her eyes at that, in a way that made him think she had known he was going to tell her that but had hoped like hell he would say something else instead. Like maybe that she and Beanie would be getting manicures together, which maybe—*maybe*—she would at least consider.

Her voice was almost nonexistent when she asked, "Why do I have to ride Beanie?"

He replied honestly. "Because it's gonna put you way outside your comfort zone."

She opened her eyes and looked at him evenly. "I'm

way outside my comfort zone just standing here on a ranch in borrowed denim."

"And look how well you've adjusted to that."

"Who says I've adjusted?"

He shrugged philosophically. "Well, you haven't done anything to get yourself written up, so I'd say you're already light-years ahead of where you were at work this time a week ago."

She glared at him. Until she realized she was glaring and forced herself to smile instead. Then, with likewise forced sweetness, she said "Gosh, Mr. Crockett, I'd really prefer to not do the horse thing today if that's okay."

His lips almost twitched at the *Mr. Crockett*. He didn't think he'd ever been called that before. "You'll be fine."

This time she did note his use of the word *fine*. She glared again. Then smiled again. All he could do was hope her constant mood shifting didn't bust a blood vessel in her brain.

"I promise you, Mia, there's nothing to it. I'll be right behind you."

Her smile brightened in a way that wasn't entirely manufactured. "Isn't there something we can do to make me uncomfortable besides putting me on a horse?" she asked hopefully. "Like… I don't know…baking cookies? I am so bad at baking. Seriously. It makes me want to have a panic attack just thinking about it. Especially chocolate-chip cookies. Chocolate is like the worst thing I can put in my body. I think I'm getting hives just thinking about it. Why don't we bake chocolate-chip cookies instead?"

He unlatched the gate as he told her, "Nice try." Then he pushed it open and made a clicking sound that was

the internationally known equine lingo for *C'mon over
here, horsey*. Beanie responded accordingly, making her
way lazily toward Silas and Mia. But with the first step
the horse took, Mia hopped off the fence and took a step
backward. And with each of Beanie's ensuing steps toward them, Mia took one in retreat. Silas shook his head.
If this kept up, she'd be backstepping herself all the way
to Missouri before the day was done.

"Stop," he said.

He'd meant the direction for the horse, but was surprised to find it worked with Mia, too. She halted in her
tracks, her eyes never leaving Beanie, still looking pet-
rified by what was to come. Beanie just gazed back at
her good-naturedly. If it was possible for a horse to grin,
that was what Beanie was doing, as if she could sense
Mia's fear and was trying to reassure her. *Oh, come on.
I'm a cream puff.*

Instead of telling Mia again that she was going to be
fine, Silas made his way to where she had retreated and
tried a different tack.

"You want to tell me why you're so afraid of horses?"

"Not really."

"But you are afraid of them, right? This isn't just an
uncertainty about doing something you've never done
before. This is like a full-blown phobia, yeah?"

She nodded. "I've been near a horse before. Once.
When I was little. Okay, it was a pony. At a birthday
party. But still. A bad thing happened to me with that
pony. It was terrifying."

A birthday party pony, Silas repeated to himself. He'd
figured she'd had some kind of major terror episode for
a first-time ride that ended up with her clinging to the

reins of a half-broke stallion raging out of control through a dark stormy night while some headless guy hurling flaming pumpkins chased after her. But the horror raging through her had been caused by a pony? Hell, she might as well have been panic-stricken by a prairie dog.

"A pony," Silas said, not quite able to hide his disgust. Hell, c'mon. It was a pony, for criminy sake.

She turned to look at him, her eyes narrowing. "It was a feral pony. Rabid, even."

"A rabid, feral pony," Silas echoed dubiously. "Yeah, you don't see too many of those. Or, you know, any."

"Especially at a birthday party for a five-year-old," she said enthusiastically, thinking he was agreeing with her. "He came at me out of nowhere."

Okay, that did sound kind of bad. "He attacked you?"

She didn't respond for a moment. Wow. Her pony PTSD must be really bad. Finally, she told him, "He... ate my party hat."

Silas waited for the rest of it. Because surely there had to be more to this story. But Mia didn't elaborate. So, he prodded, "And?"

She looked back at Beanie. "It was a really good hat. Purple foil with glitter. Purple is my favorite color."

Silas waited some more. Mia said nothing. So, he asked, "And?"

"And it pulled my hair a little when it grabbed it off my head."

"And?"

"With its teeth."

"And?"

"And the little elastic band that went under my chin

snapped and nearly hit me in the eye. I could have been blinded."

This time Silas was the one to say nothing.

"And I was next up to play Pin the Tail on the Donkey, so I was holding a cardboard tail in my hand, which may have been what triggered the pony in the first place. Like maybe it thought I was coming for its tail, too. The whole thing was very darkly ironic, really." When he still said nothing in response—because what did you say to something like that?—she added, "And terrifying."

Silas bit his lip. He would not laugh. He wouldn't. Except that he did. He couldn't help it. He could just picture a miniature Mia at some kid's birthday party, paper tail in hand, all hell breaking loose with children screaming and scrambling for their lives while a little pony chomped on a purple foil hat with glitter.

"It's not funny, Silas!" she fairly shouted at him. "It scared the hell out of me! I was only five!"

Oh, yeah. There was the anger he'd been trying to rouse in her. It came up fast and hard. Now all he had to do was help her guide it out, acknowledge it, and talk rationally about it, instead of burying it back inside herself, which she was bound to do. He could see her trying to bury it already.

"You know what I was doing when I was five?" he asked her. Then, before she could answer, since of course she didn't know that, he told her, "I was feeding cattle every morning who were five times my size, and a lot of 'em had horns as big as me, so you'll excuse me if I don't consider a hat-chomping birthday pony much of a menace."

Oh, yeah. That made her mad. This was working

great. Her eyes narrowed to near slits and her cheeks were stained red with her anger. She turned to face him fully, hands on her hips, looking way more menacing than even the horned Holsteins did to a kid who stood no higher than their knees. *You go, Mia Hawthorne. You get mad as hell.* Here it came—the dressing down he'd been hoping for.

Though maybe "dressing down" wasn't the best choice of words for this, since that made him think of Mia doing things to him that he really shouldn't be thinking about. At least not when he was trying to make her angry. A much better place and time for that would be—

Nowhere and not ever. What the hell was that kind of stuff doing in his brain in the first place? Yeah, he was trying to get something hot and heavy going with Mia at the moment, but not that kind of hot and heavy. Not yet any—

Not ever. *Damn, man. Get a hold of yourself.*

She opened her mouth as if she were going to blast him with every bad word she knew. And maybe make up a few on the spot to add to them, just for good measure. He steeled himself for the outburst to come, trying not to feel smug about how well he'd managed to bring her anger to the surface on just her second day here.

Okay, Mia Hawthorne, take your best shot, and give it to me with both barrels.

But she didn't even cock the trigger. Instead, she closed her mouth again, closed her eyes tight, and rolled her shoulders, as if she were literally trying to unload the anger that had roared up inside her. Silas could almost see the numbers tick by as she counted to ten. Then she took another step in retreat. When she opened her eyes again, the rage that had been so obvious a minute ago was gone. In fact, she looked downright serene.

She took a deep breath and released it slowly. "The pony scared me," she said simply, softly. "It was mean of you to laugh at something that scared me. It wasn't funny."

Well, hell, Silas thought. So close. He'd been so close to making her see how angry she could get over something irrational. Yeah, it hadn't been very nice of him to do it, but his end goal had been to help her out. Okay, if they couldn't deal with her anger at the moment, at least maybe he could help her put the birthday party experience into perspective.

"Were you hurt that day?" he asked her. "Was anyone hurt that day? Did the pony go nuts and bite anyone? Chase anyone? Eat anyone else's hat even?"

Grudgingly, she told him, "No."

"Did it do anything other than just stand there, chomping on your hat?"

"Oh, after nearly blinding me, you mean?" she reminded him.

"Yeah," he replied blandly. "After that."

"No," she repeated with even more, uh, grudge.

He nodded. "Then you gotta admit, Mia, it's pretty funny. I mean, picture it the way you just described it."

When he could see that she wasn't willing or able to do that, he described it to her himself, adding in the very touches that had made the image so comical in his own head, until she had no choice but to view an over-the-top cartoon version of that day complete with splashy colors and zany sound effects.

"I mean, that pony maybe even did you a favor," he

told her as he was winding it up. "That chin strap might have been the result of a manufacturer's defect. If you'd kept that hat on any longer, it might have actually blinded you in *both* eyes. Or they could've used some carcinogenic dye to make it. Maybe that pony sensed you were in danger and was trying to save your life. Did you ever think about that? Animals sense dangers we can't sometimes."

As he spoke, he could see Mia's resentment toward him easing, little by little, until, by the end, the ghost of a smile was playing about her lips. What was even better was that it was the first smile from her he'd seen that he could tell was genuine and coming from a place inside her where she felt things instead of thought them. And maybe that was an even bigger victory than bringing about her anger on day two would have been. Even if he hadn't been successful in helping her deal with her negative emotions, at least he'd put her on the path toward gaining a new perspective. Baby steps. For now, he'd take them.

She finally blew out a breath and met his gaze again. "Okay, I guess I can see how *some* people would think it was funny. To me, at the time, it was really scary."

"And that's okay, that you were scared," he told her. "But maybe, Mia, just maybe, it wasn't really the pony that was scary," he added. "Maybe something else was scary that day, and the pony was a safer thing for you to steer your fear and anger toward at the time."

Her brows arrowed down at that. "What do you mean?"

"I mean maybe there was something that had nothing to do with the pony that was actually scaring you that day. Something you didn't want to acknowledge. And maybe something inside your five-year-old self could see that the pony was harmless, and that's the real reason why you let it be the cause of your fear instead of the other thing."

"I still don't understand."

Yeah, he wasn't surprised. If what was going on with Mia and her anger was what he suspected, it might take a while for her to acknowledge it. Or, even if she acknowledged it, to admit it.

"Maybe it was safer," he said, "for you to be scared of and angry at the pony instead of the thing that was really scaring you and making you angry. Because some part of you knew the pony wouldn't really hurt you. Not like the other scary thing might."

He could tell she still couldn't—or wouldn't—understand. "That's silly. What could possibly have been scaring me when I was five other than a malevolent, hat-eating pony?"

"You tell me."

He could see that the wheels had started to turn in her brain, but they were slow and creaky and not really producing much just yet. Silas had to admit that he wasn't even sure he was on the right track with his questioning, since she was right—most five-year-olds wouldn't have a lot to be deeply angry or fearful about. Just because a question about family had made her snap a pencil in half, that didn't necessarily mean that her family had been... dysfunctional. Could have just been that the mention of family had tapped into her grief about losing them, and then oops went the pencil.

Then again, maybe not. Maybe, even when Mia was

five, there really had been something going on in her life that made her transfer her anger and fear onto a party pony. Yeah, people had legit phobias about things that other people found harmless, and Silas didn't want to belittle anyone for that. He just couldn't believe a fear would hang on into adulthood that would make her terrified of a perfectly nice horse because of the kind of isolated—and not particularly traumatic—childhood experience she'd described.

She switched her gaze from Silas to Beanie, who was still standing just inside the gate, looking harmless and gentle. Even after their back-and-forth over the party incident, Mia didn't look close to letting the horse come anywhere near her. So, Silas tried a different tack.

"Okay, look," he said as gently as he could manage. Which, okay, maybe wasn't all that gentle, but it was better than snarling, which was kind of his default conversational habit. "I'll make a deal with you. If you'll at least get yourself within a foot of Beanie, and if you'll just reach out one hand and give her a gentle pat on the neck, I'll make sure you get an extra dessert at dinner tonight."

Hey, bribery like that always worked with the camp kids. And some of them were even more skittish than Mia, hard as that was to believe.

Still watching Beanie, Mia asked, "What are they having for dessert tonight?"

Silas's superpower was that he could memorize the kitchen dessert selection for each and every day in any given month, starting on day one. "Campfire cobbler," he told her with complete confidence. "Peach this week."

He wasn't sure, but he thought he heard her mutter *Dammit* under her breath.

Just to cement the deal, he added, "With cinnamon ice cream."

Okay, that time he for sure heard the—even more emphasized—*Dammit*. She looked at Silas. Then back at Beanie. At Silas. At Beanie.

Finally, with clear reluctance, she said, "Okay. I'll do it." Then she looked at him again. "But if I get trampled to death before I have a chance to eat first or second dessert, I'm going to haunt you for the rest of your life and make sure you never enjoy another campfire cobbler again."

He nodded once. "Fair enough."

Silas made the clicking noise again, and Beanie ambled forward once more, halting just inside the gate. She was waiting a lot more patiently than Silas was for Mia to move far enough past her fear and loathing of whatever it was she truly feared and loathed to let this particular phobia go. She did the inhaling and exhaling of a few more long, fortifying breaths. And then a couple more. And then one more for good measure. Finally, she put one booted foot in front of the other and made her way slowly and deliberately toward the horse.

Not once did she take her eyes off Beanie. But Beanie never took her eyes off Mia, either. In fact, she looked as if she were already fondly anticipating the pat on the neck she knew was coming. Everyone patted Beanie on the neck. Then, eventually, everyone hugged her. Because Beanie was a sweetheart of a horse. Silas followed slowly behind Mia, but kept enough distance to give her the impression, however subconscious it might be, that it was just her and the horse.

Mia stopped when *exactly* one foot of dirt still lay between the two of them, her hands balled into tight fists at her sides. So, Silas ambled up closer for moral support. Beanie looked at her expectantly, exhaling a soft, horsey sound as if trying to convince Mia she wouldn't hurt her, then gave her head a gentle nod for good measure. Slowly, one of Mia's fists uncurled and she flexed her fingers wide before relaxing them again. Then, as slowly as a melting glacier, she lifted her hand and began to extend it toward the horse. Beanie took another step forward, as if wanting to meet halfway, and, to her credit, Mia barely flinched. She only forced her hand forward again, until it made contact—barely—with the bristly hair of Beanie's neck.

The horse nickered softly, and Mia stroked her fingers lightly downward, then back up. Then down. Then up. Beanie leaned into the strokes, taking another tiny step forward. This time, Mia didn't balk at all. She even moved a little closer herself, stroking her hand back and forth and back again.

And damned if something in Silas didn't stir to life as he watched her, seeing those fingers move so slowly and rhythmically, with such steady determination. An image exploded in his brain of her stroking her fingers over his neck instead. Then lower, over his shoulders and collarbone, then lower still, over his chest and torso, and— *Hey would you look at that?*—now he wasn't wearing a shirt in the image, and her hands were skimming over his naked body, those perfectly manicured fingernails grazing him lightly and—

"Hey, look at that," he said aloud before his thoughts could get away from him. "I think she likes you." Funny, though, how his thoughts didn't go away at all. Especially when Mia tucked her fingers under Beanie's mane to pet her some more, because that made Silas wonder what it would be like to feel her fingers in his hair, her hand cupping the back of his head as he leaned in to cover her mouth with his and—

"She's warmer and harder than I thought she'd be," Mia said softly.

Well, that made two of them, Silas thought. *Dammit.*

"I mean, I figured she'd be kind of soft and squishy, but she's all muscle, isn't she?"

Well, some of it was muscle. The rest was— Oh, wait. She was talking about the horse. *I mean,* of course*, she's talking about the horse.* What else would she be talking about?

"Yeah, horses are built pretty tough," he told her, hoping his voice didn't sound nearly as raspy and on edge to her as it did to him.

Mia gave Beanie one more pat and brought her hand back to her side. Then she turned around and covered the few steps necessary to bring her back to Silas's side. She spun around like a soldier ready to salute and said decisively, "Okay, horse fear conquered. What next?"

What was next was that Silas had to get himself under control and stop thinking about Mia in ways that he had no business considering. Best way to do that, he figured, was to rile up Mia to the point where they were at odds again and she wanted to kick him in the shins.

"What's next is that you're gonna learn to saddle her up."

Down went Mia's eyebrows again. "Why do I have to get all close up and personal with her again?"

Because the way he felt at the moment, it was either

that or get up close and personal with him. And neither one of them was gonna benefit from that.

"'Cause, like I said earlier, we're gonna go for a ride."

She looked panicked again. "What? But I don't have to ride her! I'm fine now!"

He could tell by the way she said the f-word word again that she was far from *fine*. And moving further away from *fine* with every passing second. Petting Beanie was only scratching the surface of her fear. And even though he'd made light of the incident at the birthday party to make her reconsider what her reaction might have been about, he knew her fear—of whatever she'd feared that day—wasn't truly gone. What she'd done wasn't enough. The fact that he could already feel her getting angry about doing something she didn't want to do indicated she hadn't moved past this yet. Hell, he was glad she was getting angry about it. Then she could realize, once the ride was over, that her anger had been unfounded and pointless all along. And once he showed her that, they could start working on making her see how her anger at work that day had been unfounded and pointless, too.

"C'mon," he told her as he reached for Beanie. He tilted his head toward the other side of the corral. "Tack room is over there. Rider up."

Mia gazed down at Silas from her seat atop Beanie and tried very, very, *very* hard not to get ang…annoyed. No, not annoyed. She was fine. Just a little put off. No, not even put off! She was fine. She was. She'd come a long way in the last hour where her, ah, discomfort around horses was concerned. But she wasn't exactly past it. In spite of her assurances to Silas, she knew a fear that was as deep-seated as hers was for as long as it had been didn't just go away because she petted an animal that was nice to her. But that was okay! She just needed a little more time, and she'd be totally fine.

She knew that was why Silas was insisting she go for this ride. He was supposed to be helping her work through…stuff. It was the whole reason she was here at Whispering Winds. To feel things she didn't normally feel—because she didn't normally *ever* get angry—and to learn how to handle them in the future when they came at her unexpectedly. Even if she totally had her feelings under control now. And even if she didn't—which she did!—geez, she was going to be here for two weeks. There was no reason they had to rush.

Silas cinched something tight under the horse's belly and Beanie took a step sideways. She might as well have just reared up on her hind legs and screamed, so jolting was Mia's reaction. She couldn't help it. She still didn't like horses. Even if she could agree to some extent that Silas *might* be right about that fear *possibly* being unfounded. Not that she thought a party pony had saved her from cancer, but yeah—maybe eating her hat wasn't the most terrifying thing that could have happened. She'd been five. So, sue her. Unfounded fears were still fears until they could be overcome.

But just what had Silas meant when he'd suggested that her fear of the birthday pony might have been a fear of something that wasn't the birthday pony at all? What else could there have been for her to be afraid of? That pony *was* terrifying. A lot of five-year-olds would have been scared silly. Just because not a single other child at the party had been frightened, just because they'd all laughed at the pony's antics, just because they'd all *loved* that damned pony, that didn't mean the pony was any less dangerous. What did five-year-olds know about danger? They were only five, for crying out loud.

She was about to ask Silas where the horse was that he would be riding when he suddenly launched himself up onto Beanie, too, right behind her. The horse took it in stride, but Mia stiffened, feeling as if a bolt of lightning had just shot down her spine. 'Cause a sizzle of heat followed the bolt that was nothing short of incandescent.

"What are you doing?" she managed to gasp as he made himself at home back there.

"I told you I'd be right behind you when we took Beanie out for a spin."

"Yeah, but I thought that meant you'd be on another *horse* behind me. I didn't think you'd be behind *me* on the same horse."

"Surprise," he said in the wry laconic way that rankled her more every time she heard it.

"I don't think this is going to work," she told him.

"It always works."

"So, you ride behind people on the same horse all the time?"

"Yep."

"Even big, strapping guys?"

"Yep."

"And Beanie is okay with that?"

"Yep. I told you. She's a sturdy horse, and Paints are great about that stuff."

Maybe Beanie was okay with a party going on on her back, but Mia wasn't okay with a party going on *in* her back. Which was most definitely happening every place that Silas touched her—and Silas was touching her *every* place on her back. As he settled himself more resolutely, his legs snugged tight against hers until—*Oh, my god*—he was touching every inch of that part of her body, too. Seriously, the two of them might as well have been spooning in bed.

And, *dammit*, why was that the analogy her brain chose? The way he felt back there now, it was going to be impossible for her to think about anything else. Something that became abundantly clear when he reached around her and grabbed the bridle. Now not only was he flush against her from shoulder to hip in the back and hip to shin in the front, but his arms—those incredible, muscular arms, revealed by the rolled-back sleeves of his chambray shirt—were surrounding her, too, as intimately as a lover's embrace and—

Dammit, brain. Stop that.

But her brain only got more agitated when he snapped the reins and Beanie moved forward. Because then, like the horse, their bodies were in motion. And since Mia had never been on a horse before, she had no idea what that motion was supposed to be. Silas obviously did. He was totally at home with the rocking motion of Beanie's body. But Mia couldn't quite get the hang of balancing with it. She always seemed to go up when she should be going down, leaning right when she should be leaning left. When Silas realized her struggle, he moved both reins into his right hand and guided his left to her hip.

"You want to move with the horse," he told her softly. Funny, though, how his voice seemed a little raspier than it had before. "Just feel Beanie's rhythm and go with it."

Mia tried. She really did. But all she could feel was Silas surrounding her, his warmth mingling with hers until she could scarcely tell where her body ended and his began. She could feel his breath against the back of her neck, and the hand on her hip curved tighter in a way she could only describe as possessive. He smelled like Serenity Valley, an intoxicating mix of pine trees and sunshine and denim, along with just the merest hint of campfire. She knew in that moment that even if she could force herself to someday forget about all the difficulty and discomfort these two weeks were going to bring, she would never, ever, forget the scent of Silas Crockett.

"Just go with it, Mia. You'll be fine."

Oh, she was trying to go with it. Really, she was. But for the first time in her entire adult life, she could safely say that she was *not* fine.

When the horizon before her began to swim—though whether that was because she was unaccustomed to Beanie's movements or hyperaware of Silas's—she tried to focus instead on the tattoo on his forearm, just above the hand that was holding the reins. Two long-trunked pine-ish-looking trees, one a quarter size of the other, both executed in a style that was harsh and jagged, but also somehow peaceful, too. Solid black, no flourishes, just two trees. It was so simple, but quite beautiful, really. He didn't have any other tattoos that she'd been able to see, so this one must be significant somehow, in a place where he saw it all the time. She wondered what—

Silas tugged on the reins to pull Beanie to the left, and Mia leaned that way, too. But that only moved her against the arm and hand still holding her firmly in place. Her pulse surged again, and heat swamped her. She closed her eyes and inhaled him again, going almost orgasmic at his intoxicating scent. It had been a long time since she'd been this close to a man. In a lot of ways, sitting astride a horse with Silas, a man she'd scarcely known two days, was a more intimate experience than she'd had with any of her boyfriends in the past.

"That's better," he murmured near her ear at her more natural movement.

Oh, yes. It certainly was.

"Now you take the reins."

For just the tiniest second, Mia thought he was telling her to take the reins figuratively—that she should be the one in command of whatever was happening between the two of them in that moment, a moment that had been feeling more than a little sexual. A thrill of something hot and erotic shot from her chest to her groin, stirring something deep inside her she didn't think she'd ever felt before. She'd never been with a guy who wanted her to be in control of what happened in bed. Even when the sex was good, she'd always ended up feeling like more of a receptacle for her partner's needs and desires instead of an equal participant. Guys always finished before she did, and they were never much interested in helping her over the edge afterward. For Silas to want her to be the one in control, to put her needs and desires first, ignited a fire in her that was nothing short of incandescent. She actually started to lift a hand to move it over her shoulder, to cup it around his neck and pull him closer, so he could wrap his other arm around her waist, curving it under her breast as he scraped his cheek against hers, tangling her fingers tight in his hair when he moved his other hand between her legs and—

Whoa. Whoa, whoa, whoa.

She didn't realize she'd actually spoken the words aloud until Beanie stopped moving, and she remembered she was riding on a horse, not riding Sil—

Whoa.

"Mia?" he asked from behind her. "Everything okay?"

It took her a full minute to calm herself down enough to answer. And even then, all she could manage was a nod and a strangled "Mmm-hmm."

Good God, what had come over her? Yeah, it had been a while since she'd been on anything resembling a date, but that was no reason for her libido to have gone off the way it had just then. In fact, she didn't think her libido had ever gone off the way it had just then. Not even when her libido was writhing naked beneath a guy who was actually making love to her. Or, at least, as close to love as a person could make since love didn't really exist, not for her. She didn't care how many times the college counselor had told her she was wrong about that.

"So then why did we stop?" Silas asked.

Who said she had stopped? There were still some wildly erratic—wildly erotic—thoughts tumbling around in her brain.

"I just, um, I was starting to feel a little overwhelmed," she said. Hoo boy, was that an understatement.

Silas seemed to understand, though, because he told her, "We can take a break if you want. There's a nice little watering hole just beyond those trees over there. Beanie would probably be grateful for the break, too."

Good girl, Beanie, Mia thought. *Thanks for letting me throw you under the bus.*

"Sounds perfect," she said aloud.

Not that it sounded perfect at all. Because she still couldn't quite shake the errant thoughts cartwheeling through her brain, and the object of those thoughts was still way too close for comfort.

Oh, this was not good. The last thing Mia needed was to have to battle an attraction to a man who was completely off limits. Not just because he was supposed to be helping her deal with a difficult time in her life where her emotions were raw and uncertain—not that her emotions were raw or uncertain, she hurried to add, because her emotions were just fine, and everyone else was just misunderstanding them. And it wasn't because he was such a cranky SOB, despite her libido's decision that no, no, he was *great*. It wasn't even because she was only going to be at Whispering Winds for a couple of weeks, or that Whispering Winds was a thousand miles away from St. Louis, both literally and figuratively, 'cause it wasn't real life at all. Not hers, anyway.

It was because Mia didn't do well with attractions. Attractions led to entanglements. And entanglements led to desires. Not just sexual desires, but psychological ones, too. Desires for the kind of life that she knew perfectly well she would never have. The kind that was full of love and laughter and happily-ever-after, all wrapped up in a white picket fence. Attractions like the one she was feeling for Silas always made her think that things could change. That *she* could change. And as many times as she'd tried to do that in the past, she'd never even come close.

People like her, who had only ever known what unhealthy relationships were like, were doomed to keep finding more of them. Even the ones she'd had with guys that didn't end up being as toxic as the situation she'd grown up in never felt right. Because Mia wasn't right. She'd never be right. So, she'd decided to even stop trying. Best-case scenario, she'd be cheating some decent guy out of being loved the way he deserved to be loved because she just couldn't feel that kind of thing. At worst—

Well. At worst, she'd end up in the same situation she was in as a child. Either way, someone was going to get hurt. That was why Mia was alone now. That was why she would always be alone. Because she'd learned by now that it was better to be alone than to be in a relationship—or even an entanglement—that would not end well. Silas Crockett might be cantankerous, and he might have a rough exterior—and, hey, a rough interior, too, so far as she could tell—but from everything she'd seen of him, he wasn't a bad guy. He took care of animals for a living. Hell, he was taking care of her for the next two weeks, even though that wasn't technically his job—and even though she didn't technically need caring for because she was fine. He didn't deserve an unsatisfying entanglement, either.

So, Mia was just going to have to make sure her attraction to Silas didn't get the better of her. That shouldn't be hard at all, now that she knew she had one. Misunderstanding with Perpetual Salesman of the Month Jeff Oberstrom aside, keeping a handle on her emotions was what Mia did best.

She'd had a lifetime of practice, after all.

Chapter Six

After Silas helped Mia down from the saddle, Beanie was happy to wander over to the watering hole to drink her fill. Mia, on the other hand, was clearly in no way happy. She hustled herself off in the opposite direction from the horse—and from Silas—the minute her feet hit the ground. She probably would have walked all the way back to the ranch if she didn't finally find a spot in the grass to park herself, so that she could glare first at Beanie and then at him. And also if she'd had any idea where the ranch was. But they still had the whole afternoon ahead of them, and he wasn't about to waste it. Especially since she was still steaming about her current situation—not that she would ever admit that to him *or* to herself—and he wanted to capitalize on that.

Not that he could blame her for being steamed. He wasn't in the best of moods himself at the moment. That was what happened when he had to deal with a reaction to Mia—one that was nothing short of explosive—that had come out of nowhere. He wasn't sure *what* was currently making her so angry—other than the fact that she had that pesky anger problem that was her entire reason for being here—but he definitely knew the source of his own upset. And he didn't like being sexually attracted to a woman he had no business being sexually attracted to. Especially when his feelings had the kind of ferocity he had been feeling all afternoon.

And just where the hell was that attraction coming from anyway? Silas hadn't felt this drawn, this fast, to a woman since— Damn, ever. Even with his late wife Jess, there hadn't been the immediacy and intensity there was with Mia. With Jess, it had been slow and easy and comfortable, and it had taken months for him to realize just how deep his feelings for her were. Maybe that had been because he'd never been in love before her, but still. He wasn't in love with Mia. If anything, what he felt for Mia was like the exact opposite of love. Love made a person feel...even. Steady. Satisfied. Complete. Like they'd found a piece of themself that had been missing since the day they were born. Mia had thrown him completely off-kilter. Instead of feeling complete, he felt like he was coming apart at the seams. And he sure as hell wasn't satisfied at the moment.

He told himself he really should have known better than to climb up behind a pretty woman and drop his arms around her. He'd just figured that since (A) Mia was still mostly a stranger to him, (B) she was a client of the ranch and (C) they obviously didn't even like each other much, they naturally wouldn't react to each other in any inappropriate way. Hell, as successful as Mia's mastery over her emotions was, Silas's were world-class in comparison. Even if there was a growing physical connection between them—which, yeah, okay, he guessed he shouldn't be surprised by, since they were both young and reasonably attractive—neither of them should have had a problem tamping that down and keeping it where it belonged. Certainly neither of them should have had a problem being in such close physical contact. But holy cow, his body had snapped to attention the second he was behind her.

He just hadn't been close to a woman like that for a long time, and he'd forgotten how good such a simple thing could be. He really thought he'd moved past that a long time ago, that longing for physical closeness and the feeling of well-being it could bring. It didn't even have to be a passionate, sexual closeness. Just…being close. That felt really good with the right person. But with Mia…

Well. Mia wasn't the right person, that was for damned sure. Not only did the two of them have absolutely nothing in common, she was here to get her feelings sorted out, not get them all convoluted with new ones. She was here at the ranch for a break from her real life, one that was as far removed from his as it would be if she lived at the North Pole. Hell, why was he even thinking about her life and his in one thought when he'd barely known her two days, and she'd be going home in two weeks?

Probably because she'd sure felt good up close. And she smelled good, too. Not flowery and sunshine sweet, like he would have thought a woman who didn't even own a pair of jeans would smell. But as spicy and musky as a stormy night. His body stirred again at the memory, and he ground his teeth together, willing both his body and his unruly thoughts to behave. Yeah, his reaction to Mia today was a normal one to being close to a beautiful woman who smelled like sin. But it wasn't the right time just now. Nor was it the right place. Not that any time or place would be good for getting involved with Mia. So, he just needed to stop thinking about Mia. At least in any way that didn't involve helping her get her life back on track.

He blew out an errant breath and made his way to where she was sitting, dropping himself down to sit beside her. He half thought she would get up and put some distance between them again, but she stayed put. She didn't look at him, though, and instead tilted her head back to study the sky. It was another beautiful June day in Wyoming, as much Big Sky Country as its neighbor to the north Montana was. Blue, blue, blue, as far as the eye could see, with a few wispy stretches of cloud to keep it from being too perfect. The winds were stronger this far out in the field, picking up the stray bits of her ponytail that danced around her face enough that she had to lift a hand to tuck them back behind her ears. Good thing she did, too, because Silas had been itching to do that himself.

Probably, he should look at the sky, too, instead of at Mia.

He leaned back on his elbows and tipped his head back until he could feel the warmth of the sun slathered over him. Then he took off his hat and laid down on his back completely, folding his arms to tuck his hands behind his head. He sighed heavily in contentment at the feel of the bare earth beneath him. There was nothing to make a person feel grounded again like being down on the ground. Yeah, that felt really good.

Mia surprised him by stretching out, too, though he couldn't help noticing she moved a few inches away from him before doing so. He waited for her sigh of contentment, too, but it never came. When he turned his head to look at her, he saw that her pose was identical to his, except that where pretty much all the tension had left his body the minute he'd made contact with the grass, all the tension in hers seemed to multiply.

"You okay?" he asked.

"I'm fine."

Instead of challenging her on that, he turned to look back at the sky again. A Cooper's Hawk that had been biding its time in the nearby trees took off suddenly, soaring right above them before spiraling higher and heading east, its distinctive *kac-kac-kac* following behind, making clear its irritation at being disturbed. Mia, he noted, watched it fly off intently, her gaze lingering in the direction it disappeared long after it was gone. He guessed she didn't see too many birds of prey in the city, especially hawks, and he understood her fascination. He saw them regularly, but their free-and-easy audacity always commanded attention.

He wondered what she was thinking about just then.

Instead of asking her that, he said, "So just what set you off that day at work to make you end up at Whispering Winds?"

"Nothing," she immediately answered. Too immediately. Like she knew exactly what set her off, but she wasn't about to talk about it now. Especially with Silas. He knew she was going to have to open up at some point while she was here, otherwise Miss Sylvie wasn't going to sign off on the paperwork that would keep her employed. But for now, what held his attention was the way she shut down after replying, turning her head back toward the sky above her and closing her eyes tight. "Nothing happened that day," she assured him. "It was just like any other day at work. All of it was just a misunderstanding."

Like any other day at work, Silas echoed to himself. Meaning her coworker had made it a habit to say things to her daily that might potentially set her off. Like maybe he was one of those folks who made it their life's work to provoke other people, just so they could feel powerful in their otherwise impotent lives. Someone who targeted people who were smaller and nicer and less likely to make a scene and therefore were easier to push around.

He sighed. "I think you know it wasn't a misunderstanding, Mia. And I think you also know exactly what set you off that day. You just want to pretend it never happened."

"You got the last part right, at least," she told him, eyes still closed. Still not looking at him. Still shut down. "I don't know why everyone at work can't just pretend it never happened."

"Yeah, well, the guy you went after—what was his name again?"

"Perpetual Salesman of the Month Jeff Oberstrom."

"That's a long name."

"That's what he is, though. No one else sells more cars than Perpetual Salesman of the Month Jeff Oberstrom. That's why he's Perpetual Salesman of the Month Jeff Oberstrom."

"Can't you just call him Jeff?"

"No."

He waited for her to explain why not. She didn't. So he asked, "Why not?"

"He's not a Jeff. He's a Perpetual Salesman of the Mon—"

"I get it," Silas cut her off. "Anyway, I don't think he can pretend it never happened. I think you kind of traumatized him."

She expelled a sound of derision. "I don't think sociopaths can be traumatized. And even if he was traumatized, he—"

She stopped right there and said nothing more. Probably because she was about to finish by saying he deserved it, something that would make her sound angry. And probably also because she was, you know, getting angry again, remembering what happened that day and knowing completely what it was all about instead of it being a misunderstanding.

"He what?" Silas prodded. He wasn't about to cut her any slack when she was battling the very anger she needed to acknowledge before they could start working on her getting past it.

She finally opened her eyes, but instead of looking at Silas, she continued to gaze up at the sky. All she said was, "He's not a nice guy."

"Lotta people aren't nice," he pointed out. "Do you try to make all of them relive their births by yanking them through their neckties?"

Yeah, okay, he'd finally read the HR report Miss Sylvie had emailed him before Mia's arrival. The one with the particulars he hadn't thought would be important. After realizing just how mired in denial Mia was about her anger, he'd decided maybe knowing the details of what had sent her here would give him more insight. Mostly, though, knowing the details had just confused him even more. All her coworker had said to her that day was some throwaway line he could have directed at anyone, a supposed put-down that wasn't even that insulting because it was so dumb and clichéd. His remark had barely been worthy of an eyeroll. But Mia had gone all in.

"A lot of people only come into your life occasionally," Mia said. "And if they're jerks, you only have to deal with it once or twice. You can even excuse it with people like that sometimes. You don't know them. They could just be having a bad day or going through a tough time. It's nothing personal. If they're not nice, that's on them, and they can keep it and take it with them. People like Perpetual Salesman of the Month Jeff Oberstrom make it their life's work to be not nice. Except they don't think they're being not nice. They think they're being funny as hell."

Silas said nothing in response to that. Because Mia sounded like someone who wanted to say more. He wasn't disappointed.

"'Ha, ha, Mia, it was just a joke,'" she said in bland voice that probably suited Perpetual Salesman of the Month Jeff Oberstrom perfectly. "'What, you can't take a joke? C'mon, it was hilarious. Everyone thought so.'" She returned to her regular voice when she added, "Yeah, no, Jeff, they didn't. They only laughed because they're glad I'm the one you're picking on today, not them. They're laughing because they know if they don't laugh, you'll come after them next. You're not a hilarious prankster, you're a sadistic bully who makes himself feel better about his own miserable life by making other people more miserable. Who makes himself feel strong and smart by making other people feel small and worthless."

Wow. Had Silas thought she just wanted to say more? He hadn't known the half of it. Looked like she had a whole storm brewing inside. He sensed a rant coming now. 'Cause that same anger he'd felt simmering just below her surface when he first met her was about to boil over. Hard. He could feel its heat and ferocity blistering up around them like a river of wild magma.

"Why are there even people like that in the world?" she continued, her voice gaining both volume and speed. "I mean I know it takes all kinds to make one and all that, but why does that have to include bullies? Talk about small and worthless. That's what they are. They're just mean and stupid and malignant, and they spread ugliness and hatefulness wherever they go. They find the weakest, most defenseless, least deserving person in the room—the person they know won't put up a fight, because bullies are cowards—and they go after them with a bitterness and relentlessness that can only come from someone who is just an absolute scumbag."

Something about the way she was talking now made Silas think Mia wasn't talking only about Jeff Oberstrom. There seemed to be someone else—maybe more than one someone else—taking up an awful lot of the space in her head just then.

"And you can't hide from them. They make it impossible. They know all the places you go to escape them. The janitor's closet by the women's room only three of us even use. Behind the mainframe room that's been empty for two decades because, hey, mainframe. The very back of the closet behind the soccer gear they stuck in there because *It doesn't fit in your brothers' closet, Mia, and nobody cares about what fits in your room,* and under the bed, which is a lame place to hide anyway, but try telling that to a three-year-old."

Oh, yeah. Definitely talking about someone besides Jeff now. And since she was referring to herself as a three-year-old, it was kinda easy to guess who the bully or bullies she was thinking about were now.

"And then," she continued relentlessly, "when that weakest, most defenseless, least deserving person doesn't or can't defend herself, that just makes the bully feel even better about themself. That just makes them bolder and makes them hurt you even more. Because they're scumbags. They're horrible, despicable people, who never should have had children in the first place, and they—"

She suddenly seemed to realize just how vehemently she was speaking—how vehemently she was feeling—because she suddenly stopped talking. Or maybe she stopped talking because of how much she had just revealed. This morning, she'd told him she didn't have any family. He'd assumed that meant she was an only child who had lost her parents. But there were other reasons for having no family. Sounded like maybe Mia Hawthorne fell into that latter category.

"And they what?" he asked in an effort to draw her out. Because he was starting to get a sense about where her anger might be coming from, and its origins had nothing to do with Jeff. But working with someone who was like her parents, day in and day out, for years, had finally made that anger untenable. And if her anger was as old as it was beginning to seem, they had more work cut out for them than he'd first thought.

Mia closed her eyes again. She inhaled slowly and exhaled the same way, then did it again. And again. And again. Finally, very softly, she said, "Nothing. They do nothing. They are nothing. Nothing is wrong. Everything is fine. I'm fine."

Silas bit back an oath. If he lived to be a hundred, he never wanted to hear that word again.

"You're not fine, Mia," he told her flat out. "That's why you're here. The sooner you admit you're not fine, the sooner you can start working on getting to a place where you actually are fine."

"I'm fine."

Silas figured he had two choices. He could keep needling her until they wound up in an *am-not-are-so* war as if they were preschoolers, or he could cede the battle for now and try again later. He told himself he had made some progress with her today. She had spoken about something personal, even if it had been unintentional, and even if she was pretending now that she'd never said a word of significance about anything. If she'd come from a home with parents who had been at best cold and neglectful and at worst abusive...

He felt his own anger bubble up at the thought of that. He knew there were people out there who hurt their kids. He was also certain there was a special place in hell for them. He just wished he could get his hands on them before they got there, to give them a little preview here on earth of what their eternal damnation would involve.

His gaze fell on Mia again, still lying beneath the sun with her eyes closed tight. Although he'd naturally noticed upon meeting her yesterday that she was a good bit smaller than he was, there had been nothing weak or fragile in her demeanor at all. On the contrary, she'd come across as gutsy and sturdy, in spite of her obvious struggles with her emotions. Looking at her now, though, she seemed… Well. Not gutsy or sturdy at all. In fact, he could almost see the three-year-old hiding under the bed.

And he wanted very badly to get his hands on whoever had driven her there.

Chapter Seven

Mia made her way to the big house for breakfast on her third day at Whispering Winds, wondering what fresh hell Silas had in store for her today. They'd barely spoken at dinner last night, though that was probably her fault for speaking way too much during their ride yesterday afternoon. At dinner, she'd tried to keep it light—and, okay, perky—by asking him the kind of fun, airy questions that kept a dialogue…well, fun and airy. What was his favorite food? What was his favorite color? What was his favorite song? If he could be any animal in the world, what would he be? All he'd offered in reply—to every single question—was a glare. Fine. If he didn't want to talk about how cool it would be to be a nar-whal—her own choice for that last—then he was the one missing out.

But just what on earth had all her word spewing yes-terday been about, anyway? she wondered for probably the millionth time since it happened. She never talked about her life as a child. To anyone. Certainly not to someone she'd basically just met. That was all in the past. Water under the bridge. A ship sailed. A page turned. A slate cleaned. Whatever cliché Mia had been able to conjure to put her past in the past and keep it there, she had done it. No need crying over spilled milk.

None of that had anything to do with who she was now. She didn't even think about that part of her life anymore. There was no point. She was done with it. So why had it shouldered its way into her brain and out of her mouth yesterday?

All she could do was hope Silas thought she had been talking about someone else in all her for-instances, and not her own family. Especially since she'd done her best to make clear yesterday morning that she did *not* have a family. Because she didn't. Would that she had never had a family to begin with. If that had been the case, her life would have been much easier. Silas was a smart guy, though. Unless he hadn't been paying attention—another big if, since he was also clearly super observant—he'd probably figured out enough. Certainly more than she wanted him to know.

She found him waiting for her outside the dining room entrance, but instead of gesturing her through the door—instead of even telling her good morning—he picked up a cardboard tray holding two covered cups of coffee and a bag of what she assumed was going to be today's break-fast. Obviously, he already had plans for their morning. Which meant that, obviously, so did she.

"We're gonna try something different today," he told her.

"Different from riding a horse?" she asked. "Sign me up."

"Yeah, different from that. Though we'll be doing that, too."

Damn. Missed it by *that* much.

"You're also gonna help me out with some of my chores."

Although that certainly sounded different, it didn't sound like something Mia wanted to do, which, of course, was precisely why Silas was going to make her do it. He wanted her out of her comfort zone. He wanted to make her angry. Well, the joke was on him. Even ranch chores wouldn't make her angry. After what happened yesterday, she was more determined than ever to do her *Forget Your Troubles, C'mon Get Happy* dance. Judy Garland had nothing on her, mister. She was just fine, dammit. So there.

Even so, she asked warily, "What kind of chores?"

"The kind I did before I needed a college degree to do my job."

Well, that sounded pretty manual. "Do any of these chores involve a pitchfork?" she asked.

He narrowed his eyes at the question. "Why do you sound so hopeful when you ask that? If I give you a pitchfork, is it gonna wind up in my back?"

"Of course not."

Pitchforks? Please. Her preferred method of menace and revenge was Tom Ford neckties purchased for full price from Nieman Marcus. Everyone knew that.

She was horrified by the thought the minute it entered her head. Mia Hawthorne was not a menacing or vengeful person. Only angry people were menacing and vengeful. And that was most certainly not her. If Silas handed her a pitchfork this morning, she would use it for its intended purpose and nothing more. She just hoped that purpose involved hay, the stuff that went into a cow's mouth, and not, um, the stuff the hay was turned into after it came out of the other end of the animal. And even if it did involve that version, that was okay! It was. She would manage just like she always did when life, um, threw manure in her general direction.

Silas, however, didn't look convinced by her assertion. "Yeah, well, maybe today we'll focus on the non-pitchfork jobs," he told her. "Start small and all that."

Which was how Mia found herself an hour later taking on one of those "small" tasks that was in no way small. Oh, sure, the calf in question was small*ish*—at least in comparison to the grown-up cows milling about the barn where she and Silas were working—but it was still half as big as she was. And the bottle he'd given her to feed it was the size of the liter bottle she filled with water to take to work every day. And wow, was Tim the baby cow thirsty.

And who named a cow Tim anyway?

"It's short for Tiny Tim," Silas told her, as if reading her mind. Again. Why was he so good at doing that? Except for the part about him always thinking she was angry, since he couldn't be more wrong about that. "He was born with a messed-up leg, like the kid in *A Christmas Carol*. It's pretty much fine now, but it was bad enough when he was born that his mother rejected him, and I had to start hand-feeding him."

The comment hit Mia a lot harder than it should have, tightening her belly and stinging her eyes enough to prick tears. What the heck was that about? It was just a cow. And it was hardly a surprise to her that animals could be jerks. Mothers rejecting their young for stupid reasons wasn't exactly uncommon in the animal world. Nature was a bitch and all that. There was no reason why she should be so affected by something that probably happened with some regularity in the world of farm life. Then she looked at the fuzzy-faced little cow drinking hungrily from the bottle in her hand, at his enormous eyes and eyelashes long enough to put every influencer out there to shame, and she just wanted to…hug it. Hard.

Which was super weird. As big a people-pleaser as Mia was, and as well as she got along with people—except Perpetual Salesman of the Month Jeff Oberstrom—she wasn't the type to care for and love a pet. She liked animals, the same way she liked—most—people. When she saw dogs in the park, she petted them. One summer, when there was a feral cat frequenting the alley behind her apartment, she left food and water for it until it stopped coming around. But to actually commit to caring for another living creature day after day? To love another living creature day after day?

Talk about being outside her comfort zone.

As she grew more comfortable feeding Tim, though, she started to see why maybe some people liked being around animals for more than superficial reasons. Not her, of course, but some people. Silas, for instance, she thought as she looked up to find him looking back at her. It was his job to make sure the cattle were cared for. Funny, since he didn't give the impression of being any more caring of other creatures than she was. Then again, there were people out there who got along fine with animals and not so much with people. She guessed he was just one of those.

"I think Tim likes you," he said now.

She looked at the calf, who had finished drinking for long enough to gaze at her with adoring eyes. And to also drool a little onto her borrowed jeans. She started to feel bad about that, then reminded herself these jeans had probably been drooled on by cows more than once. And she was kind of surprised to realize that baby cow drool didn't bother her as much as she would have thought it would if she were sitting in her office in St. Louis and someone was telling her a story about how they got drooled on by a baby cow.

Still looking at Tim, she asked Silas, "How do you know he likes me?"

"He stopped eating long enough to give you the time of day," he told her.

Tim made a little muffled sound with his baby cow nose and shook his baby cow head. Then he grabbed the bottle in his baby cow mouth again and went back to consuming his breakfast. Mia couldn't help the smile that curled her own mouth. In spite of his sloppiness, he was pretty cute.

"He seems like a nice enough cow," she said. "I guess I kind of like him, too."

Once Tim drank his fill, Mia followed Silas to the next chore on their list—checking a hundred miles of fencing to be sure it was all intact. Okay, okay, maybe it wasn't quite a hundred miles. Maybe it was more like one mile. Ish. It sure felt like a hundred miles, because Mia had to get on Beanie again. Alone this time, because Silas took his own horse, a gigantic copper-colored quarter horse named Jasper. Okay, maybe he wasn't exactly *gigantic*. In fact, he wasn't that much bigger than Beanie. But he *was* bigger, and since Mia still wasn't all that comfortable with any horse, he might as well have been gigantic. Even so, he and Beanie seemed to be pretty good friends, because the two horses got along great. Maybe that was why Beanie seemed a lot easier to handle today than she had yesterday. It was always good to be with friends.

At least, that was what Mia had always heard. She didn't really have a lot of friends to help her find that out firsthand. Friends were like animals—they required that pesky care and peskier love, too. Life was just easier not trying to be something she wasn't. Colleagues and co-workers she did fine with. Well, except for…you know. Honest-to-God friends were a whole 'nother thing. One she wasn't particularly interested in pursuing. Her life was fine the way it was.

After the fence-checking on Silas's chore list came equipment maintenance. That had sounded like just another thing to anger her by putting her in the uncomfortable position of not knowing what she was doing, because she was thinking about equipment being stuff like agricultural tools or horse and cattle paraphernalia or something. Instead, Silas led her to what looked from the outside like yet another barn but was actually a receptacle for a lot of the ranch's vehicles. Trucks mostly, a couple of SUVs, and a station wagon that was probably older than her and Silas put together.

Okay then. Now they were getting somewhere. For the first time since coming to the ranch, Mia felt right at home. Because she wasn't just the service advisor at Carrigan Auto. She'd learned a thing or two—or twenty—about vehicle maintenance herself over the years. Enough that she could work on just about any vehicle herself in a pinch. Enough that she'd even applied for the mechanics' assistant job at work whenever one was posted, in the hope of working her way up to actual mechanic someday. But those jobs always went to someone else, often a kid—a male kid—just out of high school. And whenever she'd objected, it was always *Don't be silly, Mia, it has nothing to do with you having ovaries.* Even though she was fairly certain that was precisely the reason she was never hired.

Anyway, she was happy to see her good friends, The Vehicles.

Without waiting for Silas to tell her what to do, she went straight to the newest of the SUVs—which was none too new—and lifted the hood. Then she went to tinkering. Silas followed her over and watched as she checked and topped off all the fluids, then replaced an air filter that was long overdue. She found everything she needed without having to ask, because one thing about people who took care of vehicles was that they always had a shoddy, rusting metal cabinet or two somewhere that held everything they needed. Like fluids and filters and—hey, whattaya know—some spark plugs, a few taillights, and a tire gauge, which she could use, too.

One by one, Mia made her way through all the ranch's modes of transportation, until every single one of them was in as good a shape as she could get it with what she had to work with. The tractor, combine and baler would have to wait for another day. If she was going to be here a couple months instead of weeks, she could have mastered them all, but even the ATV didn't give her a problem today. Silas just sat back and observed as she went about her work, arms crossed over his chest, heels dug into the straw-covered ground, looking as grumpy as ever. Though there was one time when she glanced up that he might, possibly, perhaps have been looking kind of impressed. Hard to tell when even on the handful of occasions when he hadn't been in a particularly cranky mood—few though they'd been—he'd always looked pretty cranky.

Today was no exception.

"I thought you were just the service manager at your dealership," he said as she lowered the hood on the ancient station wagon. "Not one of the mechanics."

"I'm the service advisor," she corrected him. Even though it wasn't a correction, because she was essentially the service manager, even if they didn't want to call her that, because then they'd have to pay her as much as the other managers, all of whom also didn't have ovaries.

She smiled as she added, "But that's so sweet of you to remember."

His mouth set in a flat line at her—dare she say it?— perky reply.

"I'm a naturally curious person," she told him. "I've learned a lot about the actual parts and servicing of cars over the years, in addition to being the person who organizes all the parts and service."

He nodded. "Well, if you lose your job back in St. Louis for trying to birth another one of your coworkers through their belt loop or something, you should come back here and hit up Miss Sylvie to get hired on. Since our fleet manager retired, we don't have anyone on the ranch who really takes an interest in these things."

As she wiped her hands on a rag she'd also found in the ratty metal cabinet, she tried not to be too smug. "Yeah, I can tell. Want me to retorque the tires on all of them while I'm at it?"

His eyebrows shot up. "Is that really necessary?"

It wasn't. She just wanted to show off and impress him some more. Just why she would want to impress him, though, eluded her. Maybe it was only because she liked having gotten his dander up with her perkiness and wanted to push the envelope a little more.

"Not really," she said. "I can do it another time if we have more stuff we need to get done today."

"We do," he told her. "We still need to check on the livestock in the pasture, see how the hay meadow is doing, and refill water and feed before we call it a day."

Mia had never really thought about how much work must go into running a ranch or farm or any other kind of agribusiness. That sort of thing just wasn't on the radar of a typical city dweller who took it for granted that there would always be food at the grocery store or farmers' markets for them to buy and never wondered about where it all actually came from or how it ended up for purchase.

Then another thought struck her. Agribusinesses generally produced foodstuffs. The cattle on Whispering Winds must ultimately be intended for the very grocery stores she'd just been thinking about. Some of the cattle they were about to check on out on the range might very well wind up in the meat case at her local Schnuks. And if one of those cattle could wind up in the meat case at Schnuks, then what about—

"Tiny Tim," she said suddenly.

Silas looked confused by the sudden change of subject. "What about him?"

She bit back the panic growing in the pit of her stomach. "I mean, Whispering Winds is a cattle ranch, right?"

He nodded, still clearly at a loss for where this was

going. "For the most part. Except for the dude side of things."

"So that means Whispering Winds produces...beef?"

He nodded again. "Ye-ah." He strung the word into the next time zone, still obviously not sure what she was worked up about.

It had honestly never occurred to Mia to think about the plastic-wrapped portions in the meat case that she bought at the grocery store as ever being anything but plastic-wrapped portions. Sure, they were meat. Just like carrots were carrots and bananas were bananas. But carrots and bananas didn't need to be bottle fed at any point in their life—and they sure as hell didn't have eye-lashes—while plastic-wrapped portions...

"Is Tiny Tim going to wind up on someone's dinner plate?" she blurted out. She couldn't help it. She couldn't get past that thought until she had an answer to that question.

Now Silas threw her a funny look, as if wondering why she should care. "I mean...probably? He's a beef product like the rest of the herd."

"No," she said adamantly. "No, no, no, no, no. Promise me, Silas. Promise me Tiny Tim will never, ever, be shipped off to Trader Joe's."

"Well, it could be H-E-B or Kroger or—"

"*No!*" She nearly shouted. "You can't send him any-where to become someone's dinner!"

He looked stunned by her vehemence. She didn't blame him. She was stunned by her vehemence, too. He was right. Tiny Tim was a product as far as Whispering Winds was concerned. Why couldn't she consider him a product, too?

"It's not up to me, Mia," Silas told her. "I don't handle that side of the business. You're gonna have to take that up with Miss Sylvie."

And she would, too. First thing in the morning. Mia didn't know why it was so important to her. She'd been a meat-eater all her life, including beef. She didn't plan to stop eating beef in the future. Beef was delicious. And nutritious. But beef was meat. Tiny Tim was—

What? she asked herself. He was part of a giant herd of cattle. Who were all being raised to feed people, because beef was what was for dinner while Aaron Copeland music played in the background, and Madison Avenue patted itself on the back for a hugely successful beef campaign because, decades later, people still said "It's What's for Dinner" when they took it off the grill. *Of course* Tim was going to wind up on someone's dinner plate. That was his whole reason for being born. Why did Mia care? She loved a good tri-tip as much as the next person.

She'd just never thought about a tri-tip drooling on her jeans in a way that was kind of adorable. Okay, she might have to give up tri-tips from here on out. And maybe other beef cuts, too. She was still going to eat chicken, though. Probably.

"Does Whispering Winds raise chickens?" she asked Silas.

He threw her another confused look. "Yeah. I don't really have much to do with them, but I can take you over to the henhouse if you want to meet—"

"No!" she told him vehemently. "I do not want to meet the hens."

"We don't breed them for meat," Silas told her. "We just like the eggs. So do our guests."

Well, that was something, she supposed. She still didn't want to meet them.

Silas seemed to understand, because he stopped looking confused and started looking sympathetic. He didn't look happy about being sympathetic, but he did look sympathetic. Kind of.

"Look, Mia, it's the whole circle of life thing. To people who don't grow up on farms or ranches, it's a hard awakening when they realize the things they eat drew breath at one point in one way or another. But a lot of animals exist to just be nourishment for other animals. People may not be apex predators like tigers or sharks, but meat's always been a big part of the human diet. It has been since the beginning. It has nutrition we need to survive that's hard for us to get from other places. I totally respect anyone who doesn't want to eat meat for whatever reason. But if it weren't for us omnivores eating meat, the whole food chain would go out of whack. Eat what you want. Enjoy what you eat. Don't judge others for doing the same. It's pretty simple."

"But Tiny Tim…"

He almost grinned at that. Almost. "Yeah, I guess it's hard once you get to know your dinner personally."

"He's not going to be my dinner."

"Well, he might. You never—"

"Silas, stop it. You have to make sure he doesn't…you know…go to market."

"What else is he supposed to do, Mia? It's not like we can put him in charge of the motor pool. Cattle aren't exactly cheap to raise, and if left to their own devices, they can live fifteen or twenty years. Even longer sometimes."

For one brief, insane moment, she wondered if she would have room in her apartment in St. Louis for a baby cow. But she quickly came to her senses. Not only was there no way she could raise a cow, it was none of her business what happened to Tim. Mia was in no position to tell anyone at Whispering Winds how to do their job or which animals should be designated for which fates. She was a pragmatic person. Mostly. One who knew what needed to be done and did it. One who, on normal days, lived and let live. So what was the big damned deal?

"You're right," she told him. "It's none of my business."

"I didn't mean it like th—"

"No, I know. But it isn't. I'll just try not to think about it."

He barked out a sound of derision at that. "Oh, right. Just add that to the long list of things you already don't think about. Shouldn't be a problem at all."

Now Mia was the one to narrow her eyes. "And just what's that supposed to mean?"

"Exactly what I said. Your life's work is not thinking about the things that bother you. You've buried them so deep, even my best efforts to bring 'em to the fore are useless."

She bit back a growl. "Oh, here we go again. My anger issues. Which don't even exist. How many times do I have to tell you people that *I'm...not...angry!*"

"You sure as hell sound angry."

"Well, I'm *not* angry," she told him angrily. No! Not angrily! She told him with much annoyance. That was bad enough. She didn't like getting annoyed. It too often led to ang—

"I'm *fine*."

Instead of challenging her on the word she used to deliberately make *him* angry, he only studied her in silence for a moment. Finally, he asked, "You know what happens to people who don't learn how to manage their anger?"

Gee, he should know, since he seemed to be carrying around enough of it himself. She said nothing, though, only looked at him in anticipation of his diagnosis.

"A host of physical stuff, for starters," he told her. "High blood pressure, heart disease, neurological disorders." When she didn't react to any of his scary analysis—hey, she had annual physicals, and none of her vital signs had ever been out of whack...much—he added, "Digestive issues, abdominal pain—"

Again, no worries. At this point, Mia actually lifted her hand to roll her finger in the internationally recognized sign language for *Move along*.

Silas glared at her. What a shocker. "Eczema," he said. "Psoriasis."

Okay, that did make her stop with the finger rolling and instead move her hand to her face. Then into her hair to test her scalp. So she was shallow enough to worry about her looks. So, sue her. But everything was obviously under control there, too. That just went to show that she didn't have any unmanaged anger. She didn't have *any* anger. She was fine.

"What happened at work that day that set you off?" he asked. Just as he'd asked every day since her arrival. "I'm not going to let this go, Mia. Today, you're going to give me an answer. We're not leaving here until you tell me what set you off so badly."

She expelled a restless breath. Although it was Miss Sylvie who would be signing off on the progress Mia made—or didn't make—during her stay here at Whispering Winds, she would be taking her cues from Silas's observations and opinions. If, by the end of Mia's two weeks, either of them decided she was still too angry to go back to work—as silly as that was, since Mia wasn't angry—she could lose her job. Both her boss and Patsy in HR had made that clear. Looking at him now, Mia could see he meant what he said. Either she told him what exactly had happened that day, or she better find a good place to sleep among the vehicles in the motor pool.

Fine. She would tell him. At least he would finally hear her version of it, and not just the step-by-step details that must be in the HR report. And he would finally have no choice but to realize that it all really was just a misunderstanding.

"Before I start," she said, "there's something you need to know about Perpetual Salesman of the Month Jeff Oberstrom."

"That he's a jackass?"

Okay, so he *had* been listening to her diatribe yesterday. "In addition to that," she told him.

He said nothing, only studied her in his usual stony silence.

"He also hates women. Like…a lot."

Silas looked in no way surprised by that, either.

"Of course, that doesn't stop him from putting his hands on the women who work there whenever he feels like it," she continued. "All three of us. But since we're so outnumbered, and our boss isn't exactly a feminist ally, we don't really have much choice but to either deal with it ourselves or quit. Since jobs are hard to come by these days, and we all have to keep a roof over our heads and food on our table, we don't quit."

Though Mia would probably be saving some money now that she'd decided to forgo ingesting members of Tim's family, it wasn't enough of a savings for her to be able to look for something else.

"So then you three should just deal with it yourselves."

Mia actually laughed at that. Not the perky laugh she usually went to when she was laughing at something— the one she'd spent years practicing and had perfected like a pro—but the laugh all women laughed when men told them to *just deal with* the sexist, misogynistic behavior of other men. The men who were bigger than them, and had more power than them, and were more menacing than them. The men who knew what time they walked out to their cars and where they lived once they got home and whether or not they lived alone.

But all she said was, "Yeah, well, there are those who would say that's kinda what I did that day at work. And look where that landed me."

When she looked at Silas again, his stony demeanor had somehow become even stonier. Wow. She wouldn't have thought that was possible.

"Did he put his hands on you that day?" he asked, his voice icy. "Is that what set you off?"

Mia shook her head. "Not on that day. He started to, but that was when I…" She paused, inhaling deeply before releasing her breath again.

"When you…dealt with it yourself."

She nodded. "The threat of him patting my ass wasn't what did it, though," she told him. "He patted my ass every chance he got—he did that to all of us every chance he got—and I never went after him those times. I just tried to ignore him. It was easier that way."

"Easier to be manhandled than to just tell him to knock it off?"

She laughed the wry laugh again. "Right. Spoken like someone who tops six feet and is a solid wall of muscle and, oh, yeah, is also a guy. Not to mention someone who can walk to his car after hours and not have to constantly look over his shoulder and hold his keys pointy side out between his fingers because brass knuckles are illegal in a lot of places."

Now he looked stonier still. Actually, now he looked like someone who wanted to birth a perpetual salesman of the month through his necktie. But all he said was, "Then what made you go after him that time?"

Mia sighed wearily. "Divya and Lauren and I—those are my two woman coworkers—were in the break room, talking about our families," she began. "Well, they were talking about their families, and I was listening, since I don't have a family to talk about. And Divya was saying something about how messy her toddler was and how hard it was to keep the house clean, but you could tell she wasn't complaining, because, oh my God, she loves that kid. Then Lauren chimed in about how her husband was the same way, basically an overgrown toddler, and then I said something about more power to both of them, they were braver women than me because no way was I ever going to have a spouse or any kids to clean up after, 'cause that was the *last* thing I wanted."

She stopped talking long enough to gather her thoughts—she really hated thinking about that day—and Silas continued to study her in silence. Actually, she didn't like thinking about most days at work, now that she thought about it. But who did, right?

When she didn't start talking again, Silas asked, "And where does this Jeff guy fit into all this?"

Mia closed her eyes and started talking again. "He walked into the break room just as I was saying it. I was standing up at the time, and he walked over to where we were, and he laughed that stupid laugh of his and very loudly announced that it was a good thing I wanted to end up as a single, childless cat lady, because no way would any family ever want me anyway."

She opened her eyes again, because they were starting to feel wet, and she didn't need any of that crap right now. "Then he stuck out his hand to pat me on the ass, as if it was the most natural thing in the world for him to do, and I just…"

She shook her head. She honestly didn't remember much after that until the part where two of the other salesmen were wrestling her off Jeff's back while the rest of the room looked on in horror. Well, except for Divya and Lauren. Mia still couldn't quite shake the memory of them cheering her on, but, in hindsight, she was pretty sure she was only imagining that.

"I lost it," she said. "I guess I was just so tired of all his crap that I'd finally had enough. Did I overreact? For sure. But at the time, it somehow felt like I was doing what I had to do to survive."

Silas studied her in more silence for several long minutes. Then he told her, "That doesn't sound like a mis-understanding."

Well, maybe not the way she was telling it. But she wasn't good at storytelling. Maybe it was one of those *you had to be there* things.

"I mean," he continued, "you yourself had just an-nounced to the whole room that being a single, child-less cat lady was exactly what you had planned for your future."

"I didn't say anything about a cat," she objected. "And I wasn't talking to the room at large. I was standing by a table, talking with two of my coworkers."

"Did you make the comment loud enough to be heard by everyone else in there?"

"Yes, but—"

"So, technically, Jeff was just agreeing with you."

"Yeah, but he didn't have to be so—"

"And then you went all birth-by-necktie on him."

"Well, there was a little more to it than—"

"So, what was the big deal, Mia?" Silas challenged. And he had definitely moved beyond curiosity to chal-lenging her now. "How did anything Jeff said that day provoke a response in you that was so over-the-top? It couldn't have been much different from anything he'd said to you on any other day. Yeah, the guy is an ass-hole, but we all have those at work. We just ignore them and move on."

Mia told herself he was being obtuse on purpose, just to get a rise out of her. Just to make her angry. It was the same thing she'd told herself about Jeff that day at work. That he was only saying what he did to get a reaction out of her that would make him feel smug and satisfied that he had that much control over her. Rationally, she knew she should just ignore Silas now, the way she had told herself to ignore Jeff that day at work. But just as had happened that day at work with Jeff, her rational mind took a back seat to her emotions. The more Silas needled her, the angrier...um, the more irritated she got. Because it wasn't Silas's voice or words that started bouncing around her brain just then. The same way it wasn't Jeff's voice or words that had echoed in her mind that day at work. It was her own voice. Her own words.

No one could possibly ever love you, Mia. That's why you live the life you live and why you're planning the future you are. No one loves you now, and no one will ever love you. No one has ever loved you. Because no one ever could *love you. You're just unlovable. And you're not worthy of love, either.*

She closed her eyes again, willing tears not to come. It really had been a misunderstanding that day. She hadn't been lying about that part—to herself or anyone else. She'd just never elaborated on how it hadn't been Jeff who misunderstood. Or anyone else. It had been her. Before Jeff's comment, she had been thinking that day—as she'd thought every day—that her future living a solitary life would be by choice. The same way her present living a solitary life was by choice. That day, though, with her own words bouncing around in her head in response to his, she'd been forced to realize how badly she had indeed been lying to herself. Not just that day, but every day. Truth was, she was alone and would always be alone not because it was her decision, but because there was nothing about her that made others want to include her in their lives long-term. Or even short-term. She was likeable enough. She knew that because she'd worked hard to make herself likeable by doing all the things she'd seen likeable people do. But loveable? Enough to make people want to keep her around forever? Enough to make some-one want to build a life and create a family with her?

Nah. That wasn't Mia at all. And it never would be. Because no one could possibly ever love her.

"Excuse me," she told Silas as she jumped up and headed toward the barn door. "I need to get some air."

But instead of stopping once she got outside, Mia just kept walking. She didn't know where she was going. She didn't care. She just knew she needed to be someplace where she would be left alone.

Funny, though, how she suddenly realized now that that could be anywhere in the world.

Chapter Eight

And so it went for the rest of Mia's first week at Whispering Winds. Every morning, Silas awoke with the single usual item on his agenda: Make Mia mad. And every morning, Mia woke up with one item on her agenda, too: Stay as bright and chipper as a mountain bluebird. She showed up at breakfast with a perky smile. She went about their daily activities with a perky smile. She ate lunch with a perky smile. Afternoon chores, dinner, after-dinner social events... All of it with a perky smile. Even her nightly *See ya tomorrow* was delivered with a perky smile.

Silas would have found all of it damned irritating if it hadn't been for the fact that her smiles and perkiness were so half-assed after the day she'd finally talked about what happened at work. And although she'd gotten angrier talking about it than he'd seen her this week, now she just seemed to be...sad. Sad and tired. Even the chipper mountain bluebird act couldn't hide it. It was like she was just going through some motions she'd spent a lifetime perfecting to the point where she was certain everyone would believe the act, even when it was half-assed.

Her sadness bothered Silas more than her anger did. Maybe because, where she was still in denial about the anger, she seemed to have accepted the sadness as a natural part of who she was. And although sadness was as legitimate an emotion as anger was, and it had its uses…

Silas didn't know where he was going with thoughts like those. He just saw a big change in Mia after that day. A change that wasn't necessarily for the better. And he still didn't know what to do to get her on track.

One thing at a time, he'd finally decided. Anger had been the first thing he'd noticed about her. So they would deal with that first. And if that opened the door to why she felt sad and tired, too, then, hey, bonus.

By the end of the week, though, Silas was getting frustrated. He'd tried everything he could think of since that afternoon to make her mad, from making her get up at 4:00 a.m. to help him muck out the new calves' stalls to hosing and bathing Beanie—who she was still afraid of, even if she pretended not to be. From disagreeing with everything she said, no matter how ridiculous it made him seem, to taking everything she said personally and trying to pick a fight that way.

He'd even tried some of the old school, surefire irritants like staring at her forehead when she was talking to him instead of looking her in the eye. And although that one did get a little bit of a rise out of her—especially when he told her he couldn't help it because she was just so doggone short—she'd still managed to mostly keep her cool. At this point, he was starting to run out of ideas. Soon, it was going to be summer-camp pranks like putting baloney slices in her boots or short-sheeting her bed.

Anyway, nothing had worked. No matter how subtle or how outrageous he was, she was just determined to not get angry and stay as fake perky and faux upbeat as she could. Because, as she kept telling him, over and over and over again, she *wasn't* angry. She was *fine.*

He blew out an exasperated breath as he left his house before dawn, completely out of ideas. Then he settled his Stetson on his head, and headed off to Mia's cabin for round... What day was this? Saturday. Round six.

Honestly, if it hadn't kept him from doing his job—and, you know, been really annoying—he would have found Mia's staunch insistence on staying so positive in the face of so much adversity admirable. But it really did keep him from doing his job, and it was, you know, really annoying. So there was that.

Maybe he should try something different, he thought as he made his way toward her cabin. She was half-way through her stay and they'd barely made any progress, save for some insight into her childhood he'd only managed to glean by default. And yeah, it sounded like her childhood had left a lot to be desired. But plenty of people had had crappy childhoods and did just fine as adults. In fact—

He halted himself when he realized he'd just used the word he hated so much. Did just *fine* as adults. He was beginning to realize just what a wide-ranging word that was and how often it got misused as a catch-all term that could mean...well, anything. Maybe, in some ways, Mia really was just fine. The same way he was fine himself, in spite of what he'd gone through with the tragedy of losing Jess and—

Then again, he switched tracks before he got too far down the one that was way too damaged to travel, his childhood had included the loss of a parent, hadn't it? The loss of both parents, really, even though he'd never known his father. He still had a lot of happy, comforting memories to temper the bad ones of losing his mom. Because he'd still gotten a lot of love and support from other people during her illness and after her death. Those memories outweighed the bad and had kept the big picture in perspective. They had kept him from becoming so callous and uncaring that he had to lie to himself all the time that he was *fine*. Didn't sound like Mia had many happy memories from her childhood to do that for her.

He thought about her with Tiny Tim the other day, how careful and concerned she'd been while she fed him. And yeah, some of that might have just been the result of her not knowing what the hell she was doing. But he also sensed there was something instinctual and innate inside her that made caring for another creature natural. That was pretty amazing, since it sounded like she hadn't received much care from others when she was growing up.

Then she'd discovered the new litter of kittens in one of the barns yesterday, and she'd had to check those out, too. Their mama had showed up on the ranch out of nowhere a month ago, doubtless after being dumped there by her owner once they realized she was pregnant. That happened with some regularity in rural places like Serenity Valley. Silas would ensure she was spayed once the kittens were weaned, and they'd keep the whole family. Barn cats earned their keep ten times over with the disposal of marauding rodents and reptiles both, and it had been a while since Whispering Winds had a whole passel of them like this. After he'd explained all that to Mia—well, actually *while* he was explaining all that to Mia—she'd knelt by the stall the cats currently called home and reached in to stroke each one. Even though, he recalled, she hadn't seemed overly comfortable doing it, she'd done it anyway, as if she hadn't been able to help herself. And when he'd gotten to the part about the mama cat being abandoned, and she'd looked up at him with a stricken expression, well…

It was clear that Mia wasn't callous and uncaring, even coming from what sounded like a background that would have justified her being both. He just wished he knew what to do to help her start letting go of the childhood anger she still hadn't dealt with as an adult. What was it going to take to bring it out into the open so she could look at it for what it was and turn it into something productive?

Maybe it was time for a new approach. Maybe he should stop trying to elicit her anger and instead just see if it was possible to talk it out. Not that he was some kind of shrink who specialized in talk therapy, but maybe if he could just get Mia started, she'd work through everything herself. For some people, talking helped a lot. Not Silas, of course. Miss Sylvie had tried that with him after everything that had happened with Jess, and talking had been the last thing he'd wanted to do. He wasn't a sharer. Not with words, not with feelings. But Mia, he was beginning to realize, had more feelings than probably either of them had realized. She might be okay delving deeper. It was worth a shot.

And why did he suddenly kind of hope she would share more of herself with him for reasons other than managing her anger? Why did he suddenly just kind of want to learn more about her? And maybe share things about himself with her while they were at it? Hell, hadn't he just been thinking he *wasn't* a sharer?

Coffee. Obviously, he needed some coffee. Badly.

As the sun began to creep over the mountains, he continued to make his way to her cabin. He'd told her last night they were going have breakfast at the big house, then…do something he hadn't figured out yet. Not that he'd told her he hadn't figured it out yet, because that would have given her the upper hand. Silas never let anyone have the upper hand because upper hands were hard to get back. He *did* tell her they were going to do something today. But when he knocked on her door, there was no answer from inside. He peered through one of the open windows and called out to her, but it was obviously she wasn't there.

Where the hell had she gone before the sun even came up? She didn't know her way around the ranch except for the handful of places he'd taken her, none of which—save the motor pool—had she seemed to want to return to again. Even in the big house, which was as homey as it got, she always seemed uneasy, her gaze darting from one place to another.

He had begun to suspect that nowhere in the world was comfortable for Mia Hawthorne. Except maybe—maybe—her own place back in St. Louis. But she never talked about St. Louis, even when he'd asked her pointed questions about the place where she lived and worked and had grown up. She'd assured him that she liked St. Louis a lot. Funny, though, how she never really told him why she liked it or described any of the places she enjoyed visiting or any of the people she might hang out with there.

He waited a few more minutes to see if she'd maybe taken a quick walk because she couldn't sleep, then headed for the big house. It was still a little early for guest breakfast—he'd been planning on making Mia fix her own, just to get her off on the right grumpy foot— but she wasn't at the big house, either.

Where the hell was she?

He headed back out to the front porch, hesitating at the top of the steps to look left, then right, then left again. The sky was smudged with the lavenders and ambers of early dawn, pink clouds streaking across it like cotton candy. Some of the hands were already out with the cattle, guiding them toward a pond that was the ranch's main watering hole. A soft breeze blew across the yard, stirring up dust and a few aspen leaves, whispering past his ears in the way that had given the ranch its name. It was as peaceful a morning as he had ever seen in Serenity Valley. So why was peaceful the last thing he was feeling?

Where the hell was she?

A strange feeling bubbled up inside him. At first, he didn't recognize it, but gradually the name of it dawned on him. Fear. Fear for someone other than himself. It had been so long since he'd felt it, he'd almost forgotten what it was like. Almost. There was a reason why some of the paths in his brain were impassable. He was the one who'd dug the ruts and thrown down the stones, because the last thing he wanted to do was to travel down them again. There had been days during his time with Jess when he'd known a fear of losing her that could be crippling if he didn't keep it under tabs. Especially after she'd gotten pregnant, and the stakes doubled. After losing her and their unborn baby both...

Nope. Not gonna go there. Not even after the passage of twelve years. Suffice it to say that since his time with Jess, there just hadn't been anyone who could rouse that kind of fear in Silas again. He'd made absolutely, positively, hands-down certain of that. You couldn't feel fear for people if you kept them at arm's length all the time, that was for damned sure. Feeling fear again now—for Mia, of all people—coming out of nowhere like this...

Ah, hell. Feeling it again now, he hated it even more than he had in the past. Before, whenever he'd feared the worst that could happen, the rational side of his brain would always eventually kick in at some point and remind him that the odds of the worst happening were pretty slim. Then the worst *had* happened, and he'd realized the rational side of his brain was wrong. Horribly, excruciatingly, wrong. And it had nearly destroyed him. Since then, he'd learned not to trust the rational side of his brain. It couldn't kick in anymore and tell him he was being ridiculous. Terrible things could happen, even against all odds. Screw rationality. The fear was real.

But Whispering Winds wasn't a dangerous place— not like the city was—and Mia was a grown woman, capable of taking care of herself. As evidenced by how she took on a bully twice her size without hesitation and might have even knocked him out if her coworkers hadn't pulled her off him before she had the chance. She was still in Silas's care while she was here at Whispering Winds. The same way Jess had been in his care when she—

He pushed the thought away again, before it could enter his brain. Thinking about that would only make him angry. Okay, angri*er*. And then he wouldn't be any good to anyone. Especially Mia.

Where the hell was she?

He scanned the yard again and his gaze lit on the storage barn on the other side of the main corral. There was no reason for her to want to go there for anything. All it held was the stuff they only needed from time to time and a surplus of stuff they might need in the future, and…

And also the mama cat and her kittens. Mia had told him that day filling out the questionnaires that she'd never had pets and wasn't the pet mom type. That was okay. A lot of people weren't. Himself included. There was nothing wrong with looking out for number one. Sometimes, that was the only way a person could survive.

Himself included.

He'd taken Mia at her word that morning, but he'd seen for himself since then that what she'd claimed about not being the pet mom type wasn't necessarily true, no matter what she thought.

He made his way in that direction. The sun had crept a bit higher now, staining the tops of the mountains with pink and gold, too. The breeze hit him harder after he left the shelter of the porch, so he hitched up the collar of his denim jacket around his neck. He hadn't been lying to Mia when he'd told her it could still get cold in Serenity Valley in the summer. The mountains even got snow from time to time, it got so cold up there, and a person had to—

A light bulb went off in Silas's head at that, and he suddenly knew exactly what he and Mia would be doing today. And tonight. And tomorrow. There was nothing like an overnight up in the Tetons, sleeping on the ground in near-freezing temperatures to bring up the dander of a city slicker. Of course, he'd have to find that city slicker first.

The storage barn was dark when he got there, but there

was enough early dawn spilling through the few windows for him to see Mia. She wasn't kneeling beside the kittens this time, though. She was inside the stall with them.

He made his way in that direction, scraping his boots over the hay-strewn dirt to make enough noise so that he wouldn't startle her when he got to where she was sitting. But even though she had to note his arrival—he was standing right outside the stall—she kept her attention on the single, tiny ginger tabby she had cradled in one arm. The one that was sleeping soundly on its back with all four legs extended upward and one paw over its eyes.

"What are you doing out here before the sun's even up?" Silas asked softly.

Still looking at the kitten instead of at him, she said, "I just needed to check on them."

"They look fine to me. How about some breakfast?" He tried to sound as crisp as he could when he spoke. Still might not hurt to at least try and make Mia a little bit mad. Even if his heart really wasn't in it anymore.

But Mia didn't get mad at all. She just lifted her free hand to crook her index finger over the kitten's nose and give it a little caress. "I had a bad dream about them," she said. "That they were out there on the range all alone and couldn't find their mom. When I woke up, I had to come make sure they were okay."

"And they are. Let's eat," he said, again, still striving for a cool tone of voice. He couldn't help thinking, though, that he instead sounded kind of...tenderhearted? Oh, God no. Not that. Silas Crockett did not do tender. Or heart, for that matter.

He was about to ask her why she hadn't gone back to bed once she knew it had just been a dream, but the way she was holding the kitten—the runt of the litter, he couldn't help noticing—it was kind of obvious. She wasn't done making sure they were okay. At least, she wasn't done making sure this one was.

"Her two brothers were picking on her," she said, as if she hadn't even heard him speak. Hopefully that meant she didn't have any kind of delusions about tenderheartedness in him. "She was hungry and wanted to get closer to her mother, but they kept pushing her out. So I moved them to the corner of the stall for a bit so that Mimi could have as big a breakfast as she wanted."

Silas almost smiled at that but managed to stop himself. That felt weird, too. Not the stopping-himself-from-smiling part. The smiling part itself. He didn't smile at anything these days. Weird that it would be an angry woman from St. Louis that would stir one in him now.

"Mimi?" he echoed. "You named her?"

She nodded but said nothing. The pronouncement seemed significant, though. Like maybe Mia had a thing about names. Or, at least, about not having a name. He couldn't help noticing the similarities between the kitten's name and her own. Or the part about Mimi being a homophone of *me me*. It didn't take Freud to figure out a bond had been established here in the wee hours of the morning.

"Did you name her brothers?"

She nodded again. "Leopold and Loeb."

Yep. Definitely some Freudian stuff going on at Whispering Winds this morning. He remembered her outburst by the watering hole had included a brief mention of brothers. Guess it wasn't just Mia's parents who had been villains in her life when she was a child.

"Have you eaten anything since you woke up?" he asked her. For some reason, he didn't feel like being crisp or cool anymore. Now he just felt... Well. Probably best not to dwell on that.

"No," she said. "There was no one up yet when I left the cabin. I don't know how to make coffee in one of those big urn things, and there were no Pop-Tarts in the kitchen last time I checked."

Last time I checked, he echoed to himself. He wondered how many mornings she'd woken up before everyone else this week and gone looking for breakfast. Obviously, she still wasn't sleeping well, even after being here nearly a week.

"Yeah, Miss Sylvie's not big on processed foods," he told her. "She says artificial additives don't belong in a place like Serenity Valley."

And she wasn't just talking about food in that, either, Silas knew. Miss Sylvie was as real a person as anyone he'd ever met, and she didn't tolerate artificiality in people, either. She was certain everybody would be happier if they would just be honest with themselves about who they were and what they wanted. And, of course, not be a jerk about it. Probably another reason she wanted to keep the dude side of the ranch going. To help others find their real selves.

"Come on," he told Mia. "I'll rustle us up some breakfast."

She finally looked up at that, and Silas's breath hitched in his throat at the sight of her face. She looked so...sad. So deeply, profoundly, sad. He could almost feel the melancholy creep across the space between them to work its way into his gut and up to his chest.

"Thanks," she told him. In a voice that was as far from perky as a voice could be.

The kitten stirred in her lap and opened its eyes, so she held it up to eye level, then pulled it forward to touch its nose to the tip of her own. But the gesture was as awkward as it was affectionate, as if she wasn't used to doing things like that in her everyday life. Silas sympathized. He wasn't one for affectionate gestures, either—not anymore. Even if he'd enjoyed them a lot once upon a time.

He shut down his thoughts *again* before they got away from him. What the hell was up with him this morning? He did his best to ignore the rolling tumult in his belly, one he'd had to battle for more than a decade. Nothing good came of bad memories. No way was he letting those into his head again. Ever.

Mia put the kitten back into the crate with her mother and brothers, but not before admonishing the latter to be nice to their sister. When she stood, Silas extended a hand to help her climb over the stall, even though she'd obviously managed fine without him getting in there. She tucked her palm into his automatically, though, welcoming his help without even seeming to think about it. He should have marveled at how that was a major development in her progress. But he couldn't marvel at that just now, because he was too busy enjoying the sensation of her hand in his, her skin warm and smooth against the cool roughness of his own. It had been a long time since he'd enjoyed something like that, too—a simple touch from another human being. Even if this touch didn't feel particularly simple at the moment.

She climbed over the barrier and landed squarely on her feet, but Silas had misjudged the distance between himself and the stall, and she ended up settled a lot closer to him than he'd planned. Close enough that it wasn't just the softness of her hand that he noticed. Close enough that he noticed how soft the rest of her was, too. And how warm. And how she smelled really good, like a mix of hay and mountain air and something vaguely spicy that wasn't a part of his normal world but was enticing and welcoming and comforting all the same. And how well her body fit against his, and how incredibly good it felt having her close the way she was. And the next thing he knew, he was dipping his head toward hers, as if he were going to kiss her. As if kissing Mia would be the most natural thing in the world to do when it was just the two of them alone in a barn, early in the morning, with the sun cresting the horizon and a whole day ahead of them. A day they could spend together doing whatever they wanted, whenever they wanted to, like kissing in a barn in the early morning and—

And what the hell was he thinking?

Somehow, Silas managed to rein himself in and pull his head away from Mia's before getting too close. But not before noticing how she had tipped her head back and started to rise up on tiptoe, as if there was some part of her that intended to meet him halfway. Or maybe he just imagined that. Or hoped for it. Or something. Because she came to her senses as quickly as he did, dropping back down firmly to earth and gently disengaging herself from him to take a few steps away.

For a moment, neither of them said a word, and Silas silently willed both of them to forget what had just happened. Or, at least, pretend it had never happened, since he was pretty sure he, at least, wasn't going to be able to truly forget it any time soon. Thankfully, Mia forced one of her no-longer-perky smiles and stuffed her hands deep into her pockets.

"So what's for breakfast?" she asked.

Then, thankfully, the moment was gone, and Silas could almost convince himself it had never happened. Almost.

Too much thinking this morning, he told himself. Too many thoughts about Jess and the baby he never knew and how, once upon a time, he might have had the very life he had just imagined, kissing a woman he loved in a barn in the early morning light, since that was the most natural thing in the world to do—because that was the life the two of them were meant to share.

But he wasn't in love with Mia. And their lives weren't meant to be shared. Not beyond two weeks one summer while she got her own life back on track.

"Not sure yet," he told her. "Let's see what's what."

Let's see what's what, he repeated to himself. He knew his brain hadn't just been thinking about breakfast when it put those words in his mouth. But Mia seemed not to realize that, because she only nodded and spun on her heel to head for the barn door. By the time they made it back to the big house, the staff of Whispering Winds was stirring, and a number of them had made their way to the kitchen. The activity was enough to shake loose the last of the weird feelings he'd been having.

Miss Abby, who'd been running the kitchen since Silas's de facto grandmother retired, was bustling about and offered to put something together for them. He assured her he could manage for him and Mia and to go about her usual morning routine. The coffee was ready, though, thankfully, so he poured them both a cup. Then he got Mia settled at a small table in the corner—the chef's table, everyone joked—and got to work. When he was finished, he set a plate of eggs, bacon, hash browns and biscuits in front of Mia, all of which—save the biscuits, which he'd fortuitously timed perfectly to coincide with Miss Abby's first batch out of the oven—were made by his own two hands. But he might as well have just poured a pile of the crown jewels in front of her, so grateful did she look for the meal.

"This looks amazing," she said reverently. "And I'm starving. I never eat like this back in St. Louis."

"Breakfast is easy," he told her. "Just throw everything into a skillet and give it an occasional turn 'til it's done."

"Easy for you, maybe, but I never got the hang of cooking. Especially breakfast."

Unspoken in that comment was the part about her never having been taught how to cook by anyone who cared enough to teach her. But Silas heard it anyway. He himself had learned from his mother as soon as he was old enough to stand beside her on a step stool by the stove. Because, as she'd told him while he was growing up, cooking—and cleaning and laundry and every other damned thing that needed doing around the house—was something all grown-ups should be comfortable with.

He sent a thought skyward for her. *Thanks, Mom.* Not just because, yeah, it was good to know how to take care of himself. But also because, even though cooking wasn't something he usually enjoyed, this morning, he'd kind of enjoyed cooking for Mia.

"Not to mention," she added as she slathered a generous chunk of butter—also made here in the ranch kitchen—onto one half of her biscuit, "I don't have time to do something like this every morning."

Okay, fair point. Silas didn't cook like this for himself every day, either. Like everyone else who worked on the ranch, he generally came to the big house in the morning to grab what someone else was paid to cook for the hands and guests.

"Much easier," she continued, "to just to grab a Pop-Tart from the cupboard and hit Kaldi's for coffee on the way to work. It can get a little hectic some mornings when you've forgotten to do laundry all week, and then you remember the strap broke on your favorite pair of shoes so you have to go dig out another pair from the closet, and then you can't find your travel mug, which always ends up being right on the counter where you left it after washing it, and how could you possibly forget that every…single…morning? But that's okay," she hurried to add. In a tone of voice that didn't exactly reek of okayness. "Lots of people have trouble getting to work on time in the morning."

It was the first time she'd made a specific enough comment about her life in St. Louis for Silas to actually get a picture of it. Maybe not a great one, since she hadn't exactly sounded enthusiastic—or happy—about her morning routine in St. Louis, but still. And why did it sound like she kind of made it a habit to not get to work on time every…single…morning, even though, as she'd mentioned, she was never late to work? Like maybe her subconscious was doing its best to keep her from having to do a job she'd been doing for years? But maybe he was reading too much into it. Plenty of people had to work someplace that wasn't their first choice of employment or career.

Not for the first time, Silas was grateful to have a job doing something he loved. Everyone should be so lucky. He wished there was something in St. Louis that made Mia happy outside her job. Or, at least, content.

Sounded like maybe this break from work would be helpful to her for more than just managing her anger. Sounded like maybe she needed something, even if for only a little while, that would make her feel less like she was living a life that wasn't exactly what she wanted it to be.

Another good reason to take her up into the mountains for an overnight. Getting her away from the ranch and out where things were really quiet and rugged and beautiful, she'd get a taste of how important other stuff was. Who needed Pop-Tarts and travel mugs when you woke up under a twilit, star-spattered sky to coffee percolating on an open flame? Now that was a way to start the day.

They fell into companionable silence as they ate their breakfast, and Silas couldn't help thinking how both the silence and the companionship had been pretty absent in their relationship before now. Not that what the two of them had was a relationship, he hurried to remind himself. At least, not the kind of relationship that was normally referred to as a *relationship* where a couple was concerned. Not that they were a couple, either. But silence and companionship had been a stranger to them this week. He would have thought it would feel weird to have them now. What was weird, though, was that the presence of both felt kind of...nice.

That was the weirdest thing of all. Silas hadn't felt...

nice...with another person this way for a long time. Because there hadn't been any people this way—this quiet, companionable way—in his life for a long time. Not since Jess. And, of course, the promise of their impending familyhood that would come with their new—

Anyway, it was a weird morning. But not an unpleasant one. As long as he focused on the present and not the past.

At least it was pleasant until he told Mia how they were going to saddle up Beanie and Jasper, toss a couple of packs of provisions onto the animals' backs, and then ride into the Tetons. It wasn't like they had anything else planned for the next couple of days. Except try to find a path into Mia's issues and then another path to follow out again. And the Tetons were full of paths. Sure, some were treacherous for greenhorns, but hey, who wanted to be a greenhorn for the rest of their life? That was something else he pointed out to Mia. By the time he finished laying out his intentions, though, she was looking at him as if he'd just intended for them to drink hemlock for dessert.

"But I don't like the great outdoors," she told him.

Well, this was news to Silas. Okay, fine, he could admit that she had made that clear her first day at the ranch. And on day two, come to think of it. She'd also made clear on day one that she was a city girl through and through and was in no way suited to ranch life. And yeah, those first couple of days, she'd obviously not been in her element. But once she'd gotten more used to being away from that element, she'd really seemed to take to the way things were around here. She hadn't balked at rising before the sun every morning and getting right to work. She'd even tackled the most menial, mundane jobs with an enthusiasm that had surprised—and, okay, impressed—him.

At first, Silas had thought she was only doing those things because she was so damned perky and approached everything with an unrealistically happy attitude as a result. Little by little, though, he'd had to admit she seemed to genuinely enjoy the physical labor and satisfaction that came with a job well done. She'd mostly stopped being intimidated by the animals and—as just evidenced a little while ago with the kitten—started embracing them. Literally. Hell, she was even getting along with Beanie now in spite of her residual fear and was riding with a lot more ease. The horse clearly liked her, too, always making her way toward Mia whenever she saw the two of them coming, completely ignoring Silas.

And as for the great outdoors? Well, *dayumm*. From what Silas had observed of her for the latter part of the week, she'd seemed as at home out in the great wide open as the birds were in the sky and the fish were in a stream. More than once, he'd seen her just standing still with her head tipped back, inhaling and exhaling a deep sigh as if she needed the clean air to survive, letting the sun wash over her and the wind dance with her hair as if she were a part of the elements herself. She didn't even seem to mind the borrowed denim and leather anymore and looked like she felt totally at home in both.

Ultimately, Silas had decided the reason she had thought she didn't like the great outdoors before coming to Whispering Winds was just a result of never having spent any time there. And now that she was, she was discovering a genuine love of all the things she'd been so sure she would dread. Familiarity had bred not contempt, but contentment for her. Where the hell was she getting this *I don't like the great outdoors* stuff? When it came to being out in nature, Mia Hawthorne was... well, a natural.

"Since when?" he asked her.

She looked at him as if he'd just grown a third eye. "I told you that on day one."

"Yeah, but this is day six."

"And I still don't like the great outdoors."

Wow. Clearly it wasn't just her anger and sadness that Mia was good at denying. She denied herself the good things, too. She could pretend all she wanted, but actions spoke louder than words. Mia liked it at Whispering Winds. And she was perfectly suited to the kind of life they led here. He'd bet good money that when she got back to St. Louis, she was going to miss Whispering Winds. A lot. Hell, she might even start planning a trip back for next summer as soon as she got home. Miss Sylvie hadn't been lying that first day when she told Mia that there were people who'd come here once because they'd been forced to and then came back annually to keep themselves on the good path they'd found for themselves here. Mia wasn't the first person, by far, who suddenly found themselves without even realizing they were lost. And discovered things about themselves they'd never known before.

He understood wanting to pretend the bad stuff in your life and your head didn't exist. Hell, he understood that better than most. But to pretend the good you'd found someplace wasn't real, either? Someone—or, he was learning, multiple someones—had really done a number on Mia when she was a kid. They'd somehow convinced her she wasn't good enough for...well, anything. And that she didn't deserve anything that would make her happy.

Oh, yeah. They were definitely spending the weekend up in the mountains. Silas would take her to his favorite place where, with any luck, she'd come to understand that there was a lot more going on inside her than she realized. And, with just a little more luck, maybe once she dealt with it, she'd start letting a lot of it go. The same way he had.

"Well, that's too damned bad," he told her. And he wasn't just talking about her insistence that she didn't like being outdoors. "'Cause once you finish up your breakfast, we're gonna stuff a couple of packs with what we'll need for the next two days, and we're hitting the trail."

"*Two days*?" she echoed.

"Maybe three. We'll see how it goes."

He thought she would glare at him when she heard that. And she did, for a couple of seconds. Then she only looked kind of resigned. And tired. She looked really, really, tired.

The fight was starting to go out of her, he realized. And that wasn't good. Silas had never meant to wear her down so far that she stayed down. He'd tried to wear her down so she'd spring back up again, even stronger. Strong enough to finally face the things she needed to face and move past them. Truth be told, though, he didn't think he was the one who had brought her to this point. Something inside Mia seemed to be doing that all by itself.

"Fine," she said softly.

Too softly. As irritating as it had been for him to hear

that word all week, her tone when she said it now was way worse. Before, there had been a part of her that actually believed she was fine. Now, she sounded like she knew she wasn't fine, but she had no idea what to do about that, so she would just keep being not fine and pretending everything was okay.

Yeah, the sooner he got her out into the great outdoors—out into her element—the better. Once they were under an open sky with the sun shining down and the winds whispering around them, Mia should be fine. Really fine. Not the fake fine she'd insisted she was the day she arrived or the resigned not-fine she seemed to be now. At least, that was what Silas hoped. Looking at her now, though...

Well. He just hoped they both survived the weekend intact.

Chapter Nine

Mia heard a familiar *kee-kee-kee* and looked into the trees towering over her just in time to glimpse the black, gray and white wings of a kestrel. She and Silas must have startled it as they rode down the narrow trail between two rows of dense-growing cottonwoods. She congratulated herself for her knowledge of the local fauna and flora, even if it was the kind of knowledge she would never use again once she got back to St. Louis.

After finishing her Hank Stallard Western in one evening, she'd found some books at the big house about the landscape and wildlife of the Grand Tetons in general and Serenity Valley in particular. Whenever she and Silas were out and about, she'd tested herself on identifying as much of the local plant life as she could. A couple of times, she'd even caught sight of some animals, as well. There had been a wandering garter snake—not venomous, Silas had assured her—and a long-tailed weasel, and for one breathtaking moment, a lone pronghorn hopping off in the distance, presumably in search of the rest of its herd. And, of course, there had been all kinds of birds.

During her brief moments away from his company— uh, she meant out from under his thumb, of course— she'd ambled around the ranch before dawn or after dusk,

inspecting the trees and flowers and scrub, and famil-
iarizing herself with those, too. She hadn't been able to
help herself. She didn't see that many trees or flowers
in St. Louis that hadn't been planted with aesthetics in
mind. And scrub? Forget about it. There was no scrub in
St. Louis—at least not in the part where she lived—and
Mia had found herself kind of liking scrub. Scrub was
tough and hardy, a survivor in a challenging and unfor-
giving landscape. She felt a kinship to scrub. She wished
there was some way she could take some scrub back to
St. Louis with her when she returned.

But only because she wanted to remind herself of how
tough and hardy people had to be to survive in the world.
Not to remind her of the time she had spent in Serenity
Valley with a certain cantankerous cowboy. Especially
since said cantankerous cowboy was currently making
her butt hurt. Like, literally. Because her butt was hurt-
ing really bad after doing so much riding all at once.
Geez, she'd only been riding at all for a matter of days,
and just brief stretches at a time. She and Silas had been
on the trail for hours today. Just how much farther was
he planning to go?

"Can we take a break?" she called to him now.

He was a good five or six horse lengths ahead of her,
but at her words, he reined in Jasper and turned both the
horse and himself around to look at her. It was all Mia
could do not to swoon at the sight. The sunlight filtering
through the trees cast him in gold and dappled him with
shadows, giving him the look of something otherworldly.
A fierce paladin from a fairy-tale land sent to save Mia
from a dark, menacing ogre. The vicious monster named
Jeffromsales, whose sole weakness was the stouthearted

Silas of the Valley Serene. Only the cowboy hat on Silas's head kept him from looking like an Arthurian knight, but the way he sat astride Jasper, so bold and handsome and imperious, she could almost see the shimmer and hear the carillon of his enchanted armor.

Oh, yeah. She'd definitely been on Beanie way too long today.

"Are you serious?" her paladin called back in that irritated tone of voice that pulled her firmly out of fairytale land. Ah, well. It was nice while it lasted. "We've barely gotten started."

Was *he* serious? Just where was he planning on setting up camp tonight? Saskatchewan?

"I need to stretch my legs," she told him. Not a lie. But also, her butt hurt.

He shook his head at her. "There's a clearing up ahead. We'll stop there for a bit. It's almost lunchtime anyway."

He must be pretty familiar with this trail if he knew there was a clearing nearby. Mia had no idea how far they'd traveled. The landscape hadn't changed one iota since they'd crossed from the pasture into the woods. He must only know where they were because he came up here a lot, by this very path, and knew exactly where he was going. That should have been a relief, except she would rather he knew exactly where he was going back down at Whispering Winds Ranch, because even though they'd just been there this morning, she was starting to—

Huh. That was weird. She was almost thinking she missed the place. The place where she'd been in residence for barely a week. The place that actually wasn't even her residence. So why was that the word she chose just then in reference to it? And all that aside, in case she'd forgotten, she was totally unsuited to life outside the city. Had she forgotten there were no museums or theaters in Serenity Valley? No gourmet—but not too expensive—restaurants? No coffee shops to pop into for her morning cuppa? No boutiques or department stores she could pillage for great deals?

Huh. That was even weirder. She was almost thinking like she *didn't* miss any of those. Then again, Miss Abby's coffee in the kitchen was really good…

She shook her head to clear it. Whispering Winds Ranch and Serenity Valley were both beautiful, peaceful places. Of course she would miss them when she went back to St. Louis. For a little while. But it wouldn't be long before she settled back into her usual routine there and remembered her time here as a brief respite from her real life. This place wasn't real life. Not for her. It was too beautiful and too peaceful to be real life. So yes, she would miss it. But that was okay. She'd make the best of it.

Unfortunately, the platitudes that had always reassured her in the past were in no way reassuring today. Where before they had always sounded like a pep talk in her brain, today they sounded like…well…a platitude.

She looked down the trail toward Silas again, only to find he'd started riding ahead without her. So she gave Beanie a soft click of her heels and followed. Sure enough, it wasn't long before they broke through the trees and into a small clearing, one with a small stream running through the middle of it. Silas pulled up Jasper near the water's edge and dismounted, and the horse headed straight for the water to take a drink. Mia followed suit, alighting from Beanie with a lot more grace than she had her first few times, and watched as the horse joined her buddy for refreshment.

Silas pulled a bag out of one of the packs he'd tossed across Jasper and headed toward a group of rocks a little bit upstream from where the horses were drinking, as if he wanted to give them a little time to be alone—she had definitely been too long on the trail if she was thinking things like that—then opened it to pull out two apples, a bag of almonds, a tube of multigrain crackers, a wedge of Parmesan, and two collapsible water bottles currently uncollapsed and filled to their brims. There was also one of those big bars of dark chocolate for them to split for dessert.

She couldn't help thinking it was the kind of lunch a couple might have packed for an afternoon at Lafayette Park, to enjoy a picnic by the lake as they watched the swans and soaked up some rays. Even if she and Silas were by no means a couple, and this trek was nothing like a stroll through Lafayette Park. It still felt kind of… nice…being here with him on a quiet afternoon. She'd helped him fill the packs on both their horses earlier, so she knew what else was on the menu for the weekend: More fruit and nuts, some raw veggies, canned tuna, jerky, granola, ramen, oatmeal. He'd even grabbed a little percolator to make coffee over the campfire from water they collected from the stream. Save for the oatmeal and dirty-water coffee—that, okay, wouldn't be dirty after they boiled the water within an inch of its life first—the selections were a far cry from the hardtack and rawhide she'd been so sure cowboys gnawed on when they were away from home. He did sometimes seem like the kind of guy who'd actually prefer hardtack and rawhide and dirty-water coffee. He'd probably be the one killing the germs the minute they entered his body, not the other way around.

Nah, she immediately chastised herself. She'd learned enough this week to know he wasn't as crotchety as he led people to think. Okay, maybe he was that crotchety. But she'd come to suspect his crustiness came from a place where he just got impatient with life and other people sometimes. Silas Crockett wasn't a bad guy. He was just a little rough around the edges. Okay, a lot rough around the edges. There was nothing wrong with that. Sometimes rough edges were the softest part of the fabric.

For some reason, that made her think about their... odd moment...in the barn that morning. The almost-but-not-quite kiss that never happened. She had told herself a dozen times since then that she'd only imagined the whole thing. It had barely lasted a few seconds, after all, and why would Silas want to kiss her? What she knew she hadn't imagined, though, was her own response. She'd wanted to kiss him. She'd totally set herself up for it—literally and emotionally. Even if the emotion involved had doubtless only been lust because it had been so long since she—

Anyway, although she was certain now that she had imagined the desire on Silas's part, her own desire for him had been one-hundred-percent real. She just had no idea where it came from, unless it was a response to her own lack of social life. Nor did she have any idea what to do about it. Because even though the moment had thankfully passed without her embarrassing herself, it had only made her realize how long it had been since she... Well, it had made her realize how much she missed...

She sighed. Fine. It had made her horny. And she didn't know where to put that feeling, since it wasn't exactly going away. And now she and the man she'd wanted to kiss this morning were going into the mountains together alone, to spend the night, and, well... It was just a good thing he didn't want her the way she wanted him. The last thing she needed was a one-night stand with a sexy cowboy haunting her dreams after she got back to St. Louis, where sexy cowboys weren't exactly in ample supply.

And just when had she started thinking cowboys were sexy anyway? Her sexual fantasies had always been about men who were suave and clean-cut and wealthy, wearing thousand-dollar suits and riding around in the back seats of limousines where the two of them had enough room to spend hours having—

Um, anyway, she never fantasized about cowboys. And yet, suddenly, all she could think about was having sex with cowboys. No, not cowboys, plural. Cowboy, singular. All she could think about was having sex with Silas Crockett.

Now she had to walk over to where he was sitting and pretend like she hadn't been thinking about him that way at all. Which actually stopped being a problem the minute she saw that he was sitting on a rock, not the poofy silk pillow her sore butt would much prefer. He looked up when he realized she wasn't planning to fold herself down beside him, a silent question in his expression. That question being something along the lines of *WTF, Mia?* With a sigh of resignation, she slowly lowered herself until she was perched beside him. He extended one of the water bottles toward her, and she took it, uncapped it, and enjoyed a couple of long swallows. Then she reached for one of the apples and a hunk of the cheese that he'd sliced off with his pocketknife and enjoyed a bite of those, too.

"It's nice up here," she said after a few minutes.

She'd meant for the comment to be polite conversation, but as soon as the words were out, she realized she'd really meant them. She'd had no idea she would like the quiet so much. There had never been quiet in her life. At work, they played a barrage of canned Top Forties music, and at home, she always had her TV tuned to something soft and unobtrusive in the background, because her apartment had always seemed too quiet without it. In between, there was the clatter of the car radio, the buzz of conversation in whatever establishment she entered, the hum of traffic and thump of clubbing on the street outside. City sounds. Not bad. Not good. Just there. All the time.

Here, though, there were nature sounds. The clatter of Jasper's reins as he tossed his head. The buzz of a bee flitting from flower to flower. The hum of the breeze as it tangled with her hair. All good. No bad. There all the time, too. But where Mia could always tune out the city sounds—and she did always tune out the city sounds— here, she wanted to savor every one of them. She never would have guessed that ordinary sounds, especially such soft ones, could have such an effect on a person.

"What are you thinking about?"

Silas's question seemed to come from a million miles away. It was one he'd asked her a lot this week whenever he'd caught her in deep thought about something. But where before, his tone had been rough and demanding, as if anything she said was going to wind up in his report to Miss Sylvie, now it was soft and curious, as if he wanted to know for himself.

"Nothing," she said. "Everything. Wyoming is just so different from St. Louis."

"You said the same thing on your first day here," he reminded her. "But that day, you sounded like you were complaining, and today you sound…"

"What?" she asked when he didn't finish. Because she had been complaining that first day. And now she felt a lot more—

"Content," he said as the same word unwound in her brain. "You sound more content now."

She wished she could tell him that was true. That she was more content. But at the moment, she was feeling so many things, she couldn't identify any of them. So, she only told him, "Well, I'm not complaining anymore. That's for sure true. This place is…"

"What?" he was the one to ask this time, when she didn't finish.

But Mia just shook her head. She wasn't sure a word existed that could describe what she was thinking—how she was feeling—just then. So, she only smiled and said, "Pass the crackers."

They ate the rest of their lunch in silence, as if they both just wanted to listen to sounds that were more intimate than conversation. Then they packed up what was left for later. By the time Mia was sitting astride Beanie again—and she took pride in how well she was able to manage that by herself now…mostly—she was a little more comfortable in the saddle. For the rest of the day, they rode higher into the Tetons, the vegetation going from dense to sparse to dense again, their conversation staying mostly in the sparse category.

But they didn't really need to talk. They'd talked a lot this week. It was nice not to have words interfering for a change. That was the absolute only reason why Mia never once asked the question, *How much longer till we get there?* It had nothing to do with the fact that she kind of didn't care when they got there. The journey was enough. More than enough, really. For the first time she could ever remember, Mia just sat back and enjoyed the moment. Because moments, for Mia, had never really been something to enjoy. Her moments in St. Louis had always been things she had to tolerate. Or endure. Or survive. While moments here in Wyoming were...

Well. Filled with whispering winds and serene valleys and sexy cowboys. For now, even if they were only temporary, her moments were just fine.

The sun was dipping low over the mountaintops when Silas pulled Jasper to a halt at the edge of his most favorite place in the world—a clearing in the middle of nowhere just high enough in the Tetons to make it feel like he was the only person in the whole wide world. He'd stumbled upon it a few months after Jess's death, when he'd been at the peak of his grief and completely uncertain about how he was supposed to go on without her and the baby he never got to know. Discovering this place and wandering into it, feeling as if he was the last human being on the planet, had somehow made him feel a little less chaotic, a little more peaceful, a little less likely to do himself or anyone else harm. Although it wasn't likely, he'd felt then that he was the first person seeing this place, and something about that had steadied him. It had made him feel as if finding this new place could be a new beginning of sorts for him.

And it had been. Mostly. Even after twelve years, he'd never gotten back to the place where he was before he met Jess, and he knew he never would be, since a part of that man died with her. But after a few days in this place, he'd started to regain some perspective. The planet Earth was billions of years old. The Tetons were millions of years old. That first time he came here, he watched the sun set over the mountains one day after another, only to rise again over the opposite horizon the following morning. Over and over again. Day in and day out. He'd watched a black bear lumber along the tree line at twilight and a bald eagle circle overhead at noon. He'd heard the trumpeting of a distant herd of elk at dawn and the howl of a lonesome wolf at midnight. He'd inhaled the scent of sagebrush and larkspur and pine, felt the warm sun on his face, fallen asleep to the sizzle of drizzle on a dying campfire. Then he'd awoken in the morning to the rustle of a snowshoe hare grazing a few feet away while a great grey owl watched from one of the aspens, thinking about making that critter his own breakfast.

So much life and death had passed through these parts before Silas ever came along. And it would continue long after he was gone. The universe was a vast, awesome thing. He and Jess were both just blips on a timeline that stretched to virtual infinity in both directions. Even if her time had been cut cruelly short, she would live on his memory as long as he lived himself. Until the time he took his last breath, he would just do what he had to do to get from one day to the next to the next. There was still beauty to be had in this world—he'd realized that first time he was here. There was still life. There were still things worth getting out of bed for in the morning. Still things to make living worthwhile. Still things that could make him content in some small way. Maybe even things that could make him happy someday, in some small way. It was why he came back up here whenever he could. Because a lot of those small happinesses were here in this little clearing in the Tetons that recharged him whenever he needed recharging.

For some reason, that made him turn in his saddle to look for Mia. She was right behind him, having stayed close for their ride since lunchtime. She looked tired, but also gratified, though whether that was because they'd finally stopped someplace or because she was proud of herself for having lasted as long as she had, he couldn't have said. Maybe it was a little bit of both.

"Are we there yet?" she asked when she pulled up beside him. But there was a smile on her face when she asked it, and something about that made Silas smile back.

"Yeah," he told her. "We're finally there."

And why that sounded so meaningful—felt so meaningful—he had no idea.

Instead of wondering about that any longer, since wondering about it made gears start turning in his head that he wasn't sure should be turning, he swung himself off Jasper and turned to help Mia off Beanie. But she did that all by herself, as she had been doing for a few days. She stumbled a bit when she got both feet on the ground, but righted herself again just fine. In hindsight, he guessed this was a pretty ambitious ride for someone who, a week

ago, had never even been on a horse, but she'd risen to
the challenge impressively. Once again, he marveled at
just how quickly she had taken to a lifestyle completely
different from the one she normally lived.

They unsaddled the horses and got them fed and
watered and settled before going about settling themselves. The same stream they'd enjoyed lunch by gur-
gled through the middle of this clearing, too, only it was
much wider up here. Not far from it was a springy patch
of sagebrush and moss where Silas always pitched his
sleeping bag. He'd dug a shallow firepit there, too, a decade ago, complete with metal grate and a ring of rocks
to keep it all in place. Some of the stones had been disturbed since the last time he was here, probably by a
bobcat or badger who'd gotten a whiff of the remnants
of his last breakfast, but they were easily restored to their
rightful position.

"Just how often do you come up here?" she asked
when she saw what he was doing.

"Every chance I get," he told her. "Though not nearly
as much as I'd like to."

She spun in a slow circle, taking it all in. "It's really beautiful. Even more beautiful than Serenity Valley. Quieter, too."

"That's my favorite part," Silas told her.

She nodded. "Yeah, brains can get pretty noisy sometimes. It's nice when you can find a place that makes
them quiet down."

She'd just put into words the thing he'd never been
able to explain to anyone before. Not that there had really been anyone to explain stuff like that to, since most
people thought when he left the ranch that he needed to

get away because he didn't like being around anybody. But Miss Sylvie sure had asked him often enough over the years what was bugging him so much that he had to make himself so scarce sometimes, and all he'd ever been able to reply was that he didn't know. And then she'd always just glare at him like she was sure he could have told her if he wanted to, he was just too ornery to do it. Next time she asked, he was going to tell her it was because his brain was being noisy and he needed to go someplace quiet. And if she pointed out that Serenity Valley was one of the quietest places around, he'd just tell her it wasn't that kind of noisy and let her figure out the rest of it herself.

And she probably would. She'd lost someone she loved, too, when her husband Rye died.

"We need to get a few things done before it gets too dark," he told Mia. "Collect some firewood, unpack our bags, catch some dinner and—"

For the first time since they'd left the ranch, she looked a little panicky. It was a new record for her. She'd gone almost a full day without being alarmed by something. That was a major milestone.

"*Catch* some dinner?" she asked warily.

"Yep." He suddenly wanted to see how long her apprehension would last. This weekend was supposed to be one long teachable moment, after all.

Her eyebrows knit downward. "We're not going to… catch…anything with eyelashes, are we?"

"Nope," he told her. "But I might name mine Tony the Trout before I gut him."

"Silas!"

He laughed at her reaction. Not loud or boisterous or

anything. Hell, it was barely a few chuckles. But holy crap, did that come as a surprise. He couldn't remember the last time he'd laughed out loud at anything. It actually felt kind of weird physically to experience. Weird and...good. It felt really good. He'd genuinely forgotten what that was like.

Mia grinned at his reaction, and the warmth that had erupted in his belly with his laughter spread into his chest. As perky and upbeat as she'd done her best to be this week, not once had she smiled in the way she was smiling now. And there was something in that smile that...

Wow. Had he thought he felt good before? 'Cause that reaction had nothing on the one he felt seeing Mia smile an honest-to-God real smile for the very first time.

"You're grinning," she said, her voice laced with mystification, as if she were as surprised by this turn of events as he was.

"So are you," he pointed out.

"Yeah, but I smile all the time. You almost never do. For sure never like you are now."

He was about to tell her that her smiles were never real, like the one she was wearing now, but he feared doing so would make her real smile falter. And he didn't want to see this first real smile from her interrupted for anything. He didn't point it out for the sake of progress, he told himself. Just another major milestone to note in Mia Hawthorne's anger management journey.

"Circle of life," he told her, reminding her of their previous conversation. "Fish gotta swim, birds gotta fly, people gotta eat."

She still didn't look comfortable about catching dinner. Even without eyelashes.

"Fine," he conceded. He almost laughed again at his choice of word. "I'll do the catching and cleaning. You can do the cooking."

She balked for another moment, then her expression cleared. "As long as you don't do any naming."

"Deal," he said. He knew, though, that when he looked back on this evening after Mia was gone, he would always think of the dinner they were about to enjoy as Tony the Trout.

Together, they collected wood for their fire, finding an ample supply of kindling, limbs, and logs, all of it ripe for burning since they hadn't had any rain for more than a week. There were a lot of things Silas loved about the mountains, but the main one was how they always provided whatever he needed whenever he needed it. Not just food and water and warmth, but other kinds of sustenance, too. Sustenance for the soul. Sustenance for the mind. Sustenance for just about anything a person could need.

For some reason, that thought made him look at Mia, too. He had dropped a match into the firepit to light the kindling, and now she was poking it gently to get it started. Although the flames lurched and receded a few times, she kept them going nicely. Once they were burning steadily, he settled the metal grate over the fire and made his way to the stream to invite Tony the Trout to join them, and to hopefully bring his girlfriend Tina with him. In no time at all, Mia was turning a couple of decent-sized fish filets in the frying pan they'd packed for this very purpose. Then they dropped some raw carrots and a handful of crackers onto their plates and sat back to enjoy their dinner.

"Now this is what I call eating out," Mia said before forking her first bite into her mouth.

Silas grinned at that. He was grinning like an idiot tonight. "Yeah, I guess al fresco in Wyoming is a little different from al fresco in St. Louis."

"You got that right. And even in summer when restaurants move tables outside, a lot of times, it's just too hot to eat on the street."

As if cued by her comment, a chilly breeze blew across the firepit, startling the flames and sending one log bumping into another, stirring a flurry of orange sparks into the air.

"Yeah, you're not gonna have that problem up here," he told her.

They ate in silence for a few minutes, then Mia looked around again. "I just can't believe that this time last weekend, I was sitting in my apartment, listening to the air conditioner humming, feeling the thump-thump-thump of a live band playing in a bar up the street, while I waited for the microwave to ding on the leftover bibimbap I DoorDashed the night before. How can I be in the same country I was then? Or in the same universe?"

Silas tried not to think about how she was going to be in another universe again this time next weekend. Instead, he just told her, "Yeah, sorry, but bibimbap isn't something Miss Abby puts on the dining calendar at Whispering Winds Ranch very often. Or, you know, ever."

He hoped she would say something about how that

was okay, she could live without bibimbap, then wondered why a thought like that would even enter his head.

To his relief, she moved on to a different subject entirely, asking him if Miss Sylvie had ever thought about starting a camp for young mechanics. And although Silas had no clue where a question like that would come from, it set them off on a conversation about cars that led to conversations about everything else the two of them could think to talk about, which ended up being a lot.

At some point over the course of the evening, Silas wasn't sure when, it struck him that the two of them were getting along like old friends who shared a history that spanned decades. Mia could have been one of the ranch hands he'd grown up with on Whispering Winds instead of some visiting city slicker, so natural did it feel for her to be up here with him talking the way they were.

Just when had their sole purpose in life stopped being an effort to provoke and grate on each other and started being... Something else? Not becoming friends, necessarily, but not staying enemies, either. And he kept coming back to the afternoon when she finally went into detail about what had happened at work that day with her good buddy Perpetual Salesman of the Month Jeff Oberstrom. The edges of Mia's perkiness had blunted after that, and her cheerfulness had become tainted with sadness. She seemed to be swinging back again tonight, though. Not perky so much—thank God—but not as sad as she'd seemed when he found her with the kittens this morning, either.

Silas, too, had tempered himself after that day, acting less cranky. Being less cranky. Feeling less cranky. Maybe because... Well, he still wasn't sure what the source of his own about-face was. But he was suddenly kind of glad now that it had happened. He just couldn't help wondering how long it was going to last.

And he couldn't help thinking how this evening wasn't turning out to be anything like he'd planned...

Chapter Ten

Mia had never viewed a night sky like the one above the Wyoming mountains. There must be a trillion stars up there, at least. And the sky behind them wasn't quite black. It was blue. A dark, rich, blue like the feathers of a grackle when the sunlight hit it just the right way. A midnight-blue wing spattered with diamonds. That was what the sky looked like up here.

After cleaning up the remains of their dinner, Silas had stoked the fire in the firepit and they'd laid out their sleeping bags beside it. When he told her this morning they'd be sleeping on the ground, without so much as a tent to protect them, she had been appalled. No way did she want to sleep out in the open. Her idea of roughing it was a hotel without room service. But after the day's low-key activity and conversation—and dare she say camaraderie?—with Silas, it hadn't felt weird at all to unroll what would be her bed for the night. Now, lying here this way beneath this sky, their heads nearly touching in the corner of the L-shape they'd positioned their bags in…

Well. She could definitely see the attraction.

"The sky up here is amazing," she said. "I'm going to miss it a lot when I go back to St. Louis."

Still looking up at the sky, too, he said, "You always

say 'When I go back to St. Louis' and never say, 'When I go home.' Why is that?"

Mia turned her head as well as she could to look at him. "I do?"

He nodded. "Whenever you've mentioned going back, that's how you've said it. 'St. Louis.' Not 'home.'"

She thought about that, shaking her head. "No, I'm sure you're wrong. I say it a lot."

"Say what a lot?"

"When I'm away from St. Louis, I always say, 'When I get back—'"

But she halted before uttering the crucial word. "When I get back *home*," she forced herself to say. But she did have to force herself to say it. And it didn't feel right saying it at all. But going back to St. Louis *was* going home, she insisted to herself. Naturally, she didn't think of the house where she grew up as home. But her apartment? The one she'd picked out by herself and furnished to be a reflection of the person she was now? That was her home. Wasn't it? So why did it feel weird to think of it that way? Why did she have so much trouble calling it that?

Silas turned to look at her, too, for a minute, then looked back up at the sky. "Even having grown up here," he continued, "and seeing this sky nearly every damned day of my life, it's never been anything but awesome."

Nearly every day, Mia echoed to herself. Meaning there had been some days in his life when he hadn't been riding around Serenity Valley doing all the things that seemed to come so naturally to him. But, of course, he would have left the ranch from time to time for one reason or another. College, for instance. She remembered him saying he'd gone to University of Wyoming in Laramie, which was clear on the other side of the state. Even so, she couldn't imagine him anywhere but here. He really did seem like a primordial part of this place. A man of the earth in an almost literal sense. He just felt that rooted to Whispering Winds. He just seemed that *at home* here.

It occurred to her then that, even after spending so much time with him this week, she still didn't know a whole lot about him. She knew some of his personal history, but not much about his thoughts and dreams and feelings. He was too good at hiding those. Then again, she hadn't exactly shared many of her own thoughts and dreams and feelings with him, had she? She'd kept her own hidden, too. Something about being up here, though, away from society and people, where it felt as if the two of them were the only people in the world, had her feeling more of a connection to him.

"Did you always want to be a cowboy?" she asked impulsively.

This time he sat up to look at her, drawing his legs up before himself and draping his arms over his knees. "Where did that come from?"

She sat up, too, to look at him, sitting pretzel-fashion to lean back on her flattened hands. "I don't know. It just occurred to me that lots of little kids say they want to be cowboys or cowgirls when they grow up, but then they become software developers or graphic designers instead. And here you are, an actual cowboy, who maybe wanted to be a software developer or graphic designer when he was a little boy."

He grinned at that. Another one of his rare, genuine grins that made something inside Mia go all warm and mushy. She'd only seen that grin from him a handful of times this week, and every time she did, something inside her just…melted. She didn't know any other way to describe it. Those first couple of days with him, she would have sworn the man was made of ice and cactus, so cold and prickly had he been. But the more time she'd spent with him, the more she'd come to see that those things were only on the outside. No one could smile the way he did, infrequently though it was, and be cold and jagged inside. And looking at him now, his features softened by the campfire, his bottle-green eyes shining like the stars above them…

The heat in her belly swirled outward, into her chest and womb and beyond, scalding her warm thoughts and making her want things she hadn't wanted for a very long time. She'd begun to think this evening that maybe coming up here had been a good idea after all. That maybe Silas had been right to show her this place. Because she'd been calmer up here than she could remember ever being anywhere. But now, she was going back to her original way of thinking. It was a bad idea. Not because of the potential for unsafe water or accidentally pitching her sleeping bag on top of a scorpion. Now, it was because being here with Silas, in this otherworldly place, feeling these unfamiliar feelings and thinking…lusty…thoughts like she'd been having earlier…

Well, anyway, maybe they should have stayed down at the ranch. Then again, if they'd done that, she wouldn't be looking at one of his genuine smiles right now, would she? And she wouldn't have heard that even rarer chuckle from him earlier. She wouldn't be seeing this softer side of him that she was really—really—getting to like. And the thought of leaving this place not having seen this softer side of Silas just felt wrong somehow.

"I didn't even know what a software developer was when I was a kid," he told her. "Hell, I don't know what one is now."

Now she was the one to chuckle. "Me, neither. And I work with software every day."

He studied her in silence for a moment, as if he were seeing something in her, too, that he'd never seen before. Then he turned his head to look back up at the sky. "But, nah, I never wanted to do anything but ranch work. Miss Sylvie tried with me when she sent me off to college. She wanted me to study medicine or law, or hell, medieval literature. Anything to get me *out* of ranch work. But I ended up declaring my major as animal and veterinary science."

"Well, that's kind of like going into medicine."

"Not with a minor in agricultural business and livestock management, it's not."

"Sounds a lot like you majored in Cowboy."

"Yep."

"And minored in Cowboy."

"Yep."

He turned to grin at her again, and somehow, she kept herself from swooning. And also from crawling across the small space that lay between them to trace that smile with her fingertips. And then drag her fingertips over his rugged cheekbones and down his elegant nose, and back to his mouth. And then cover his mouth with hers to just kiss him and kiss him and kiss him and—

Anyway, somehow, she kept herself in check. Which was pretty amazing, considering how much time they'd spent this week on making her *not* tamp down and ignore her feelings. Oh, sure. *Now* those lessons about letting herself feel her authentic feelings were sinking in. The last thing she should be feeling authentic about was—

Um, never mind.

They sat in silence for a moment, just staring at the sky. A great gray owl hooted somewhere close by—she recognized the sound, because she'd heard it nightly at Whispering Winds, and Silas had told her that was what it was—followed by a rustle in the grass from something small and furry. Mia waited for the feeling of wanting to be somewhere else to creep up inside her, since sitting on a sleeping bag under the stars was even more foreign to her than sleeping on a squeaky bed in a cabin on a ranch. But that feeling never came. The owl hooted again, and something about the sound comforted her. Calmed her. Made her wish she could take it home with her to listen to every night.

She actually had been sleeping better in Serenity Valley than she did in St. Louis, once she'd gotten used to her new surroundings. And she'd woken up feeling fairly well rested, even after those nights when she'd only gotten in a few hours. Weird, because in St. Louis, even on those rare nights when she slept solidly, she still always woke up feeling groggy until she had her first cup of coffee. Then she spent the rest of the day wanting a nap and more coffee. She couldn't remember the last time she'd actually felt truly rested. Maybe she never had. At least not until coming here.

"How about you?" Silas asked. "When you were a little girl, did you want to be a… What is it they call you at work again?"

This time she was the one to smile. "I'm the service advisor." Not the service manager, according to her title—even though that was absolutely the job she was doing. But God forbid they would call her that, because then they'd have to pay her what they paid the rest of the—all male—managers, who actually did have that word in their job description It really wasn't okay that she wasn't being paid what she was worth. And when she got back to St. Louis, she was going to see about doing something to rectify that.

"So, you majored in Auto Service Advisory in college?" Silas asked.

She laughed. "No, I majored in business administration. I kinda planned to own my own business someday, and I figured it might come in handy to know how to run one."

"What kind of business?"

"I don't know," she answered honestly. "I never really got that far in my planning. I just knew I wanted to be the one in charge for a change."

"You wanted to be in control."

Now she turned to look at him. "You make that sound like a bad thing. Everyone wants to be in control."

"Not everyone," he said cryptically. "But yeah, wanting to be in control isn't always a good thing. Depends on the circumstances."

"Well, I wanted to be in control of a business," she assured him. "At least, I thought I did when I started college. Instead, I ended up as the go-between for the customers who come in to get their cars worked on and the guys who do the work on their cars. I take care of all the paperwork, do all the scheduling, order parts when they're needed, that kind of thing."

Strangely, the realization now that she wasn't running her own business didn't bother Mia as much as it used to. And it suddenly didn't seem so imperative to work toward that goal. She wasn't sure when the change had happened. It had been a while since she'd thought about the business-owning thing. But now that she did, it just didn't seem that important anymore to be the one in charge. To be the one in control. What did seem important was doing work that made her happy. And she had to admit that Carrigan Auto wasn't a place that was exactly rife with joy. Maybe she'd look into doing something about that, too, when she got back to the city.

Her thoughts scattered when Silas asked, "So, did you want to be a paper pusher and scheduler and car parts orderer when you were a little girl?"

She laughed lightly again, marveling at how good that felt. When was the last time she'd actually laughed at something, even lightly? Even something small that someone at work said in passing? She honestly couldn't remember. Watching funny movies and videos, she never laughed out loud. She never even chuckled. Why was that? How could anyone go through life not laughing at things? *Why* would anyone go through life not laughing at things?

"No," she told him. "I didn't want to be any of those things when I was a little girl."

"Then what did you want to be?"

The word was out of her mouth before she could stop it. "Invisible. I wanted to be invisible when I was a little girl."

She wanted to be invisible as an adult, too, actually. But it was easier to be invisible when you were a small child who didn't have to be out and about in the world. All you had to do was make sure there was enough room between the floor and the mattress to scoot under the bed. Or enough clothes in the closet to hide behind. Or, at the worst times, enough dirty laundry to conceal her in that one corner of the basement that was dark and smelly and scary—but not nearly as scary as what was going on upstairs.

There was a long moment of silence from Silas. Mia was almost afraid to look at him. Not because of what she might see in his expression. But because of what he might see in hers. She never talked about this stuff. Never. There was no reason to. Not only did no one want to hear about her unhappy childhood, but she didn't trust anyone not to take it the wrong way if she did talk about it. Besides, it wasn't important. It was all in the past. She'd moved beyond it, she was sure of that. She should just change the subject right now so they could talk about something else—anything else—instead.

Before she had the chance to do that, though, Silas asked, "Why did you want to be invisible when you were a little girl, Mia?"

Somewhere deep down inside herself, she had known it was going to come to this—that she would have to talk about more than just what happened at work that day with Jeff. Because somewhere deep down inside herself, she'd known that what happened at work that day with Jeff had had nothing to do with work or Jeff. Even after spending her entire adult life assuring herself that her past was in the past. That nothing that had happened then affected her now. That she didn't even think about it anymore so it couldn't possibly affect her now…

Somewhere deep down inside herself, Mia had known, all along, that she was lying to herself about all of it.

"The reason I wanted to be invisible when I was a little girl," she said softly, carefully, "was because, if they couldn't see me, they couldn't…scare me. They couldn't yell at me. They couldn't hit me."

Silas turned to look at her fully, stretching his arms over the tops of his knees now, almost as if he were reaching out to her somehow. Mia sensed more than saw the motion, but she finally turned her head to look at him, too. She only got one part of his position wrong. She'd thought that he would look at her with pity. Instead, he seemed angrier than she'd ever seen him. Though that anger clearly wasn't aimed at her.

"Your parents hit you?" he said. His voice was quiet and even, completely at odds with his expression.

"Yes. They hit my older brothers, too. And each other. They weren't nice people."

His dark brows knit downward. He said nothing for a moment, but she could tell what he was thinking. And what he was feeling. Silas wasn't as good at hiding his feelings from her now as he'd been her first few days at the ranch. Or maybe he just wasn't bothering to hide them right now. And she was surprised to realize that what he was feeling wasn't pity for her. It was anger at her parents. But even more so, contempt for them. That was fine, though, since Mia felt enough anger at her parents for her and Silas both.

All he said, though, was, "Yeah, I kinda figured out

eventually that you weren't an only child like you said that day in Miss Sylvie's office."

"I never said I was an only child. You just assumed."

Even though she'd known he would assume that, and she had been careful not to correct him. She just hadn't wanted to lie to Silas, even then. Bad enough she had been lying to herself all that time.

"So, are your brothers still around?" he asked.

She nodded. "They're both still in St. Louis. My parents, too, last time I heard. But I don't go out of my way to keep up with any of them."

"Your parents, I get. But not your brothers. Sometimes kids in a situation like that grow closer. Kind of a strength-in-numbers survival thing."

"Not in my family. My brothers hit me, too. And each other. And, once they got big enough, my parents. There was a lot of hitting in my family. A lot of yelling. A lot of…" *Just say it, Mia.* "A lot of anger."

He only nodded in response to that, as if he now understood. Or maybe he'd understood long before now. If so, that put him way ahead of her. Mia didn't understand any of it. So, she did what she always did on those rare occasions when something about her childhood intruded into her thoughts. Into her life. She did everything she could to push them away.

She appreciated Silas's matter-of-fact reaction to her revelation. A lot of people would have felt sorry for her and tried to make her feel better. Tell her how much they admired her for surviving all that. How the things that don't kill us make us stronger. How she was doubtless a more empathetic person now for what she went through back then. Blah-blah-blah. *Survivor* was one of those words that had been thrown about too much, in too many ways. To Mia, it was nothing but a T-shirt slogan now: I Survived Spring Break. I Survived Burning Man. I Survived the Sixties. And hey, everyone had a sucky childhood in some way that leant itself to some kind of survival, right? I Survived Narcissist Parents. I Survived Home Schooling. I Survived Brussels Sprouts. Everyone had at least a few survivor T-shirts in their emotional closet.

"It wasn't your fault, Mia. You know that, right?"

She did, actually. On some level. Somewhere. Probably.

"The way your family was…" Silas continued, as if he wasn't sure she knew what he meant. "You weren't responsible for any of that."

She looked at him again. "But I was there."

He nodded. "Yeah, you were. And now I think we might finally know where all your anger comes from."

Again, she tried to deny it. It was all so long ago. She'd lived an entirely different life since then. One completely free of adversity and animosity, because she did whatever it took to make sure adversity and animosity never, *ever*, entered her life. Everything Mia did every day—*every* thing, *every* day—was geared toward avoiding conflict and anger. The moment she woke up in the morning, she pushed aside the bad dreams of the night before and the existential dread of a new day, shoving both as deep down into her soul as she could. She watched funny videos while she ate her breakfast, played happy music on her drive to Carrigan Auto, and worked in a space filled with positive affirmation posters and whimsical desk tchotchkes. Then she played more happy music on the way home and watched nothing but romantic comedies and cozy mysteries at night.

Nothing in her life so much as whispered *anger*. So how could she still be so angry after all this time?

"But how is that even possible?" she said. Though, whether she was asking the question of Silas or herself, she had no idea. "I haven't seen anyone in my family for more than ten years. I've barely even *thought* about them. How can I still be so...so..." She expelled an almost feral growl. "How, after all this time, can I still be so *angry* at them?"

She suddenly felt restless, so she scrambled up from the sleeping bag to... What? she asked herself when she was standing. Just where was she planning to go? To look for an Anger Anonymous meeting? She made a quick circuit around the campfire. Then another one. And another one. When that didn't help, she widened her circumference and belabored her tread, until she was stomping around and away from where they'd pitched their bags. Silas stood, too, and followed her, his own pace steady and unhurried. She finally stopped at the banks of the stream, both because there was no further to go without getting wet and because the sound of the water calmed her somewhat. Still, she said nothing, though. Because she truly had no idea what to say. Or think. Or feel. Too many thoughts were battering at the edges of her brain for her to make sense of any of them. Too many emotions were swarming in her chest for her to address even one. She felt like she was going to explode if she couldn't do *something* to make them all stop.

As if from a very great distance, she heard Silas say, "At least you're not denying that you're angry anymore."

She started to shout at him she was *fine.* That was what she always said whenever anyone suggested she was anything else.

You seem tired, Mia.

I'm fine.

Everything okay, Mia? You look unhappy about something.

I'm fine.

You don't look so hot today, Mia. Maybe you should go to the doctor.

I'm fine.

She looked up at the sky again. It was like someone had just opened fire with buckshot on a dark curtain over a window, and now little peeps of the light inside the house were struggling to shine through. Like someone had hung those curtains—long, thick, black-as-night curtains—over those windows so that no one would ever be able to see what was going on on the other side. Like the house beyond those windows was so cluttered, so disorganized, so ugly, that it had to be hidden from view. But now the merest light was shining through, as if trying to say, *Hey, there's some stuff in here that might be useful. That's kind of nice, even. And, possibly, valuable. Anybody interested in seeing inside?*

Mia realized in that moment that she wasn't fine. She hadn't been fine for a very long time. She'd probably never been fine, not really. So maybe it was time that she stopped saying—stopped pretending—she was fine. And if she did that, then maybe, like the house she saw in the sky, somewhere inside herself, she might find some stuff that could be useful, too. Some stuff that might be kind of nice. Some stuff that might possibly even be valuable. She just had to figure out what it was and how to find it.

"No, I'm not denying that I'm angry," she told Silas just as softly.

He hesitated, as if he were waiting for her to say more.

Good luck with that, she thought. Because she had no idea what else to say. Kinda hard to figure out how to express yourself when you just realized you'd been lying to yourself your entire your life about…oh, everything.

Finally, he said, "Is this the part where you tell me—and yourself—that you're fine?"

She looked at him full-on. "No. I'm not going to do that."

"And why is that?"

She inhaled a deep breath and released it on a shaky sigh. "Because I'm not fine."

He nodded once. Not in smug satisfaction that he'd been right all along, but sympathetically, as if he'd been down this road himself and understood how much it took to admit what she had just admitted.

"Well then, Mia Hawthorne, what are you going to do about that?"

Unbidden, her eyes filled with tears. "I don't know."

Her restlessness exploded then, turning into something resembling panic. She dropped down to the ground on her fanny, scrubbed a closed fist over each eye to wipe away the dampness, then pulled her knees up snug against her chest and wrapped her arms fiercely around them. It was the same position she'd assumed as a child when she was also starting to panic, doing whatever she could to make herself invisible. If she could just wad herself up tight enough, and small enough, maybe no one would see her. If she just stayed quiet and didn't move, maybe she could make it through the next minute. Then the next. And the next. And if she stayed that way long enough, the chaos outside her bedroom, or upstairs from the basement, or inside the house, would finally stop. Then she could dart as quick and quiet as a mouse to a safer place.

But there had never been a safer place. Even on those occasions when she could escape the house, she'd always known she would have to go back again eventually, and the abuse would continue until she could escape again. That was why, when she'd left that house for the last time, when she'd finally freed herself from all the turbulence and fear and rage, she had been so sure she would finally, finally be...

Well, fine.

She dipped her head and pressed her forehead to her knees, trying hard—so hard—not to cry. But the tears still came. They came silently, though, the way they had when she was a child, back when she knew better than to make a sound and give away her hiding place. When she felt a hand on her back, she automatically lurched away from it, so lost in her memories that she forgot it was Silas, not her parents and brothers. Not realizing at first that the touch was gentle, not cruel. When he opened his palm over her back again, even more gently this time, she relaxed a little. But the tears only came harder.

"You're okay, Mia," he told her gently. "You're in a safe place. I promise. No one here is gonna hurt you."

Her face still pressed to her knees, she nodded. She knew that. But her instincts still screamed at her to jump up and run away as fast and as far as she could. For long moments, she kept herself scrunched up small, until the tears finally stopped and she had some tiny handle on her emotions. She didn't try to push them back down inside this time, though. There were too many of them, and they were too big, and she didn't think she had enough room inside anymore to keep them all confined. She knew she would have to confront them at some point. For now, though, she just tried to calm them as best she could. She would try to figure out how to sort them all later.

When she finally lifted her head, it was to see that Silas wasn't crouched beside her anymore. He wasn't even standing near her. She swiveled her head until she saw him, a little way down the stream, on top of a rock formation that lifted him a few feet higher off the ground. She suspected he had moved away because he understood her need for boundaries—even if they only extended a little way down a stream—and that he was going to respect them until she wanted to cross them herself or invite him into her space.

She realized then she was ready to do that very thing. Which was pretty major, because Mia had never been entirely comfortable allowing people anywhere near her space. Even with boyfriends, there had always been something—some strange, unidentifiable thing—that had prevented her from feeling at ease when she was with them the way she did when she was alone with herself. For some reason, though, she didn't mind Silas crossing her boundaries to come into her space. It felt totally normal to want that. Totally natural. As if he had already been a frequent visitor to her space. As if, in some way, he had actually become a part of it.

She made her way down the stream until she stood at

the foot of the rocks. "Everything okay up there?" she asked him.

She tried not to notice how raspy her voice was or how jerky her motions had been as she'd moved closer to him, as if the strain of the last several minutes had infiltrated every part of her, right down to the way she moved and sounded.

Silas didn't reply, only looked down and extended a hand toward her, as if inviting her into his space in return. Mia placed her hand in his automatically, and he hauled her up beside him. The promontory was narrow and craggy, just precarious enough that she didn't let go of his hand once she was beside him. He didn't let go of hers, either, even though he seemed perfectly at ease up here.

"You wanna know the real reason why I brought you up into the mountains today?" he asked.

She sniffled and swiped her free hand across her eyes one final time. "I figured it was to introduce some more adversity into my life and make me angry," she told him. Though her voice was less raspy now and her footing was more solid. Maybe because she felt less raspy now. And she somehow felt more solid.

"Besides that," he told her. "Since that didn't seem to be working anyway on account of you've seemed to be totally at ease since we got here, and you haven't been very angry, even just now, talking about your anger."

He was right. Before her outburst, and in spite of her earlier misgivings about the outing, Mia had felt weirdly comfortable while they were making camp and dinner earlier. And *comfortable* was a condition she could safely say didn't take up much room in her emotional locker.

Maybe it was because this place was so far removed from her life in St. Louis and bore no resemblance to anything that had ever created discord in her life. She looked at Silas. Or maybe she'd been feeling that way for another reason entirely.

"The *real* reason I brought you up here," he continued, "is because this place can be very…" He inhaled deeply and released the breath slowly. "Very therapeutic. And you don't have to pay hourly rates for it, and you don't have to answer questions like, 'How did that make you feel?' and 'Can we explore that some more?'"

Wow. Sounded like Mia wasn't the only one who'd tried the therapy route. She wondered if it had worked for Silas. Then she remembered how cranky he'd been this week and how much he buried his feelings, too. She was going to go out on a limb and say, *Maybe not so much*. And she wondered what had put him in therapy to begin with.

"And how is this place therapeutic?" she asked. Not that she disagreed. She'd already found it to be pretty damned therapeutic. She just hadn't realized that until he said it.

Instead of giving her a direct answer, Silas looked up at the sky again. "You know what I like to do up here in the mountains on a night like this, when it feels like the whole damned universe wants to see me crushed and broken under its fist like sandstone?"

That was a feeling Mia knew well, too. She said nothing, though. Silas sounded like he was going to tell her the answer whether she wanted to hear it or not.

"Whenever that happens, it makes me want to tell the

whole damned universe to piss right off. 'Cause I'm not gonna be crushed."

To prove that, he looked back up at the sky and released Mia's hand so that he could cup both of his around his mouth. Then he shouted with all his might that the universe wasn't as big and bad and scary as it tried to make itself, and he was *not* going to let it tell him what to do. In fact, he added, shouting even louder, the universe could go and, um, do something to itself that was in no way polite. Then he called the universe a few bad names. Then he told it to do some other things that were pretty much anatomically impossible—and not just because the universe didn't have an anatomy—and then reiterated that it should go and, um…

Anyway, he really told the universe off. A lot. When he was finished, he dropped his hands to his sides again, expelled a long, ragged sound, and looked at Mia.

"Damn, that felt good."

She never would have guessed. He'd seemed super angry when he was doing it. Funny, though, how he didn't seem angry at all now.

"You should give it a try," he told her.

"Oh, no," Mia said. "No, no, no, no, no. I am not a shouter. And I am not a confronter. I don't care how much crap the universe throws at me, I'm not going to risk its wrath more by telling it to, um…do what you just told it to do."

"And how has that worked out for you so far?" Silas asked. "The 'not shouting' and 'not confronting' part?"

She started to tell him it had worked out fine. But she knew better. For one thing, he would just laugh at her. For another, she was done lying to herself.

"I don't like shouting," she told him. "It brings back too many bad memories."

"There's nothing wrong with shouting at the universe, Mia, as long as there's a good reason for it and it makes you feel better. Hell, most times, the universe isn't listening to us, anyway. And maybe shouting at it yourself will take the power of the shout away from the people you've given it to and put back into your hands."

As convoluted as all that sounded, it made sense to Mia.

"I don't like confrontations," she told him. "Those bring back even worse memories."

"Confrontations aren't always a bad thing, either," he told her. "The right kind of confrontations, *handled appropriately*," he added meaningfully, "can lead to really positive results sometimes."

She eyed him thoughtfully. "You sure I'm not going to be billed for this session?" she asked, striving to inject some lightheartedness into what was beginning to feel kind of like... well, a confrontation.

"Just try it," he said. "If you could tell the universe anything you wanted right now, what would it be? You don't have to shout it. Just say it in your normal voice, if that's easier."

Oh, where to start? Mia thought. She went with the most obvious. "I would tell it to stop producing so many mean people."

Silas smiled at that. Then he pointed upward. "Don't tell me. Tell the universe."

Mia looked at the sky. At the universe. It was so beautiful. How could it possibly allow so much ugliness to exist? "Stop producing so many mean people," she told it quietly.

"Good," Silas said. "What else do you want to tell it?"

Mia sighed. "Stop being so unfair," she said a little more loudly. "Stop rewarding horrible people with wealth and power and quit punishing good people by making them sick and hungry."

"Excellent," Silas said. "What else?"

Mia took another breath. More loudly this time, she told the universe it needed to do a better job protecting people who couldn't take care of themselves. And that it should stop ignoring the indigent and frail and disenfranchised. And while it was at it, could it please inject a little compassion and empathy into people who had none? Could it make people be a little more generous? A little more kind? A little less likely to hurt others? And what about disease? And poverty? What was up with those? Why did they even exist? Was the universe even *trying*? Geez.

Oh, yeah. She was just getting warmed up.

For the next...frankly, she lost track of time at that point... Mia went after the universe for every infraction it had ever caused or allowed, her voice growing bolder and louder with each new charge. By the time she was finished, she was shouting even louder than Silas had been, and she was telling the universe to do all the things to itself that he had told it to do. Silas was even joining in the chorus by then. Together, they took on every societal woe there was, every political injustice, every abuse of power, every natural disaster, the hoarding of wealth, and the scarcity of decency, not to mention the absolute freaking unfairness of life.

Mia was nearly spent by the time she finished. But, wow, did she feel better than she'd ever felt in her life. She felt more *alive* than she'd ever felt in her life. Her heart pounded like a freight train, and she could *feel* her blood rushing to every cell in her body. Her head spun with the awareness of everything around her—the vastness of the sky, the tumult of the wind, the screech of a night creature, the sharp scent of the woodsmoke. A commotion unlike anything she had felt before roared up inside her, as if every emotion, every impression, every response she'd ever buried deep inside suddenly broke free of its bindings and raged free throughout her system.

All her life, she had been afraid to express her true feelings—express her true *self*—because she'd been terrified of drawing attention to herself and exposing vulnerabilities that would make her a target. Or because, even worse, she might find that her true self was made of the same vicious, violent fabric as the rest of her family. But that fear was fleeing now with all the other emotions she was letting go of. There was *so much* inside her in that moment that she never knew she could feel. But there was no violence in her. No viciousness. Nothing remotely like whatever had driven her parents to be the monsters they were. There was only relief. And elation. And absolute, utter, liberation. The freedom to feel whatever she wanted to feel. To do whatever she wanted to do. To *be* whoever she wanted to be.

Herself. Mia realized in that moment that she could feel and do and be all the things she'd never allowed herself to feel or do or be before. And that doing those things would bring into her life not turmoil, but joy.

So ferocious was her exhilaration that she jumped

down from the rocks and started pacing again, making a dozen circuits around the clearing before returning to stand by Silas. Even then, she was still gasping for breath and groping for coherent thought. When he jumped down from the promontory to stand beside her, he was grinning, more broadly now than she had ever seen him grin. And, *oh my God,* was he beautiful when he did that. Beautiful and breathtaking and very, *very* hot. It was all she could do not to throw herself at him and kiss him to within an inch of his life. Within an inch of her life. Within an inch of both their lives. She just wanted *him*. In a way she'd never wanted anything—anyone—before.

The next thing she knew, her fingers were tangled in his hair, his arms were wrapped around her waist, and their mouths were pressed together hard. All Mia could think after that was that Silas had been right about another thing, too. Maybe some confrontations could indeed lead to very good things...

Chapter Eleven

It was a glorious kiss. All the need, all the want, all the desire, all the *passion* Mia had tamped down for so long came roaring back up again, and there was just so much of it, she couldn't keep it all to herself, so she had to give some of it to Silas. But he didn't seem to be minding much. In fact, he seemed to have a lot going on in himself, too. Because he kissed her back with the same kind of relentlessness, as if something had taken hold of him, too, and neither of them seemed to know what to do about it except…surrender to it.

For a long time, they only stood at the water's edge, entwined together until it was hard for her to tell where her body ended and his began. Where she ended and he began. It felt then as if the two of them had become one being. One feeling. A completion of hearts and minds and souls that had been separated for too long.

It was Silas who finally seemed to realize what was happening. He tore his mouth from Mia's, but he didn't let her go. He only looked down at her as if he had forgotten everything except the two of them and was just now becoming aware of their surroundings. But he said nothing at first. Probably because, like Mia, he had no idea what to say. There were no words for what she was feeling. It was something she had never felt before.

Finally, quietly, he said, "This probably shouldn't be happening."

She shook her head. How could he think that? This felt like the most obvious thing in the world to her. "Why shouldn't it be happening?"

He muttered a sound that was at once poignant and playful. "Because it isn't exactly part of the program you came to the ranch for."

"I thought there wasn't an official program for that," she reminded him.

"Yeah, well, there's not. But if there was, I'm reasonably sure that this wouldn't be included in it."

"And what exactly is this, Silas?"

He studied her in silence for another moment. Then he repeated, "It's something that probably shouldn't be happening."

Their breathing was still coming out labored and rough, and both of them were still clinging to each other as if they never, ever, intended to let go. She wasn't sure she could put an easy label on what was happening between them, either. But whatever it was, it sure felt like it was going to happen, whether they wanted it to or not.

"At work," she said, "they told me they were sending me to Whispering Winds because it was a place where I could take a break, find myself, and put my life back on track. But I don't think my life was ever on any track in the first place. And how can I find myself again if I never knew where I was to begin with? I think whatever this is happening—" Here, she pushed herself up on tiptoe again to press her mouth fiercely against his. "Is me doing that," she finished afterward. "Because what I'm feeling now…" she expelled a long, shaky breath "…this is the first thing I've ever felt in my life that's coming from a real, honest place inside me. A place I didn't manufacture. A place I haven't repressed or tried to control."

Silas kissed her back, but gently, brushing his mouth lightly over hers before tracing soft butterfly kisses along her cheek, her jaw and her throat before pulling away again. "I still don't think it's a good idea," he said softly. "My job is to help you figure out what's wrong in your life and show you how to work through the things you need to work through. Not create more problems for you by—"

"That's not your job," she interrupted him. "Your job is to manage the animals on a ranch. You're not a therapist. You're not a babysitter. You're a guy I met while I was taking a break from work to do a little soul-searching, and we hit it off, and now we're responding to each other the same way two people meeting on a cruise ship or at a ski resort would if they hit it off together."

"It's not the same," he told her.

"It's exactly the same."

"I still don't think we should—"

"I don't care," she interrupted him again.

And for the first time in her life, she meant it. She truly wasn't thinking about the repercussions of anything just then. All she knew was that what she felt in this moment was more real and more honest than anything she'd ever felt before. She and Silas were two unhappy people, and they'd been reaching out to each other all week in one way or another, trying to make a connection of some kind. There had been moments when they were almost close enough to touch, but one or the other of them had pulled back. Tonight, they had finally reached each other. Tonight, they were connecting. And, like two people who'd been drowning, they were clinging to each other as if their very lives depended on it.

"Silas, we couldn't have avoided what's happening right now if we'd thrown a bale of barbed wire between us. Maybe you're right that it's not a good idea. But maybe, just maybe, it is *exactly* what's supposed to be happening. To me, it feels totally natural and absolutely right."

His dark brows arrowed down at that, but she could no more tell what he was thinking than she could have counted the stars in the sky. She only knew she wanted him. She *needed* him. And man, oh, man, whether he wanted to admit it or not, right now, he needed her, too. She could see that plainly, even if he couldn't. The same way he'd seen her anger when she'd been blind to it herself, she could see his need for…something. Something she couldn't identify, but something so strong, she could feel it shuddering from the core of him.

For a moment, he said nothing, only searched her face as if looking for the answers to so many questions, he didn't know where to begin. Then, slowly, he lowered his head to hers again. Their kiss this time was slower, gentler, more tender. Another brush of his mouth over hers before he traced the outline of her lips with his tongue. Then he went in for another deeper, more leisurely, taste of her. Mia melted into him, curling the fingers of one hand into the silky hair at his nape, splaying the other open over his shirt above his heart. She felt his pulse quicken against her palm, loving how it mirrored the beat of her own heart, and she pushed herself up on tiptoe so that she could savor the taste and feel of him, too. When she did, he scooped her up in his arms and, still kissing her, carried her back to their sleeping bags by the fire. Then he knelt and placed her gently atop her bag, stretching himself out beside and atop her to press their bodies close again.

A log on the fire crackled and shifted, sending up a spray of embers and a shimmer of heat. It was nothing, though, compared to the conflagration growing in Mia. For a long time, they only kissed and cuddled and caressed, each getting to know how the other felt and responded and reacted. As she kissed him, she traced her fingers over his rough jaw and along the strong column of his throat, then dipped lower to skim her fingertips over his elegant collarbones. She undid the buttons of his shirt one by one, tucking her hand inside to run them over the bumps and ridges of his hard, hot torso, then pushed the garment back over one shoulder to palm the curves of his salient biceps. Then she pulled her mouth away from his to send her mouth on the same journey her fingers had taken, tasting the brine of his skin, and losing herself in his heat and his scent.

Silas stroked his hands over her thighs and hips and back as she did, then moved lower to cup the curve of her ass over her jeans, jerking her body closer to his until his thigh was pressed hard against the hot feminine core of her. Mia gasped at the contact, closing more intimately around him to move her body back and forth along his leg, creating a delicious friction that sparked the fire inside her even hotter. As she did, he moved one hand between them to unfasten the buttons of her shirt, tug-

ging the garment free when he reached the waistband
of her jeans.

Then he was pushing her shirt open and reaching behind her, deftly freeing the hooks of her bra and pushing that aside, too. When he covered her bare breast with
his warm palm, she cried out, his rough calluses rous-
ing a response on her tender flesh that sent a spiral of
pleasure through her. He moved his mouth to her other
breast, tracing the lower curve with his tongue before
drawing its plump peak fully into his mouth, easing her
backward until Mia was flat on her back beneath him.

She moved a hand to the fastening of her jeans and
freed it, then tucked her hand inside to move her fingers
between her legs. When he realized what she was doing,
he lifted her hips enough to push the garment down over
her hips and moved his hand between her legs to join
her. Together they stroked her tender flesh, Silas stopping their hands just short of penetrating her, as if he
had plans for that part of her later. So, Mia withdrew her
hand, unbuttoned his fly and tugged down his jeans, too,
moving her fingers down the length of his solid shaft and
back up again, until he was hard and swollen and damp
against her palm. Somehow, she found the wherewithal
to toe off one boot then the other, until, together, they
were able to strip off her jeans completely. Then Silas
moved his hand back to her, and she spread her legs wide
enough for him to…

Oh. Oh, yeah. Right *there*. He thumbed that most
sensitive part of her gently, then dipped two long fingers slowly, deeply, inside her. Mia bucked against him
to drive him deeper, but even that wasn't enough. She

wanted more. She wanted all of him. And she wanted all of him *now*.

"I need to feel you inside me," she told him breathlessly.

He was lying beside her now, his head tucked under her chin, his own breath hot and damp against her neck. He looked up at her words, his expression frantic. "Mia, I didn't exactly come up here prepared for a party like this."

Right. Condom. It had been so long for her, she'd forgotten she was supposed to take precautions for some things. For other things, though... "I have an IUD," she told him. "And I know I'm healthy. It's been a while since I've been with anyone. Like a *long* while since I've been with anyone."

His gaze darkened. "For me, too."

"I want you inside me," she told him again.

She didn't have to tell him twice. Silas lay down fully beside her, rolling onto his back and lifting her until she was astride him. She guided him inside her, then lowered herself on top of him, taking him deeper, deeper, and deeper still, until he completely filled her. Oh, yes. That was what she needed. To feel complete. To feel, finally, as if she were whole. For a long moment, she didn't move, only savored the perfect union of their bodies. Then she slowly rose up on her knees and down again. Silas groaned with satisfaction when she did, anchoring a hand on each of her hips to pace her motions, bucking against her hard with every descent to fill her even more.

Little by little, their motions grew faster and more frenzied. Mia leaned forward to kiss him again, her tongue tangling with his. Then she was the one on her back, with Silas kneeling before her. He circled her ankles with sure fingers and lifted her hips from the ground, opening her legs wide so that he could drive himself into her even deeper. Within minutes, Mia was riding the crest of her orgasm like a tidal wave and Silas was joining her, spilling himself hotly inside her. Then they were both lying on the bag again, side by side, gasping for breath and groping for coherence. After a few minutes, they somehow found both, and they smiled.

"Wow," Mia said with much understatement.

"Wow," Silas agreed.

"I never knew it could be like that."

He looked at her for a long time, as if he were thinking very hard about something. Then, very softly, he told her, "I never knew it could be like that, either."

And there was something in the statement that made Mia think he was talking about a lot more than sex. But what had just happened had been more than sex for her, too. What, exactly, it was, she honestly didn't know yet. It was too new, too foreign, too fragile, for her to put a name on it. She only knew that whatever it was made her feel good. Really good. It made her feel, for the first time, as if she were…well, finding herself. Or, at least, a part of herself. And for the first time, too, she actually wanted to look deeper inside herself to find out what else was in there.

Besides Silas Crockett, she meant. Because he, for sure, was a part of her now. She just wasn't sure yet where to put him. Like herself in that moment, she just wasn't sure where he belonged.

Silas awoke as he had a million times before in his life, under the wide-open sky of Wyoming just before dawn. Maybe he didn't get up into the mountains as often as he used to, but it wasn't uncommon for him to open his eyes and see the dawn blooming above him, staining the sky with pink and lavender and yellow. What was uncommon—an anomaly, really—was that this time, he wasn't waking up alone. Mia still slept beside him, turned on her side to face him. Due to the cold, they'd gotten dressed again after the second time they came together, then they'd zipped their two sleeping bags up over themselves to turn them into one. At some point during the night, she'd covered his waist with her arm and curled her fingers over his biceps, and now he never wanted to move again.

He'd forgotten what it was like to wake up next to someone. The few women he'd dated since Jess's death had never ended up being more than a way to pass some time and expend some energy—the same way, he was pretty certain, he had been for them. With Mia, though… The way the two of them had responded to each other last night… All that fire, all that demand, all that urgency, all that *passion*…

It had never been like that for Silas. With any woman. Including Jess. And it just felt so damn good after all this time to be this close to someone who was starting to actually mean something to him. Just what that *something* was, though…

He shook off the thought before it could get out of hand. He told himself he should be bothered by what had happened last night and that it never should've happened in the first place. But another part of him knew it had been inevitable. He and Mia had just recognized and responded to something in each other that neither had wanted—or maybe hadn't known how—to acknowledge before last night. Hell, the second they'd met they'd created an immediate—and ultimately intense—bond. They'd both been carrying around ugly burdens for way too long, though both had managed to convince themselves that those burdens were of no consequence anymore. They'd reassured themselves they were managing just fine with the crappy hands life had dealt them, that they'd in fact moved past them to live as full a life as was possible. Now he knew that wasn't true at all. He'd known it wasn't true for Mia the minute he met her. But he hadn't realized how much he'd been lying to himself, too.

He wasn't any more fine than she was. He was still as full of rage about his own past as she was about hers. He'd been telling himself he was managing it, but was he really? Or had he just been burying it, too, the same was she had? Ignoring it while it still festered inside him? Even after coming up here to scream at the universe for more than a decade, he was no closer to moving past his anger now than he'd been when he first lost Jess and their baby.

He looked at Mia, still sleeping so peacefully beside him. His anger wasn't quite so horrible this morning, though. It made a difference, having someone beside him who could maybe help him out.

As gently as he could, he disengaged himself without waking her, then rose to build a fire from the smoldering embers. It was still cold this morning, but his memories of the night before went a long way toward keeping him warm, and the fire that caught quickly did the rest. He started a pot of coffee and dug out the precooked bacon and a couple of eggs he'd grabbed fresh from the hen-house, so he could fix them some breakfast once they got hungry. There was nowhere they needed to be, no fixed schedule they had to maintain. They could stay up here enjoying themselves—and enjoying each other—for as long as they wanted. The world beyond their immediate surroundings might as well not have existed right now. It just wasn't important. Not the way other things were.

Once the coffee was percolating, Silas went back to the bedroll and tucked himself in next to Mia again. When he did, she stirred, her eyes fluttering open to the same sky he'd been looking at himself, though it was a bit brighter now. It took her a minute to remember where she was and why she wasn't at home in her own bed—or at least in her cabin down at Whispering Winds—and he waited for her to look as disconcerted as he'd told himself he should be a little while ago. Instead, when her gaze lit on his, she smiled, looking as if she was right where she wanted—where she needed—to be. The same way he felt himself.

"Good morning," she told him.

"Mornin'," he greeted her back.

"Coffee smells good."

"It'll be done in just a bit."

She inhaled a deep sigh and slowly let it go, sound-ing as satisfied and contented as Silas was, then pulled her arms out from under the covers to stretch them high above her head. When she was done, she pushed her body close to his, wrapping one arm around his waist again and resting her head on his shoulder. Silas roped an arm across her, too, pulling her closer still, and settled his chin on the crown of her head. She felt so good there beside him, a perfect fit. As if the two of them had been cut from the same cloth at some point and were finally being seamed back together again.

He sighed deeply. Resolutely. He guessed he should have seen this coming before last night. He and Mia might have only known each other a week, but it felt like a lot longer, as if the two of them had been together forever. Maybe because, after last night, he knew all the most important things about her, because she'd shared all those most important things with him. Not just her memories and her emotions, but herself, too. Over the course of the week, he'd seen so many sides of her—her smarts, her adaptability, her wit, her compassion. Hell, no wonder he was halfway falling in—

Hell, no wonder he felt like he knew her so well.

But there was so much she didn't know about him. Because he *hadn't* shared anything with her, save a few hours of coupling that, as gratifying as it had been, had been more physical than anything else. Mia had shared the most important parts of herself with him last night—physically, psychologically, emotionally. It was time he shared the most important parts of himself with her. The physical part had been easy. The rest of it?

He blew out an errant breath. Well, that was going to be a little more difficult. For both of them.

"What are you thinking about?" Mia asked softly. "You look really pensive all of a sudden."

He grinned at that. Damn. Another grin. He'd had more of those in the last twenty-four hours than he'd had in the twelve years that preceded them. This grin wasn't so much happy, though, as it was wry, because she was so in tune with what was going on in his head.

"I'll tell you over coffee," he said. "I think it's about done."

They climbed out of the sleeping bag, but instead of rolling it up afterward, which Silas normally would have been sure to do, because he didn't like leaving things undone, he decided to leave it for now. Other things took precedence. Like coffee with a woman who'd come to mean more to him than he should probably allow himself to—

Like coffee with Mia. That was pretty much the most important thing in the world at the moment.

It was a glorious morning, as was always the case this high up in the mountains, especially this time of year. The sun had crested the trees by now and was already beginning to warm the chilly air, and the only sounds were the crackle of the fire and the murmur of the wind as it threaded its way through the leaves.

He and Mia made small talk as they settled down by the fire—how, if he were back on the ranch, he'd be doing his weekly paperwork about now, even though it was Sunday and technically a day off, and how she would be sleeping late back in St. Louis, or at least trying to, because Sunday was the one day she gave herself permission to loaf. He fished a couple packets of sugar and dry creamer out of his pocket to set next to her coffee, and Mia looked at both with a smile.

"You noticed how I take my coffee," she said.

He nodded. "Sorry the creamer is powdered instead of the real thing, but hauling a fridge up here, even a mini one, would have made the trip even more arduous."

She smiled. "It wasn't arduous."

He chuckled at that. "That's not the impression I got from you yesterday."

She laughed, too. "I guess I thought it was *kind of* arduous at the time, but this morning, for some reason, life feels a little easier than it did yesterday."

"Yeah, funny how letting yourself lose control once in a while can make you feel so much better the next day."

He'd been talking about the railing-at-the-universe stuff when he said that, but both of their thoughts clearly went to what happened afterward instead. Mia's cheeks bloomed with pink at her memories, while a wild heat sparked to life in Silas's belly at his. He reminded himself she'd be going home in less than a week. And he told himself that was a good thing. What the two of them had found together was amazing, for sure. But it was the result of something that had been building in both of them for a long time before they met, and it would surely run its course before long. Best if the two of them went their separate ways before that happened. Way easier to say *Take care and happy trails* and part with fond memories than it was to say *Whew, glad we got that out of our systems* and then feel awkward wondering how to end it. Though that didn't feel quite like what was happening between them, either...

Silas enjoyed a few sips of his coffee, then set down his cup and rolled up his shirt sleeve to reveal the tattoo on the inside of his forearm. It was the only tattoo he had. He wasn't one of those people who felt the need to ink their hobbies and loves and significant life moments permanently on their person. But he had done it for one. Because he'd known what it signified would be something he carried with him forever. It would be a part of him always. Although he'd known he would never forget, he'd wanted a tangible reminder anyway. Something he would see every day. Because not a day went by that he didn't think about what had happened.

"So, you asked me what I was thinking about this morning," he said as he went about the motions.

Mia was sipping her coffee, watching every move he made over the rim. But she said nothing in response to his statement. Probably because she could tell that he wasn't really asking for or expecting one.

"What I was thinking was that you've told me a lot about yourself this week, but I haven't returned the favor."

"I was supposed to tell you about myself," she said. "That's what it said in the literature HR gave me about the program at Whispering Winds. That part of the healing process would be 'exploring the source of my anger with an understanding listener.' I think that was what it said."

Yep. That was what the literature said. Though that literature had been a bit misleading in Mia's case.

"Yeah, sorry about the 'patient' part not being there," he told her. "That was Beau they were talking about, not me."

"But you have been a listener," she told him. As if to illustrate that, she held up her creamed-and-sugared coffee. "And I haven't exactly been overrun with patience myself this week. I'm glad they paired me with you instead of Beau."

He nodded once. "Me, too," he said. "But I think I speak for both of us when I say the anger management thing has sorta turned into something else."

Those two bright spots of pink appeared on her cheeks again. And the fire in Silas's belly kicked higher.

"Yeah, I think you definitely speak for both of us," she agreed.

"So then I should tell you a few things about myself, too."

Her response was once again silence. He wondered if that meant she didn't want to hear what he was going to say. She *needed* to hear it, though. And he for sure needed to share it.

He held up his arm so that Mia could see the tattoo. "I've seen you looking at this more than once this week, but you've never said anything about it, even though I'm pretty sure you wanted to."

"It's your only visible tattoo," she said, "so it must mean something super personal. I didn't want to pry."

Of course she didn't. Prying would lead to sharing, and sharing—honestly sharing—was something the old Mia never would have done. It was something the old Silas never would have done, either. But after last night…

Well, after last night, he didn't feel like the old Silas anymore. Because, after last night, he was reasonably certain he *wasn't* the same Silas anymore.

"I figured it must signify something super important, too," she added softly. "Maybe *the* most important thing. And sometimes people want to keep those things to themselves. That's what I did with my family stuff. For decades." She shrugged, smiling in a way that was both happy and sad. "Well, at least until last night."

He nodded, feeling both happy and sad himself that she understood. The tattoo did indeed signify the most important thing that had happened in his life. Or, at least,

ELIZABETH BEVARLY 235

it had been the most important thing when it happened. And for years afterward. For some reason, though, looking at those two trees on his arm now hurt a little less than it did before.

"What kind of trees are they?" she asked.

"They're aspens," he told her. "But they're a lot more than trees."

He met her gaze, but she said nothing, just silently willed him to go on when he felt up to it. It took a minute, but Silas finally did.

"The big one is for my…" He blew out a rough breath then made himself finish. "For my late wife. Jess. She died twelve years ago this fall."

Mia's eyebrows arrowed down at that, and her gray eyes went stormy. But it wasn't the angry kind of tempest he'd seen in those eyes that first day. This was more like the gray of an autumn sky, mourning the loss of summer and concerned about an uncertain winter.

"Oh, Silas. I am so sorry," she said quietly. "I had no idea."

"Of course you didn't," he told her gently. "How could you? No one around here has said a word about her for years. Including me. I made sure they all know not to."

"I'm sorry," she said again. As if she didn't know what else to say.

Silas understood. There weren't a lot of things *to* say to someone who'd lost a loved one that didn't come out sounding clichéd or insincere. Hell, how could anyone grasp the magnitude of another person's suffering in the first place? He started to tell her it was fine, then almost smiled sadly at his own reaction. Instead, because Mia was looking at him so expectantly, he told her the rest.

Well, as much as he could handle talking about the rest right now.

"Her name was Jess Penn," he said. "But the first time she introduced herself, I misunderstood and thought she was telling me her name was Aspen, so I said something like 'Pleased to meet you, Aspen.' After that, it turned into kind of a joke with us. Then it became one of those...what do you call them? Terms of endearment." Now, he did smile. And it was indeed sad. "I called her Aspen a lot."

"What happened?" Mia asked. "I mean, is it okay if I ask? You don't have to talk about this if you don't want to."

"Yeah, I do," he said. "I mean, no, I don't want to. But I have to. The same way you didn't want to but had to tell me last night about your family."

"I had to tell you those things about myself so I could work through them, and you needed to know that stuff so you could sign off on my progress and get me back to work in St. Louis."

"That wasn't the only reason I needed to know it," he told her. He hoped she could deduce the rest, because he wasn't sure he could find the words right now to explain it. He'd also needed to know about her past because it was important to her, and what was important to her was important to him. Not because he was trying to help her manage her anger and get her back to work. But because *she'd* become important to him, too. He wanted them to share their pasts with each other because he wanted them to share other things, too. He still had no idea how the two of them might manage that. But he needed her to know how he felt *right now*.

Judging by her expression then—one that softened her sadness with both affection and hope—she did understand. At least as well as Silas understood it in that moment himself.

"I met her at the University of Wyoming when I was there," he continued. "I lived on campus and got a job in the kitchen of one of the restaurants within walking distance. Jess was a barista at a coffee shop at the end of the block where I stopped every day on my way to work. We started dating when we were sophomores, and by senior year, we were living together."

It had been the oldest story in the world. Boy meets girl and all that. Then had come the second oldest story in the world.

"She discovered she was pregnant not long after we both graduated," he continued. "Her degree was in early childhood education, and she wanted to go for her master's, and neither of us wanted her pregnancy to interrupt that, so we did whatever we had to do to make it work."

He told Mia the rest. About the courthouse wedding and how Silas delayed his own master's to take a full-time job at a local feed store. About how they started socking away every cent that they could for what was to come. Once they got over the shock of how much their lives were about to change, they'd genuinely started looking forward to the future and making big plans, right down to the house with the white picket fence, the minivan and a puppy named Sparky.

As Silas recounted everything, he was overcome with memories he hadn't allowed himself to think about for a very long time. And with feelings he hadn't allowed himself to feel for a very long time. He waited for the anger—the rage—that had always been the strongest of those, knowing what was coming next. Then he was surprised to discover that even though, yes, the rage was still there, it wasn't as overwhelming as it used to be. Still, he braced himself for the rest of the story. About how they found out during her second trimester that the baby was going to be a girl, and how they started calling her Aspen 2.0 until they could decide on a name for her. That was when Silas held up his arm again and pointed to the smaller of the two trees inked there.

"This one is Aspen 2.0. Who I never got to meet in person, but who I know would have been a carbon copy of Jess." He stared at the tattoo, the only remnant he had left of what was supposed to have been his family. "A couple of months before Jess was due, she was driving home from class one night, and she was hit by a drunk driver. She and the baby both were killed instantly."

"Oh my God, Silas," Mia said. "I don't even know what to say."

But she knew what to do. As he had been telling her the story, she'd sat on the other side of the fire, her coffee cup neglected in one hand, her other hand cupped over her mouth as she listened in silence. Now she set down the cup and circled to where he was sitting, folding herself beside him to wrap both arms around his middle and press her face to his chest. He wrapped an arm around her, too—the one without the Aspens, since that one lay limp in his lap—and for a long time, neither of them said a word. Silas just let the memories tumble around in his head and the emotions bounce around in his chest until they finally, finally, settled down.

Eventually, he was able to roll down his sleeve over Jess

and the baby once more, to protect them in a way he'd not been able to protect them when they were alive. Again, he waited for the roar of the rage in his brain to deafen him, for the anguish to seize up his body like a stone. But neither of those things happened. Instead, he just felt sad. Sadder even than he'd felt when it happened, more than a decade ago. He realized then that he'd never really felt sad after their deaths. He'd only felt angry. And furious. And ready to beat the hell out of anything—anything— that got in his way. He'd never let himself be sad about losing his family. He'd never let himself grieve. Anger had been so much easier.

Now he curled his tattooed arm around Mia's waist, too, and pulled her close. The two of them sat in silence for a little longer, both lost in their thoughts and feelings and confusion. When he heard her sniffle, he knew she was crying, but somehow, he also knew that, this time, her sorrow was for him. Maybe he had become as important to her as she had become to him. Because by sharing Jess and the baby with Mia, something important in his own life was now important in hers, too.

"Anyway," he finally said, his voice rough and quiet, "now you know why I am the way I am."

She lifted her head to look at him for a long time, her eyes still damp and full of... Something he wasn't sure he should try to identify. Not when they were both in such a raw state. "And what way are you, exactly, Silas?" she asked.

He looked at her in confusion. After a week with him, shouldn't that be pretty clear to her?

He started off with the obvious. "Angry." Then he

added the rest. "Bitter. Crochety. And hell, that's just the beginning of the alphabet."

She shook her head slowly. "Okay, maybe you've been all those things at some point this week. But you know what else you've been?"

He didn't answer. There were still twenty-three letters in the alphabet to cover.

"You've also been kind and gentle and decent," she said.

No. None of those words had been in the assortment marching through his brain. "I'm none of those things," he said.

"And thoughtful," she continued. "And sympathetic. And compassionate. I could fill a thesaurus with all the good things you've been this week."

"Mia, I—"

"You've been nothing but patient with me the whole time I've been here."

He almost laughed at that. "We both know that's not true."

"But it is," she insisted. "Yeah, you've been irascible sometimes, but most of that was to try to get through to me in any way you could. You were trying to help me, and I was making your job way harder than it needed to be. I've given you a million reasons to throw up your hands and walk away. But, Silas, you never did. You stayed with me."

"It's been my job this week to make sure you stay out of trouble."

"In other words, to take care of me," she pointed out. "The same way you take care of the animals at Whispering Winds."

"It's just my job, Mia."

"Maybe it's your job for a reason. Because you're well suited to it."

"It's my job, because there was no one else to do it."

"And now you're taking care of me because there's no one else to do that, either."

It probably should have bothered him how happy it made him to hear her say that.

"You're a decent, caring human being, Silas. Yeah, okay, sometimes you're grumpy and irritable. So is everyone else on the planet. And sometimes, you're a little rough on people. But mostly, you're rough on yourself. And after everything you just told me you went through, after the losses you've had…" She shook her head, then lifted her hand to curve her palm over his jaw. "You still have it in you to be a good guy. Because that's what you are. A good guy. You're just going to have to accept that."

She moved her hand to brush a soft kiss over his cheek, then curled her arm around his waist and pressed her head to his shoulder again. "I'm so sorry about Jess and your baby," she said. "I get now why you need to yell at the universe. I just wish there was some way the universe could undo what happened."

Silas wished that, too. Every time he came up here. But the universe had always turned a deaf ear to his pleas. He looked down at Mia, at the soft silver hair spilling out of her ponytail and the stain of pink on her creamy cheeks and the damp place on his shirt where some of her tears had fallen. He felt her arm tighten around his waist and the warmth of her skin against his shirt, mixing with his own. He inhaled the campfire and coffee aroma of her, heard her soft breath mingling with the breeze in the trees.

And he thought that maybe, possibly, perhaps, even though the universe couldn't undo what had happened twelve years ago, it might maybe, possibly, perhaps, be trying to find a way to make it up to him now.

Chapter Twelve

Mia's final week at Whispering Winds passed so quickly, she felt as if she were moving at the speed of light. After coming back down to the ranch from the mountains late Sunday afternoon, she and Silas parted ways long enough to shower and change clothes before meeting again at his house on the edge of the ranch's property. He cooked dinner for both of them—chicken, Mia couldn't help noticing, not beef—then they took an after-dinner coffee out to his front porch to share quiet conversation about all the things they hadn't talked about before. Important things, not-important things, and everything in between. Once darkness fully fell, they went back inside to say their good-nights so that Silas could walk Mia back to her cabin. Except that instead of doing that, they tumbled into his bed, waking to greet the sun again in the morning. That became their pattern for the rest of the week.

They talked about their families during those evenings they spent together, too. The one Mia had left behind forever. The one Silas would never have. And although Miss Sylvie had told Mia on her first day at Whispering Winds that the program she was going into wasn't technically therapy and had assured her that anyone she met on the ranch would by no means be a therapist, that week for Mia was very—dare she say?—therapeutic.

She hoped it felt that way for Silas as much for herself. She knew they both had a long way to go in their healing. But at least they had taken the first step. They had acknowledged that they weren't fine. And they had realized that that was okay. They just needed to be sure they never lost sight of the things that were truly important and be kind to themselves along the way.

They remained inseparable for the remainder of her time at Whispering Winds. Mia spent her days shadowing Silas on whatever tasks he needed to complete and doing the things she needed to do herself—like feeding Tiny Tim and checking on Mimi the kitten to be sure her family was treating her well. Her nights she spent with Silas, either in his bed at his house or in hers at her cabin. There were times during that week when she felt as if the way she was living was the only life she'd ever known, in spite of it being as far removed from her reality as it could possibly be. Then she'd remember that no, her reality was more than a thousand miles away, and she would be going back to it soon.

Too soon. On Friday, after Mia filled out the forms and questionnaires for her outgoing from the program, Silas asked her what she wanted to do for her last evening at Whispering Winds Ranch. And it took everything she had not to tell him she wanted to go back up into the mountains with him and never come back. To spend the rest of their lives making love under the stars. She had made a promise to herself that last week that she would always be honest from now on—with other people and with herself—and that was the honest answer. Unfortunately, she had also made a promise to herself that she would always be realistic from now on, too. And spending the rest of her days in Serenity Valley was anything but that. Certainly, her life back in St. Louis wasn't exactly a dream come true, but it was real. For her, at least. And Whispering Winds was real for Silas. She just couldn't see any way—any honest, realistic way—that the two of them could combine their lives. And neither could Silas. They lived half a country and two lifestyles away from each other, and there wasn't a commute in the world that would fix that.

Even without that, though, they both still had work to do on themselves before they could think about someone else. As much progress as Mia had made during her stay at the ranch, she still had a ways to go in dealing with the trauma from her childhood that still filtered into her daily life. Silas had barely begun to grieve the deaths of a wife and child he'd lost more than a decade ago. It was going to be a while before either of them had room for something more. It was possible they would never have room enough for that. That was honest. That was realistic. That was life.

So, on Friday, her last day at Whispering Winds, she told Silas she just wanted to do what they always did— spend the day together, then finish up at the end-of-session party Miss Sylvie always threw, complete with barbecue and hayride. Which they did, as if it were any other day on the ranch. But when that day was through, and Silas walked her back to her cabin at the end of it, Mia kissed him on her porch for the last time. She knew that in the morning, before the sun came up, the shuttle would be taking her and some of the other ranch visitors to the airport in Jackson Hole to catch their respective flights back to all their real lives. Mia didn't want her last memory of the two of them together to be her rushing around the cabin in the morning while he lay in bed watching her go. Instead, she wanted to kiss him sweetly under the stars, whisper her thanks for the best two weeks of her life, and tell him...

Tell him goodbye.

So that was what they did. And less than twenty-four hours after that, Mia was turning the key to her front door in St. Louis and going back to her honest, real life.

Which immediately felt neither real nor honest. Instead, the apartment where she'd lived for almost three years felt like a hotel room she was visiting for the first time. When she went to the grocery on Sunday to restock her kitchen, the place felt like a movie set with extras pretending to pick through the produce for a film take. It was the same with her favorite coffee shop and the park where she'd enjoyed her evening walks for years. Even the library, once her literal escape from life and now her go-to for literary escape from life, felt oddly artificial when she went there to pick up some books by Hank Stallard, the Western novelist she'd discovered from Miss Sylvie's recommendation. What was really weird, though, was how the literary escape she found in those books felt infinitely more like real life to her now.

Her first day back at work came midweek after her return to St. Louis. That morning, she woke up dreading the idea of going in to work more than she had dreaded anything in her life. And considering how much she'd had to dread over her twenty-nine years, that was saying something. But she'd learned a lot of things during her two weeks in Wyoming, not the least of which was that she needed to stop pretending when something was wrong or didn't feel great.

It was okay that she dreaded going back to work, she told herself as she buttoned up her favorite wispy-lavender blouse over her favorite beige-linen trousers. Other than wanting to earn a paycheck, what reason did she have to want to go? It wasn't like her identity was wrapped up in being a service advisor at Carrigan Auto. And it wasn't like she had a ton of friends there. Or, you know, any friends there. No one at Carrigan Auto was friends. None of them saw each other after the workday ended. Few of them even ate lunch at the same table in the break room. And, of course, there was always the specter of Perpetual Salesman of the Month Jeff Oberstrom who she would have to deal with on a daily basis again.

Somehow, though, she knew it wasn't any of those things that were at the root of her dismay. Carrigan Auto just didn't feel like the place where she was supposed to be working, even after going there five days a week for more than a decade. Now that she thought about it, it was kind of a mystery why she'd stayed at Carrigan for as long as she had. It had just been easier than trying to find something else, because looking for something else could be stressful, and she'd always done her best to avoid bad feelings like stress.

But stress wasn't always a bad thing, she reminded herself. Sometimes stress could lead to good outcomes. Like new jobs. And new friends. And the solving of problems one didn't even want to admit one had. Stress could even lead to meeting handsome cowboys in beautiful places. She needed to start thinking about and acknowledging the issues in her life. Now that she understood that thinking about and acknowledging those issues didn't always have to lead to feeling bad about things, her day-to-day existence should be a lot easier to manage.

For some reason, that made her think about Silas. Hah. *For some reason,* she echoed to herself. Since returning to St. Louis, just about everything had made her think about Silas. Unlocking her front door had made her think about his crotchety mood that first day when he'd unlocked the door to her cabin. When she fixed breakfast for herself in the morning, she remembered him making her breakfast over an open fire. When she'd done her post-trip laundry, which had mostly consisted of underwear, because she'd worn borrowed clothes for nearly the entirety of her stay, all she'd been able to think about was the way his hands had felt skimming under the hook of her bra to unfasten it, and how his fingers had felt dipping beneath the fabric of her jeans and between her legs to—

Um, anyway, she'd thought a lot about Silas since her return. It was just too bad he was going to have to stay in her thoughts. Because no matter how much she might have wanted things to be different for the two of them—and Mia really did wish for that—it would never work.

Her hands got to the top button of her blouse and she realized she'd completely misaligned the two sides when she first started. How had that happened? This was her favorite shirt. She wore it all the time. Though now that she looked at herself in the mirror, she decided it, too, looked kind of off. And why did the linen trousers she'd always loved suddenly feel like they didn't quite fit right?

It was going to be A Day. She could already tell.

And it did end up being a day. Just not a capitalized one.

When she entered her office at Carrigan, it looked exactly the same as it had when she left. The files she had organized meticulously in her accordion folder were still there, and her desktop computer was full of the same spreadsheets and documents. The fluorescent bulb overhead still buzzed annoyingly. Her chair still squeaked when she took her seat. She politely acknowledged the awkward welcome-backs from her coworkers as they passed by her door, then she went right to work, her brain moving as fluidly back into what needed to be done as if she'd never been away. The day flew by until mid-afternoon rolled around, when there was a soft rap at her office door.

She looked up to see Perpetual Salesman of the Month Jeff Oberstrom standing framed by the jamb. Funny, but he seemed a lot smaller than she remembered. And a lot less…Jeff-y and salesman-y. She said nothing to greet him, only gazed at him in question. Before all of this, much of her workday had revolved around how to avoid him. But she'd barely given him a thought since coming back from Whispering Winds. And now, the only thought she spared him was an ironic one—that without him, she never would have met Silas or discovered the most beautiful place she'd ever seen. And how good it felt to move past and be free of feelings caused by people like Perpetual Salesman of the Month Jeff Oberstrom.

"Hi, Mia," he said. But instead of the overblown blo-viation his words normally carried—even the short ones like *Hi* and *Mia*—he sounded anxious. Anxious, too, was the way he moved a hand to the tie tack pinned to his necktie, as if wanting to be sure it stayed anchored in place. Huh. She'd never noticed him using a tie tack before.

"Hello," she said in response. Adding nothing. Still not sure why he was there.

He straightened a little. "Look, I, um, I wanted to apologize for what happened a few weeks ago."

"Okay."

He waited to see if she would say anything else. She didn't.

"I didn't mean anything by my comment that day."

"Yes, you did," she said calmly. "You were deliberately trying to get a rise out of me, the same way you always try to get a rise out of the people who work here. You did it because something in your pathetic, miserable life is terribly wrong, and your way of dealing with it is to pick on people you think won't fight back."

He looked stunned by the fact that she had called him out. Oh, well.

He stammered uncomfortably. "I… I was… I was just kidding."

"No, you weren't," she said. "You were being a dick. Thanks for the apology. Have a nice day."

Then she looked back at her computer screen, clicking on an icon to open another file.

But he didn't take the hint. "It's just… Look, Mia, I don't want you to think badly of me or anything. We still have to work together."

"No worries, Jeff," she said as she started to type. "I don't think about you at all."

And then she went back to work. Without another thought for Jeff.

She wasn't sure, but he may have stood in her doorway for a few more minutes, as if he were waiting for her to say or do something else. But that wasn't going to happen. Life was too short for her to let people like Jeff roam around in her head. She'd said what she'd needed to say, and now, as far as she was concerned, the conversation was over. She had better ways to spend her time. Hell, even reading about new federal vehicle guidelines was better.

And so it went for the rest of Mia's first week back at work. And her second week. And her third and her fourth. Get up in the morning. Dress in clothes that no longer felt comfortable. Go to a place where she knew what she was doing and did it well, even if it didn't bring any kind of satisfaction. Be polite and helpful to the customers and colleagues who didn't piss her off. Try not to care when Perpetual Salesman of the Month Jeff Oberstrom ended up not being Salesman of the Month for July. Their new saleswoman Naomi, hired while Mia was in Serenity Vally, outsold him by a mile, followed by Carl, their salesman who had been around forever. Both of them kicked Jeff's butt.

But Mia did kind of care—and laugh—about that. It was as if the universe had heard at least a few of the things she shouted that night on a mountaintop in Wyoming and was finally starting to do its job.

With each passing week, though, every time Mia fired up her desktop at work in the morning or crossed the threshold into her apartment after she went home, she felt less and less like she belonged there. Not that she'd ever really felt like she belonged at Carrigan Auto. Not that she'd ever really felt like she belonged in St. Louis. Silas had been pretty perceptive when he pointed out she never called it home.

But that was because no place had ever felt like home to Mia, and she'd never felt as if she belonged anywhere. Not on the handful of vacations she'd taken over the years. Not on any of the day trips to the numerous cities within a couple hours' drive of St. Louis. Not in any of the many neighborhoods that made up her hometown. Mia had just decided at some point that because she'd never known what it was like to actually have a home, she would never be able to make one anywhere.

But now even the façade of homelife that she'd created for herself didn't feel right. Every day, she clocked out from a job where she didn't belong and returned to an apartment where she didn't belong to lead a life she didn't belong in. And nothing she did or thought or told herself made it possible to recapture that sense of make-believe that everything was all right. That everything was *fine*.

But that was okay, she told herself. Her new honest reality was just something that would take her a while to get used to. And once she did, she would be… Well, kind of fine.

TGIF, she thought as she returned to her apartment at the end of…whatever week this was since her return from Wyoming. All the weeks were starting to run together, just as they had before she went to Wyoming. See? She was getting used to her new honest reality already. Dammit. As always, she thought about Silas when she turned the key in her front door. As always, she thought about Silas when she went into the kitchen to see what there was to nuke for dinner. As always, she thought about Silas when she showered and changed into pajama pants and T-shirt and sat in the corner of the sofa to see what she could stream tonight.

As always, the TV screen filled with suggestions based on her most recent viewing habits. Oh, look. More Westerns. Funny how those had completely usurped the recommendations of romantic comedies and cozy mysteries that used to show up nightly. And funny how none of the Westerns had felt any more true-to-life than the romantic comedies and cozy mysteries had.

She scrolled down until she found one that had a horse who looked like Beanie in the sample and hit Play. The movie was okay. It was even fine. But by the third sweeping panoramic shot of mountains, including one that of course reminded her of the night she and Silas spent together in the Tetons, she decided she'd had enough and turned the TV off. It wasn't okay to not be okay. It wasn't fine to not be fine. Not when she could be okay and fine both. Or actually better than okay and fine both. She knew she could, because for one brief, glorious week, she *had* been better than both. Way better. That second week of her stay in Wyoming, when she and Silas shared everything they could about themselves with each other. Their bodies, their memories, their thoughts, their souls...

Their hearts. He was the first person, the only person, she'd ever opened up to, and once she did, she'd spilled every last bit of herself at his feet. But where she'd thought he would find those bits of her kind of gross and off-putting, he'd only picked up the pieces and helped her put them back together. Then he'd pulled her close and made her feel as if—

As if she was exactly where she belonged.

That Wyoming mountaintop with Silas was the first place Mia had felt like she was home. She hadn't realized it at the time, because she'd been processing so many feelings, so many thoughts, so many memories. Looking back now, though, she finally understood. Home wasn't a physical place with walls and furniture and people coming and going. Home was a feeling. A knowledge. A sense of being. Home was when you were right where you were meant to be. And for Mia, home was with Silas Crockett.

It was why she'd felt so out of place since coming back to St. Louis. Because he wasn't here with her. Wherever he was, that was home. It didn't matter where she lived her life, as long as she lived it with him. And it didn't matter how much work they both still had to do on themselves, as long as they did that together, too. The sooner she got back to Serenity Valley, the sooner she could start living and healing. The sooner she got back to Silas, the sooner she would be home.

She headed for her bedroom and grabbed her weekender bag from the floor of her closet where she'd stowed it. Though, looking at it now, it wasn't stowed very well. There must be a part of her that had known she would be needing it again soon.

She prowled the room, looking for the things she knew she'd need for her return to Serenity Valley, then realized the only things she had here in St. Louis that were essential were pajamas, underwear and toiletries. She'd stop at the mall on her way out of town in the morning to load up on jeans and T-shirts and socks, but she'd wait until she hit Wyoming to look for boots and hats, since any she found in the big city would doubtless be more for fashion than function. Maybe Silas could help her with that, the way he'd helped her with so many other things.

She took her half-filled bag back into the living room and was headed to the kitchen to see what kind of snacks she had for the road when there was a soft knock at her front door. So soft, in fact, that she almost didn't hear it. And even when she did, she thought it was someone knocking at her neighbor's door across the hall. No one ever knocked at Mia's front door. A second round of quiet raps, however, told her there was a first time for that, too.

She moved swiftly to the peephole to look through it, and her breath hitched in her chest at what she saw. Not that peepholes were famous for offering much detail into callers. But it was enough for Mia to see that her caller, currently in profile, was wearing a Stetson. And when he turned his head to look back at the door, she knew a joy unlike any she'd felt since—

Well. Since a certain night on a certain mountain above a certain ranch with a certain cowboy.

Still afraid to believe her eyes, she left the chain in place when she opened the front door. Silas stood on the other side, looking completely out of place in his rough denim and rich leather against the pale backdrop of drywall and fluorescent lights. The man belonged in sunlight and wide-open spaces. What was he doing here?

"Hey," he said softly.

"Hi," she said just as quietly.

For a moment, they only gazed at each other in silence. Then Mia took the chain off the door and invited him inside. Silas, ever the gentleman, removed his hat before entering, and as he crossed the threshold, she noticed he was carrying a battered duffel bag in his other hand. There was another moment of silent gazing once he got inside, then he leaned forward and brushed his lips softly over her cheek before pulling awkwardly back again. As if the chaste kiss had been an untoward intimacy after everything they'd already shared together. Somehow Mia remembered to close the door behind him. But where she would usually automatically throw the bolt and replace the chain again—hey, a girl living alone in the big city and all that—this time she didn't bother. Silas was here. She wasn't alone. She was as safe as she could possibly be.

Restlessly, he crossed to her sofa and dropped the duffel bag on it, then started to turn around. But he did a double take when he saw her own weekender sitting at the other end, still open.

He looked at her again. "Are you coming or going?"

She smiled at his phrasing. She'd felt like she was coming and going ever since her return from Whispering Winds but had never known what exactly her destination was. From her apartment to work. From work to her apartment. Neither of them a place she needed or wanted to be. Until now. With Silas here, her apartment was starting to kind of feel like home.

"I was packing to come back to Serenity Valley," she told him. "I was going to leave tomorrow morning."

He grinned at that. The one she'd seen often her second week at Whispering Winds, so happy and open and carefree. The one that had made him look even more handsome, even more compelling, even more tempting.

Then she realized that no, this smile now was a little different. That one had been tempered at times with somberness. Even sadness. There wasn't any sorrow in this one. There was only joy. Something warm and wonderful blossomed in her belly to see it. Maybe because she suspected she was smiling the same way herself.

He pointed into the half-empty bag. "Looks like you still have some packing to do."

"Actually, I'm pretty much finished. I figured there wasn't much I needed to take with me, since everything I need—"

Here she stopped, because a thread of doubt wound through her. Just why was Silas here? Was it because he'd just missed her and wanted to spend a few days with her? Or was it because he'd discovered the same thing she had—that the feelings she'd been wading through for the last month included one she was still afraid to identify?

She made herself say the rest. "I didn't pack more for Serenity Valley, because I realized everything I need was already there." She smiled tentatively. "Except now it's here. So…" She took a few steps forward, until barely a foot of space separated them. "So now, I'm not sure what I should do."

He smiled back. Less tentatively. "Well, that's a funny thing," he said. "Because I came here to St. Louis, a city I've never visited before, because everything I need is right here." He nodded toward the duffel bag. "Hell, all I packed was a toothbrush and a couple changes of clothes. I was kinda hoping you might have an extra bar of soap lying around."

She took another step forward. "As long as you don't mind smelling like rosewater and glycerin," she said.

He took another step forward, too. "I've smelled like worse in my life, trust me."

She chuckled at that, and something inside her that had been wound way too tight since coming back to St. Louis completely unraveled. "Then you can stay as long as you want," she told him. "Unless you'd rather go back to Whispering Winds tomorrow with me right on your tail."

He covered what little space still separated them and looped his arms around her waist, pulling her close. She lifted her arms to drape them over his shoulders. Even a thousand miles away from it, he smelled like Serenity Valley, all pine and woodsmoke and fresh air. He smelled like home, Mia thought. He felt like home, too. She never wanted to leave his arms again.

"It honestly doesn't matter where we go," he told her. "One thing I've learned over the last month is that even the place you've called home all your life doesn't feel like home if you don't have the right people there with you." He looked around her apartment. "And a place you've never even seen before might very well feel like exactly the place you need to be." Now he looked back down at her. "As long as the right people are there with you. Look, Mia, I know you and I still have a lot to work through, but it seems to me like we could help each other out with that. The way—"

Now he was the one to interrupt himself. And he was looking as doubtful as she'd felt when she did the same thing.

"The way what?" she asked softly.

He pressed his forehead to hers. "The way family is supposed to. Neither of us really had the chance to learn that before, you know? Your family wasn't capable of it, and mine never had the chance."

The heat in Mia's belly spread up into her chest, into her heart, until it nearly overwhelmed her.

Silas bent to give her a brief, sweet kiss then pulled back again. "Both of us needed and wanted—and de-served—to have families we never got to have. We're both kind of grieving the same loss. Maybe we could do that better if we did it together."

He was right, of course. She realized now that what she'd been doing since leaving Whispering Winds was grieving, too. Not for the loss of a loved one, the way Silas was, but for a life and happiness she could have had—should have had—but was denied. Every child deserved to feel happy and safe and loved. Too many weren't. And those children, once they were adults, needed to grieve that loss if they were ever going to come to terms with it.

Silas's memory and love for his wife and daughter would always be a part of him, the same way Mia would always carry the scars of her childhood with her. But those losses and scars didn't mean they couldn't be happy. Their losses and scars didn't define them. There was so much more to both of them beyond that. There was joy. There was frustration. There was fear. There was hope. There was dismay. There was happiness. There was…

There was love. That was what she'd been feeling since leaving Whispering Winds, the emotion she'd been afraid to admit. She loved Silas. She'd probably fallen in love with him that night on the mountain. Maybe even before then. Maybe the moment they met, when the hurt, fear and anger in her recognized the hurt, fear and anger in him. On some level, she'd known even then that she needed him. And that maybe he'd needed her, too.

Just like everything else that made them who they were, that love would always be with them. And it would make everything else—everything—bearable. It didn't matter where they lived or what they carried with them. As long as they had each other.

"I love you, Mia Hawthorne," he said point-blank. "I think maybe I fell in love with you that first day, that first second, when you told me you were fine. Because I knew you were no more fine than I was. That we were two of a kind, me and you. As different as we seemed at first..." He shook his head and laughed lightly. Mia laughed with him.

"We really are two of a kind," she told him. "What you just said to me is exactly what I wanted to say to you. Right down to the 'I love you.' Because, Silas Crockett, I love you, too. And I don't care where we are, either. I just want to be with you."

As if cued by her comment, a car alarm outside began to blare incessantly, punctuated by the siren of a swiftly passing police car. Then the bass kicked up from the Friday-night featured band at the nightclub on the corner. Then the terrier upstairs began to bark.

Mia sighed melodramatically. "Though I gotta say, your place in Serenity Valley is a lot less noisy than my place here in St. Louis."

He laughed, then drove his gaze around her living room again. "Don't take this the wrong way," he said when he looked at her again, "but this place doesn't really seem like you. I mean, I'm not sure what I expected, and this is really nice and everything, but... It just doesn't feel like the Mia I know."

She looked around at her apartment—something she hadn't done for a long time. Everything had come from online or brick-and-mortar chain stores that specialized in prefab whatever to make a person's home feel like a million other people's homes. She hadn't thought too much about it as she'd furnished the place in bits and pieces over the years. She'd just bought things that matched in colors she kind of liked that looked like the sort of thing a happy family on TV would have on the soundstage set that was supposed to be their house. She'd liked it all when she bought it. But she'd barely looked at everything once she got it all into place. Silas was right— it was nice, but the two of them could have been standing in anyone's house. And in nobody's home.

"I call it Twenty-First Century American Whatever," she told him. "It's all the rage among people who have no idea where they belong."

He eyed her thoughtfully. "So, you don't think you belong here?"

She shook her head. "I know I don't belong here." She tilted her head toward her bag on the sofa. "Hence the packed weekender."

"That's only good for a weekend, though," he pointed out.

"Gosh. Guess I'll need some help figuring out what to do once I get to Serenity Valley." She stood on tiptoe long enough to give him an *I am so glad I found you* kiss. Then she lowered herself again and said, "Good thing I have family there."

He smiled at that. Then he dipped his head to kiss

her back, brushing his lips over hers, once, twice, three times, four. Enough to make her heart hammer hard in her chest and the rest of her melt into him as if she were a part of him. When he pulled back again, she was gripping his shirt in both fists as if she never intended to let him go. Because now that she'd found her family, now that she'd found her home, she was never, ever, going to leave either again.

Silas took a step away, but only far enough to open his hand, palm up, between the two of them. "Well, then, Mia," he said, "what do you say you and I go home?"

She took his hand readily in hers. But instead of heading for the front door, she turned toward her bedroom instead. "Tomorrow, cowboy," she told him as she tugged him along behind her. "I've already made plans for us tonight."

Epilogue

Silas leaned in the kitchen doorway of the house where he'd spent his childhood until his mother's death—the one that had never felt quite like home after that, even when Miss Sylvie returned the keys to him upon his return from Laramie—and watched Mia as she put away the groceries she'd just brought home from Jackson Hole. The kitten formerly known as Mimi, whose name Mia changed to Lettie after her return to Serenity Valley a few months ago—*I read somewhere that it means* happy, *Silas*—wove in and out of her denim-clad legs as she did, waiting for the treats she knew were in one of those bags. Because Mia always bought treats for Lettie. Lettie was family.

And Mia's legs were always denim-clad now. So was the rest of her most times. Denim and cotton. That was about all she owned, save the leather cowboy boots and felt Stetson that were already looking worn from her wearing them daily. Oh, and also the work gloves she wore sometimes when she was tuning up or refurbishing the ranch vehicles, since Miss Sylvie had hired her as the new motor pool manager. He wasn't sure she even owned a pair of pants that weren't denim or a shirt that wasn't cotton. She'd dropped all the heels and office work

clothes at her favorite thrift store back in St. Louis before leaving that life behind to start her new one here.
Though she'd kept the barely-pink dress she'd tried so
hard to look invisible in that first night at Whispering
Winds, in case there was a special occasion. Like her
first night back in Wyoming. And the one-week anniversary of her return to Wyoming. And the one-month
anniversary. And the two-month. And... Well, there had
just been a lot of special occasions since her return to
Serenity Valley, that was all.

A cool breeze shook the window curtains over the
sink behind her, the mountains beyond them looking
more purple now than they had in the summer months.
Tiny Tim—who Miss Sylvie had given them as a house-
warming present after Silas explained Mia's food-with-
eyelashes situation—bellowed from the yard outside for
his own treats, since she always brought home a bag of
cattle cubes for him, too.

Fall had well and truly arrived in Wyoming, which
meant snuggling in bed on frosty mornings and hot coffee around the backyard fire pit at night. Today, it also
brought Sturgill Simpson singing twangily from the
speaker atop the fridge about how life wasn't fair and
the world was mean—though, these days, life felt a lot
fairer for Silas and Mia, and the world wasn't nearly as
mean as it used to be. And there was a *no beef for me
please* stew simmering on the stove—a recipe Silas had
whipped up especially for Mia her first week back—that
filled the kitchen with the aroma of onions and rosemary.

He smiled. The house sure as hell felt like home now.
Even more than it had when he was growing up here.
There were times when he could almost feel his moth-

er's presence in the place, nodding her appreciation for how he and Mia were taking care of things and building a life together here. And there were times when he could almost feel Jess and their daughter, too, both of them happy that he'd found something else—someone else—to keep him going now that they were gone. Jess would have wanted and expected him to find someone else to love, the same way he would have wanted and expected that of her had the situation been reversed. She and the baby would always be with him. But that didn't mean he couldn't make room in his life—in his heart— for other people, too.

It was just him and Mia now, and that was all either of them needed to make a family. Oh, all right, and Lettie and Tim, too. Maybe someday they'd add to their family. Or maybe they'd always feel like this was the way it was supposed to be. Right now, it was enough. Right now, it was damned near perfect. And it would be perfect from here on out, no matter what he and Mia decided to do with their life and no matter what that life threw at them. Whenever they felt the pressures of the world descending, they could just ride up into the mountains and shout at the universe again.

Though Silas suspected he knew now what the universe would say after they were through. The universe would tell them they were just fine. That they'd been fine all along. Really. They'd just had to discover that for themselves.

* * * * *

Get up to 4 Free Books!

**We'll send you 2 free books from each series you try
PLUS a free Mystery Gift.**

Both the **Harlequin® Special Edition** and **Harlequin® Heartwarming™** series feature compelling novels filled with stories of love and strength where the bonds of friendship, family and community unite.

YES! Please send me 2 FREE novels from the Harlequin Special Edition or Harlequin Heartwarming series and my FREE Gift (gift is worth about $10 retail). I may cancel anytime by emailing ReaderServiceInfo@Harlequin.com or by calling 1-800-873-8635.If I don't cancel, I will receive 6 brand-new Harlequin Special Edition books every month and be billed just $6.39 each in the U.S. or $7.19 each in Canada, or 4 brand-new Harlequin Heartwarming Larger-Print books every month and be billed just $7.19 each in the U.S. or $7.99 each in Canada, a savings of 20% off the cover price. It's quite a bargain! Shipping and handling is just 75¢ per book in the U.S. and $1.75 per book in Canada.* I understand that accepting the free books and gift places me under no obligation to buy anything—they are mine to keep for free no matter what I decide.

Choose one:
☐ **Harlequin Special Edition**
(235/335 BPA G3CD)

☐ **Harlequin Heartwarming Larger-Print**
(161/361 BPA G3CD)

☐ **Or Try Both!**
(235/335 & 161/361 BPA G3CE)

Name (please print)

Address _____ Apt. #

City _____ State/Province _____ Zip/Postal Code

Email: Please check this box ☐ if you would like to receive newsletters and promotional emails from Harlequin Enterprises ULC and its affiliates. You can unsubscribe anytime.

Mail to the **Harlequin Reader Service:**
IN U.S.A.: P.O. Box 1341, Buffalo, NY 14240-8531
IN CANADA: P.O. Box 603, Fort Erie, Ontario L2A 5X3

Want to explore our other series or interested in ebooks? Visit www.ReaderService.com or call 1-800-873-8635.

*Terms and prices subject to change without notice. Prices do not include sales taxes, which will be charged (if applicable) based on your state or country of residence. Canadian residents will be charged applicable taxes. Offer not valid in Quebec. This offer is limited to one order per household. Books received may not be as shown. Not valid for current subscribers to the Harlequin Special Edition or Harlequin Heartwarming series. All orders subject to approval. Credit or debit balances in a customer's account(s) may be offset by any other outstanding balance owed by or to the customer. Please allow 4 to 6 weeks for delivery. Offer available while quantities last.

Your Privacy — Your information is being collected by Harlequin Enterprises ULC, operating as Harlequin Reader Service. For a complete summary of the information we collect, how we use this information and to whom it is disclosed, please visit our privacy notice located at https://corporate.harlequin.com/privacy-notice. Notice to California Residents—Under California law, you have specific rights to control and access your data. For more information on these rights and how to exercise them, visit https://corporate.harlequin.com/california-privacy. For additional information for residents of other U.S. states that provide their residents with certain rights with respect to personal data, visit https://corporate.harlequin.com/other-state-residents-privacy-rights.

HSEHW2603